STEPH

STEPHANIE'S TRIAL

Susanna Hughes

Nexus

First published in 1994 by
Nexus
332 Ladbroke Grove
London W10 5AH

Typeset by TW Typesetting, Plymouth, Devon
Printed and bound by
Cox & Wyman Ltd, Reading, Berks

ISBN 0 352 32902 5

This book is a work of fiction.
In real life, make sure you practise safe sex.

Chapter One

The Baron liked to watch. He was a big man, very tall and with an aura of physical power that belied his sixty years of age. He looked precisely what he was, a Prussian military man, his back as straight as a ramrod, his almost totally bald head held high and proud. But despite the infinite combinations available on the sexual menu at the castle, all the Baron had wanted to do was watch.

Stephanie had kept him well supplied with spectacle. The castle was designed to cater for every conceivable sexual taste and the Baron's voyeurism was no exception. There was a room specially constructed for the purpose. It was small, just big enough to contain a double bed and bedside tables. There was no other furniture. The bed was covered with silk sheets and piled with cushions and pillows. The walls on either side of the bed were made entirely of two-way mirrors from floor to ceiling. Each could be curtained off at the touch of a button on the bedside table. The view on one side was of a stone-walled dungeon, its brick vaulted ceiling hung with chains and pulleys, its walls thick with iron rings, bolts and chains and all manner of devices to fetter and restrain. On the other side the glass revealed a normal luxuriously appointed bedroom, dominated by a large double bed. The occupants of either room could only see a wall of mirror from their side. On the dungeon side there were even fixing points in the mirror itself and Stephanie once had ordered one of the female slaves spread-eagled against the glass, her breasts and belly pressed against its surface, writhing against it as she was punished for misbehaviour, the sweat from her body smeared on the mirror.

But tonight was the Baron's last night at the castle and Stephanie wanted to give him a special performance, something he'd remember. Though this was his first visit to the castle he was an old friend of Devlin's and an immensely wealthy man whom Devlin had done business with for many years. It was important that he enjoyed himself, especially as Devlin had been called away on business. But if she was truthful with herself it was not only a question of looking after an honoured guest; she found herself strangely attracted to this big man. It was something in his eyes, a stillness there, a deliberateness, a suggestion of power, that made her feel the first pangs of sexual excitement whenever she saw him.

Stephanie sat naked on the bed, the black lingerie beside her. She was facing the mirror, looking straight into it. She knew, of course, the Baron was on the other side of the glass. She knew he would be watching her, had already watched her strip out of her yellow sun-dress, white bra and tiny white panties, revealing what she hoped he had wanted to see all weekend.

She picked up a black nylon stocking and rolled it into a pouch around the toe. She raised her leg and pointed her foot, fitting the nylon over her toes, slowly rolling it up over her ankle and calf, the translucent material engulfing her creamy flesh until its black welt bisected her slim, contoured thighs. She used the palms of both hands to smooth and stretch the nylon flat against her leg. The Baron would be able to see the slit of her sex covered with her curly black pubic hair. He might even be able to see her labia and a slick of wetness there because, she knew, her juices were already oozing from her body.

Picking up the second stocking, Stephanie repeated the process. The nylon rolled out from her fingers, encasing her leg in a shiny, slippery, seamless smoothness like newly applied gloss paint. Again she leant forward to iron out any wrinkles with the palms of her hands, her firm breast touching the top of her thigh as she did so.

She lowered her leg to the floor when she was satisfied the stocking was completely smooth, and picked up the garment she had laid out next to the stockings. The black lace cami-suspender was as sheer as the stockings, a deep bra with its bottom edge scalloped at the front and side into angular crescents of material at the apex of which was the long finger of a suspender. Stephanie slipped the silky nylon over her head and down over her breasts, pulling its cups into place so they fitted snugly. She clipped the black suspenders into the tops of the stockings and fastened them securely. The black nylon welts formed thick chevrons on her thighs. The material of the cami-suspender made an arch over her navel, her belly-button exposed, the triangle of her pubic hair framed by the suspenders on each side. The lacy cups of the bra did not hide her breasts but only shaded them; her nipples and the darkness of her areola were still clearly visible.

Stephanie stood up. The tight suspenders pulled at the black lace covering her breasts and in turn on the straps of the bra on her shoulders. She enjoyed the feeling of tightness it gave her, like subtle bondage.

Looking directly into the mirror she slipped her feet into a pair of high-heel shoes. They were shiny black leather, the heels so high the top of her foot was arched out. Apart from the long black fingers of the four suspenders from the waist to the welts of the stockings she was naked, the creamy flesh in between somehow made to look softer, more alluring by contrast with the sheer black nylon that surrounded it. The high heels shaped the muscles of her calves and tilted her firm apple-shaped arse into a distinct pout. She turned her back on the mirror and examined herself over her shoulder – just as the Baron was examining her, no doubt. The two creases of her flesh where thigh met buttock were bisected by the deep cleft of her arse; it was dark in there, a darkness full of promise. Between her legs, even with them firmly closed, there was a space between her thighs, a diamond-shaped hollow immediately under the plane of her labia.

Stephanie took a hairbrush from the bedside table and walked up to within a foot of the huge mirror. She had pinned her rich black hair up to the back of her head. Now she let it fall free, brushing it out, long full strokes of her arm from the crown of her head out to the very tip of her hair, brushing out to the side, holding the hair out almost horizontally. The movement of her arm made her breasts tremble under the transparent lace, the hard buttons of her nipples pressed into the complex web of material that imprisoned them.

She thought of the Baron, a few feet away. What was he doing? The red drapes would be closed on the other wall, the dungeon side. The lights in the room would be dimmed. Was he lying naked on the bed, his big body stretched out, his cock throbbing and erect

4

as he watched her perform? Or was he still dressed, sitting on the edge of the bed, those hypnotic eyes staring at her quietly in the way they had of seeing and seeing through her at the same time? What was his cock like? Was it as big and powerful as he was?

Stephanie's body shuddered involuntarily. She felt her sex pulse. She knew it was wet. Reversing the hairbrush in her hand she ran the handle, a slim black lacquered handle, down the front of her body, down between her breasts, over the sheer black lace to the creaminess of her navel, down until it nestled in her pubic hair. She parted her legs slightly, then pushed the hairbrush down into the narrow gorge of her sex, its polished and lacquered surface immediately making contact with the hard knot of her clitoris. The contact made her groan. She leant forward, bringing her other arm up to rest against the mirror at head height, then resting her forehead on her lower arm. She stared down at her body, seeing it and its reflection at the same time. She moved the black handle in tiny circles and felt her clitoris throb like a thing apart from her, like a little animal come to life. Looking down she saw the way the long suspenders were arched out from her body, holding the stockings taut. She could see her feet in the high heels, covered by black nylon, her legs well apart. The handle of the hairbrush would make her come, she knew, if she continued what she was doing. Wanting to delay the inevitable a little longer, she moved the handle lower, bending her knees slightly to allow it to slip up between the lips of her cunt and into her sex. There was no resistance. She was soaking wet.

She raised her head and looked straight into the mirror as though trying to see through it. In her mind's eye she saw the Baron standing on the other

5

side of the mirror, his erect penis pressed against the glass exactly opposite her cunt, his hands groping at the image of her body, caressing it, squeezing it as his cock, slimed with its own secretions, left a wet sticky trail on the surface as it slid up and down, wanting to come.

Stephanie could wait no longer. She pulled the handle of the hairbrush from her body. It glistened with the sap from her sex. She brought it up to her mouth and licked it hungrily like a child licking an ice-cream. It tasted good, she tasted good. She had come to love the taste of her own body. She had tasted it many times now, on men's mouths and cocks, on women's mouths and fingers, cocks and mouths and fingers she'd sucked hungrily as she did now with the smooth glossy finish of the hairbrush. Then she threw the brush aside and turned her back on the mirror. Resting the full curves of her arse against it, she bent over.

It was exciting. She knew this would expose the whole of her sex to the Baron's view, from the neat puckered crater of her anus to the particularly fleshy slit of her outer labia, and inside, the delicate inner oval like a vertical mouth, wet and pink and crinkled like the pistil of some exotic carnivorous flower. Using her hands to spread her buttocks, she pushed back until she could feel the cold glass against her sex. Was the Baron on his knees in front of the mirror now, looking right up her cunt, into the black depths, examining every detail? She felt a strong pulse of pleasure emanating from her clitoris. This was a performance the Baron wouldn't forget.

Stephanie straightened herself up and walked over to the bed. The mirror was marked where her sex had been, almost like the marks lipstick makes after a kiss.

Now the pulses in her body were too strong to ignore. Now it was her turn, the mistress of the castle had to have her pleasure. It was a pity that the Baron, the big, powerful Baron only wanted to watch. Stephanie would have loved to be crushed under that heavy body, loved him to have stepped through the glass now and use his cock – the hard, erect, throbbing cock she could see in her mind's eye – on her, thrusting it up her and in her.

But at least she had a substitute. She pressed a small button on the bedside table to indicate she was ready, then lay back on the middle of the bed, bending her legs at the knee and opening them wide, the heels of her shoes digging into the pale peach-coloured sheets, rucking them around their tips. She raised her head and looked down her body, down the black lace and naked flesh underneath it. The suspenders on top of her thighs were hanging loose, not stretched by the position of her legs but the wide black welt of the stocking still formed a perfect chevron on her thigh. She let the fingertips of her right hand graze the black nylon of the welt, slipping to and fro, feeling the contrast between the shiny material and the soft warmth of her flesh. Then she let her hand drift down past her navel to where her pubic hair waited impatiently for attention, the animal impatiently waiting to be petted.

Her clitoris was swollen, engorged by her excitement. Stephanie teased it out from the forest of her pubic hair, nudging it with her finger not at all gently. She wasn't in the mood for gentle. She felt a sweet surge of pleasure. She could easily, so easily, have brought herself off on the idea of the Baron's greedy eyes staring at her, naked and open. But she wanted to wait. What she wanted now was cock, and she wanted it urgently.

And what Stephanie wanted Stephanie got. That was the way of the world and had been since she arrived at the castle and was begged, by Devlin, to take over. She was used to getting her own way in everything. Another moment's delay and she would have started to get angry, but just as she was beginning to think what she would do in the morning to express her wrath, the bedroom door opened.

The man was naked, his muscular body glistening with oil just as Stephanie had specified it should. His cock was oiled too and erect. That was not unusual among the slaves. In the cellars under the castle where the slaves were kept the men were all forced to wear tight leather-covered metal pouches over their genitals, chained and padlocked in place. Freedom from this constriction was so rare it produced instant bone-hard erections. Not that this cock was entirely free. A black leather harness was strapped fiercely around the base of it and under his balls. It separated each testicle and held them high on either side of the big, veined shaft. The harness was strapped on so tightly the leather bit deeply into the flesh, reddening it and increasing its size further.

Stephanie had selected the slave personally. His body was strong and hard. He was well-trained and well-behaved. He responded well to instruction. Being allowed to fuck the mistress of the castle was a rare treat. Not that he deserved it. None of the slaves in the cellars did, male or female. They were all thieves when it came down to it, all caught with their hands metaphorically in the many tills of Devlin's companies. They had all chosen to come and serve at the castle rather than be prosecuted in the courts.

'Get over here,' Stephanie ordered imperiously, finding it hard to concentrate on anything else but her

8

physical need. The words increased it: the knowledge of her absolute power gave another twist to the spiral of her desire.

The slave did not need any second bidding. He stood at the foot of the bed between Stephanie's open legs. She used her foot, sheathed in the black nylon, to prod at his cock. All the slaves wore name-tags, etched metal circles hung by a thin chain around their necks. The name on this slave's tag was JAMES.

'Well James ... You know what you're here for, don't you?'

'Yes, mistress,' he said at once. He looked down at his feet, fearing that looking at her naked body would be a punishable offence.

Stephanie opened her legs wider and arched her buttocks off the bed, pointing the long slit of her sex at him. 'You may look at me, James ...'

His eyes went straight to her cunt. She saw his cock twitch against his leather bindings.

'Do you like what you see?'

'Yes, mistress,' he said, thinking of a thousand other things he could say but not daring to go any further.

She wanted to provoke him, to make him cross the barrier of his obedience. She rolled her hips and clenched her thighs, making the lips of her sex move as though sucking some invisible cock into her body. She took both nipples in her fingers and pulled them up away from her body until her breasts were like pyramids on her chest and her nipples hurt, a hurt that turned instantly to the heat of pleasure.

James felt his cock spasm again. He had never felt it so hard, so hot. He could see into her sex, see her labia parting like the gills of a fish breathing and he could stand it no longer. He launched himself at her,

9

falling on her, devouring her, his oiled body slipping against hers, his arms wrapping around her neck, his cock slipping effortlessly straight up into the tight, hot, wet cavern of her cunt. He started hammering it into her as he felt her legs curling around his back, the shiny nylon rasping against his skin, as she used the leverage to get her cunt further down on him, impaling herself on the rod of his cock.

The feelings were too strong to do anything else but give in to them. His cock was big and very hard. It filled her completely. She managed to raise her head once to look over his shoulder, down over his plunging buttocks and into the mirror beyond. What was the Baron doing? He would be able to see everything, see the slave's cock ploughing into her, his balls strapped tightly in black leather, its shaft running with her juices. He would see the way her cunt, the lips of her cunt made thin now by being stretched, closed around the cock, just like a mouth, sucking it in. He would see her legs, up-ended, the suspenders pulling at the nylons, her feet still crammed into the black high heels. Was he wanking while he watched, bringing himself off in time to James's strokes? The idea sent another thrill coursing through Stephanie's body and she let her head fall back onto the bed.

'Fuck me,' she said unnecessarily, just wanting to hear the words.

She could think of nothing but her pleasure now. The engine of her orgasm had started to turn, a giant flywheel moving slowly at first but inexorably, gathering momentum until it spun faster and faster with unstoppable power, propelling her down deeper and deeper into her own body and her own senses, until all she could feel was herself and there was nothing in the world but the exquisite sensations of her climax.

As she came she felt the head of James's cock buried against her womb, hammering at it relentlessly, the curve of his pubic bone hard against her clitoris, the neat package of his strapped-up balls tight against her arse. It all made her come, driving her orgasm on and on, extending it, making it go on for so long she thought it would never stop.

And just as she thought it was subsiding she felt James's body tense, his muscles lock, arching his body like a bow to get his cock even deeper into her as his spunk suddenly spat uncontrollably from his spasming shaft. The feeling of his spunk filling her renewed her orgasm, made it peak again, threw her nerves into yet another rigor of pleasure.

Eventually, after what seemed like forever, her body released its grip on her mind, sensation gave way to thought, and she opened her eyes. James's cock had softened and was squeezed out of her cunt. Its departure produced a shudder in her, an aftershock, an echo of the shattering orgasm she had just experienced. It was extraordinary, she thought as James rolled off her, how her sexuality had grown and developed. Before she had started to plumb the depths of her sexual psyche, not having the slightest idea of how fathomable it would be, before she had strangely, unaccountably decided she must take a journey through the highways and byways of her own sexuality, a personal odyssey, she had had virtually nothing to do with sex. She had experienced it, but it had not moved her or bothered her or even interested her for much of the time.

All that had changed, changed suddenly and dramatically through two men. Martin, whom she had wanted more than any man in her life up to that point, had shown her that sex was more than a physi-

11

cal act and introduced her for the first time to an undergrowth of sex, to fantasy and the pleasures of the imagination. With Martin she had experienced pleasure she had never even dreamt of. Like the lightning that brought Frankenstein's monster to life, Martin's mind as well as his body had shocked Stephanie into sexual awareness. But if it had been Martin who'd opened the door for her, it was Devlin who had given her the means and the opportunity to explore the corridors and passages that lay beyond, the passages that led to where she was today.

Devlin had brought her to the castle and the cellars. Devlin had allowed her into his life and, in the end, wanted her to control it. Though he had built the castle, though he had constructed the cellars and staffed them with slaves from his vast empire, it had been Stephanie, Stephanie's imagination, that had for the first time given Devlin the sexual pleasure he craved. Stephanie was mistress of the castle now and Devlin, for all his wealth and power, was her hopeless, fawning slave.

What Stephanie had discovered for herself, on her sexual odyssey, was that she seemed to have an infinite capacity for sex, for excitement, for fantasy, for extending the boundaries of her own – and other people's – sexual awareness. She had, it appeared, an instinct, a sixth sense when it came to other people's sexuality; an ability to read their deepest sexual desires and, with the facilities of the castle, fulfil them. But at the same time, at precisely the same time she had also discovered that her own sexual feelings could be roused to fever pitch by impulses she had no idea she possessed, by the impulse to dominate, to have power, to command obedience and punish defiance.

In the last six months Stephanie's life had been

transformed. Here at the castle she lived in complete luxury, her life spent in catering for Devlin's needs and the needs of the guests who were flown to the castle, customers and business associates like the Baron, their access to the castle an inducement to continue a productive relationship with Devlin's companies. But best of all, better than all the luxury and wealth and the incredible beauty of the lake and the island, was that in satisfying Devlin and others like the Baron, she was above all satisfying herself. The orgasm she had experienced tonight, so sharp, intense and long, was all part of that, all part of knowing and controlling, of being at the centre. Knowing the Baron was watching had brought her off but it was the idea that she had constructed and orchestrated the spectacle that was really at the root of her sexual enjoyment.

The thought of the Baron reminded her that the plan for the evening was not yet complete.

'Is Molly ready?' she asked James.

'Yes mistress, she's waiting outside in the corridor.'

'Well, you'd better get her to come in.'

'Do you want me to stay, mistress?'

'No James, just tell Molly to come in and then go back to the cellars.' James was still lying on the bed. 'Now,' Stephanie prompted with a snap in her voice.

James immediately scuttled to the door. Stephanie smiled to herself. She had thought of presenting the Baron with a threesome, having Molly lick at James's balls while he was fucking his mistress, but she thought the Baron would appreciate more intimacy. He had seen orgies of sex over the weekend. Now she wanted him to watch her. That was the point. She wanted him to be excited by *her* body, *her* reaction, *her* sex. And that, in turn of course, would excite her.

13

A small, petite blonde, her hair cut in a short bob, her eyes a radiant blue, came through the bedroom door. Though not tall she was perfectly proportioned except for her big, full breasts that threatened to burst the confines of the white lacy underwired bra she wore. Her legs were sheathed in very white hold-up stockings, their welts, fashioned in thick bands of white lace, reaching so far up her thigh they almost touched the crotch of her panties. These were white and cut very high on the hip, so high in fact that the strip of material between her legs was not wide enough to cover all the flesh between her legs and managed only to conceal the central slit of her labia. Thin, wispy pubic hair was exposed at each side.

'Well, Molly,' Stephanie said. 'You know what you are going to do, don't you?'

'Yes, mistress,' Molly replied.

'Do it then.'

At once Molly knelt by the foot of the bed, the metal tag bearing her name bouncing on top of her deep cleavage.

Stephanie liked Molly. Molly had a fleshy, soft mouth and a long, probing tongue. She had used Molly before. A thrill of pleasure made Stephanie shudder unexpectedly. She scrambled down the bed and hooked her black-stockinged legs over Molly's shoulders and around her back, the heels of the black shoes digging cruelly into her back. Molly's mouth was inches from Stephanie's wet labia.

'Lick it, Molly . . . Lick the spunk out of me.' The words thrilled Stephanie because she knew the Baron could hear them. She dug her heels into Molly's back to urge her forward.

As she felt the singular pleasure of a woman's mouth lapping at the entrance of her cunt, her tongue delving inside to scoop out the white gobs of spunk that had already run down the slippery passage, she looked straight into the mirror. Can you see me, Baron? Can you see my pleasure? It was a pleasure she'd never dreamt she would enjoy. That was something else she had discovered about herself. It had never occurred to her that she would come to enjoy the pleasures of a woman, of sex with a woman, as much as the pleasures of sex with a man. But she did. As if to prove it again she felt her body shiver and her cunt contract. The giant flywheel was starting to turn again and it would not be long before the Baron saw her come again, this time on the ministrations of a woman. Would he come again too?

The speedboat was tied to the wooden jetty at the bottom of the stone steps that led from the front of the castle. The lush growth of climbing plants that overhung the steps were no longer flowering but still scented the area with a fragrant perfume. Though it was autumn the morning sun, hanging low over the calm waters of Lake Trasimeno, where the castle sat on an island, still warmed the air, although a heavy dew on the foliage was much slower to evaporate than in the heat of summer when Stephanie had first set foot on the island. The varnished wood and polished brass of the boat gleamed as it rocked gently in the very slight swell, the boatman standing ready as the servants, in smart white linen jackets, loaded the Baron's cases aboard.

Stephanie led the way down the steps, worn by four centuries of use, the Baron immediately behind her. She wore a functional black Lycra swimsuit covered by a chiffon wrap, intending to swim once she had seen the Baron off.

'Well, I hope you had a pleasant trip,' she said as they arrived at the boat. 'The plane is waiting.'

'Yes, I heard it come in.'

'And I'm sorry you missed Devlin.'

'I hope very much that you will come and visit my schloss in Bavaria. I would like to see you there. Both of you, of course.' He looked at her with those steady, unwavering eyes and Stephanie felt a little shiver of pleasure. Was he imagining what she had looked like last night?

'That would be delightful.'

'I too have some . . .' He hesitated trying to think of the right word, '. . . surprises.'

'Really?'

'Oh yes. I think you would be most interested.'

He took her hand and stooped as he brought it to his lips.

'May I say something to you, my dear?'

'Of course.'

'I would like to tell you that you are a most beautiful woman. Most beautiful. And with exceptional . . .' He sought for the right word again, '. . . talents.'

'Why thank you.' She looked up into his eyes and felt a surge of excitement. 'You should know,' she added.

'Oh yes, and I am most grateful for what you allowed me to see.'

'For myself, Baron, I was sorry that was all you wanted to do.'

The Baron smiled, an indulgent smile, like an adult smiling at a child.

'I'm an old man, my dear, set in my ways. Perhaps if you come to the schloss . . .' The words hung in the air, his eyes looking out over the water. 'If Devlin wouldn't mind.'

'I don't belong to Devlin,' Stephanie said sharply, wondering whether to add that it was Devlin who belonged to her.

'In that case . . .'

The Baron kissed her hand again and looked deeply and steadily into her eyes. Again Stephanie experienced a frisson of excitement. The Baron had a presence about him, an aura of power and masculinity that Stephanie found wholly attractive.

Bowing slightly as he relinquished her hand, the Baron climbed into the boat and the white linen-jacketed servants helped the boatman cast off the forward and aft lines. Immediately the boat drifted clear of the big rubber tyres that hung down from the side of the jetty and the boatman throttled the in-board engine up to a gentle hum and steered the boat out into the lake. Then he pulled the twin chrome throttle levers back, the note of the engine changed to a roar that echoed against the walls of the castle, and the boat surged across the water.

The Baron sat on the bench seat in the transom. He looked at Stephanie one final time, his eyes roaming her body, the swell of her breasts under the clinging black Lycra, the flatness at the junction of her thighs, her long slim legs and pinched ankles, remembering what it had looked like last night, open, exposed and in the throes of passion. He did not smile. As the boat turned he did not look back either.

A long foaming white wake stretched across the calm water in a huge sweeping curve until the boat was no more than a dot on the horizon and the water nearest the jetty had resumed its more usual motion, only the slightest hint of a wave disturbing its sun-kissed surface.

Stephanie stripped off the chiffon wrap, handed it

to the servant who had brought her a towel, and dived into the shimmering water. The temperature was cold but she didn't mind that. After a few minutes of vigorous swimming she would soon warm up. She struck out towards the centre of the lake, swimming a hard, regular front crawl, feeling the muscle power in her arms and legs that frequent exercise built up. She felt also the impact of the Baron's look as he had watched her from the boat. Would he do more than look next time? There was one thing that was certain: Stephanie definitely hoped he would.

After an hour in the lake Stephanie pulled herself up on to the jetty again and took the towel from the servant who had waited patiently for her. She rubbed her hair dry, then headed up the steps to the castle where a small shower room had been built off the vast entrance hall with its sweeping marble staircase. Pulling the tight swimsuit down she stood under the jets of the powerful shower, letting the hot water cascade off her body. Quickly she washed her long black hair then stepped from the shower stall. She glimpsed her naked body in the full-length mirror that lined the shower room door. It always surprised her. Apart from the fact it was marginally slimmer, the muscles in her legs and arms more defined, her waist that little bit more cinched, her breasts slightly higher on her chest, it was the same body that had stared back at her for all those years, innocent of the things it indulged in so regularly now. Stephanie was surprised it had not changed more, it did not look different, looked as different as it felt, because it felt and behaved and was different.

Taking the clean white towelling robe with which the shower room was always supplied and wrapping her wet hair in a small white towel turban-fashion,

Stephanie walked through to the terrace outside the dining room. Though the sun was only just high enough to clear the rich foliage that surrounded the terracotta-paved terrace it was warm enough to dry her hair and Stephanie pulled the towel off and sat at one of the white wrought-iron tables. She ordered a pot of coffee and the English newspapers that had been flown in yesterday.

The white linen-jacketed servant (the slaves were never used for domestic duties at the castle other than labouring in the orchards and extensive gardens) was soon back with a tray of white china and a silver coffee-pot. The papers were tucked under his arm. He also carried a cordless telephone.

'*Signor* Devlin, *signorina*,' he said, handing her the phone.

Stephanie pulled the aerial of the phone out of its socket as the waiter scurried away. 'Devlin . . .'

'Darling.' Devlin's voice sounded as though he were speaking from the bottom of the Atlantic Ocean.

'I can hardly hear you.'

'The lines are all terrible.'

'So how's Moscow?'

'Cold. But business is booming. I'll be back on schedule. I just called to see how you got on with the Baron.' Every other word disappeared into the ether. It took Stephanie a moment to gather what he was saying.

'I can hardly hear you, Devlin.'

'I can hear you perfectly.'

'The Baron was fine. He's an interesting man . . .'

'I thought you'd think so.'

'He's invited us to his schloss.'

'Oh . . . would . . . an experience. Did . . . entertain him?'

'Oh yes. I think he was suitably impressed. I gave him my personal attention.'

'Good ... back ... week. See you ... and ... tell me ... about it.'

'Devlin, I thought I'd go to London for a few days to do some shopping. There's no one expected here, is there?'

'No ... good ... Have a ... time. Call Venetia.'

'Did you think I wouldn't?'

'No ...'

'Devlin.' Stephanie snapped his name out this time.

'Yes ...'

'Yes what?'

'Yes, mistress.' Even over the crackling line she could hear his voice change tone just as hers had done.

'Can you hear me?'

'Yes ... tress.'

'When I get you back here, Devlin, do you know what I'm going to do with you?' She wanted to give him something to think about, something to lie in bed at night and remember. 'I'm going to have you strapped down to my bed, Devlin, strapped down so tight you can't move a muscle, not an inch. Are you listening?'

'Yes ... mistress.'

'Then I'm going to make you watch.'

'Watch mistress ...'

'Watch. Watch me as I take off all my clothes. A tight, clinging silk dress. My strapless bra. My little black panties, the tiny ones that barely cover my sex. You know the ones I mean, don't you?'

'Yes, mistress.'

'I'll pull them down over my thighs, very slowly.' Stephanie's hand slipped inside the white towelling robe, she pinched her nipple then dropped her hand

20

into her lap. 'But I'll leave my stockings on, and my suspender belt. And my high heels. I'm going to put one foot up on the bed and smooth the wrinkles out of the nylon. You know how I like my stockings to be tight against my legs, don't you?'

'Yes.'

'One leg then the other, so you'll see my pussy, won't you? If I allow you to look, that is.'

'Please let me . . .'

'Then I'm going to kneel on the bed over your cock.'

'Yes . . .' Devlin's voice was reedy and strained. She knew he would be wanking himself by now.

'But as much as you want to, I'm not going to let you fuck me. I'm going to make you watch me wank. I'll make you watch me bring myself off and you won't be able to do anything about it. You won't be able to get your cock into me because you'll be so helpless, tied up and helpless. And I'll come. I'll come on my own hand and my cunt will be all soaking wet . . .' It occurred to Stephanie that in Moscow the telephone exchange had old-fashioned operators and open lines. That was why the line crackled so much. They were all listening, all the foreign operators with smatterings of English. 'I'm going to turn round, then, with my bum towards your face, inch my way up your body . . .' Stephanie's hand slipped between her legs and up into her cunt. It was already wet. '. . . until I'm sitting on your face. Then you can lick me out, can't you?'

'Yes mistress . . .' Devlin groaned.

'And if you don't please me I'll have to have you whipped. Won't I?'

'Oh mistress . . .'

'Whip you until you beg me to stop.'

21

'Please, please . . .' Devlin's voice was only a whisper.

'Are you wanking now?'

'Yes, mistress. I can't help it . . .'

'Then come. I give you permission. Come for me, Devlin. I order you to.' Stephanie penetrated herself deeper, two fingers inside now and the thumb of her hand grinding against her clitoris. Suddenly she heard a loud groan, like a cry of pain. 'Have you come?'

'Yes, mistress.'

Stephanie smiled to herself. Even two thousand miles away Devlin was her slave, putty in her hands.

'Remember, Devlin. I always keep my promises. As soon as you get back here that's what I'm going to do.'

'Yes please, I can hardly wait.'

'Call me in London.'

'I will.'

Stephanie put the phone down and withdrew her hand from her sex with only the slightest hesitation. She was still smiling broadly. She would enjoy acting out that little scenario when Devlin came back next week just as much as Devlin would enjoy thinking about it over his next few days in Moscow. With Devlin's international commitments taking him all over the world Stephanie had got used to turning him on over the telephone. She knew him so well now, all his fantasies, all his proclivities, his whole sexuality, that it was not difficult to fuel his sexual fires until they burned out of control. Not that it didn't fuel hers as well. What she had conjured up on the phone excited her as much as it did him. The pleasure she would get from turning fantasy into reality would be as great for her as it would be for him.

She had no way of knowing that the circumstances of his return would be far from what she expected.

Chapter Two

The Learjet banked in a long wide turn out to the east of London. Stephanie stared out of the window at the vast expanse of blue skies and pure white cloud for the last time as the plane began to descend and the windows were soon enveloped in thick, featureless grey. She could not suppress a shiver. After months of Italian sun on the island the prospect of the damp and cold of an autumnal London made her feel suddenly thoroughly chilled.

But despite the temperature difference she was looking forward to four or five days in the city. There would be lots to do, shops and restaurants and exploring the mysteries of Devlin's London house. The latter in particular was an interesting prospect, considering what she had found there on her last visit.

She had never quite got accustomed to travelling on the private Learjet. Its interior was roomy with four big leather armchairs, a large leather sofa and a bar at one end. There was a fully equipped shower room and a galley big enough to prepare most meals. It was definitely the way to travel.

With the English climate in mind she had used the shower room to change from the light linen suit she was wearing to a black wool skirt and a creamy cashmere sweater.

'We're coming into land, madam.' Susie, the Malaysian flight attendant on Devlin's private jet, had appeared from the forward cabin. As usual she was wearing a rough silk Kheong-Sam, high to the neck but split to the thigh, this one in a jade green that matched her eyes. Her jet-black hair was parted down the middle of her head and cut short, a style that perfectly suited her rather oval face. 'Do you wish for anything else?'

Stephanie had made it a little tradition to have a vodka martini whenever she travelled on the Lear. Susie made them very dry and very cold but one was quite enough today. 'No thanks, Susie.'

'Very well.'

Susie left the main cabin without a smile. Since Stephanie had been introduced to Devlin's ménage her relations with Susie had been frosty. On her first trip on the jet Stephanie had refused to accept Susie's prohibition against interfering with a human cargo the plane was carrying and ever since Stephanie had felt that Susie regarded her with disdain.

As the plane decelerated and sunk lower through the thick cloud the memory of that first trip was very distinct. Though the last six months had produced a series of bizarre and extraordinary events in her life, from her introduction to Devlin and the strange painting that hung in his bedroom, to being drugged and kidnapped by one of Devlin's business associates who had become obsessed with her, to her revenge on him with the help of the beautiful and black Jasmina, let alone all that had happened in the cellars at the castle with the guests, Stephanie remembered everything that had happened in graphic detail. She remembered the way Devlin had fingered and fucked her for the first time, with his banana-sized fingers and his monstrous and gnarled cock, while he stared at the painting that was dominated by a crimson vulva that seemed to be alive. She remembered Venetia and their first experience together, the first time she had been alone with a woman, and the way they had made love since with such passion. But here, on the plane, was the start of an even bigger adventure, her first hint of what lay ahead for her as it had flown her to the castle for the first time. She had wandered into the cargo hold in the rear cabin to find a masked man there, gagged and tied securely to the bulkhead wall.

She could not suppress a grin as she thought about it. Even then, she thought, before she knew anything about the cellars and the slaves, before she had more than scratched the surface of her sexuality, her first response to this bizarre spectacle had not been shock but lust, a surge of lust stronger than anything she'd experienced before.

The double clunk of the landing-gear being lowered snapped her out of her reverie. She checked that her seat-belt was securely fastened and looked down into her lap. The skirt of the black suit revealed an inch or two of slim thigh sheathed in sheer smoke-coloured nylon. Out of curiosity she pulled her skirt up further to reveal the black suspenders that held her stockings and her little black panties. She ran a finger down between her legs over the silky nylon of the panties. As she thought they would be, her reminiscences had made them distinctly damp.

Fifteen minutes later, with no customs or immigration formalities to complete, Stephanie was striding towards the black Mercedes coupé that waited by the Portakabin that served for an arrival hall at the private airfield. Venetia stood by the waiting car, her face breaking into a smile as Stephanie appeared.

It had been some weeks since Stephanie had seen

Venetia. She was struck, as always, by her sculpted beauty. Venetia was tall, her long fair hair pinned tightly to the back of her head in a French pleat, her figure displayed to perfection by a tight red jersey dress that hugged her large, full breasts, clung to her waspy waist and was filled again by the long rich curves of her buttocks. Stephanie felt an immediate pulse of desire, a desire born of knowledge, knowledge of the way the contours of this magnificent body felt against her own, knowledge of Venetia's expertise in womanly love.

'Darling . . .' Stephanie said, kissing Venetia on both cheeks as she held her by the arms.

'You look wonderful,' Venetia said, stepping back to admire Stephanie.

'And so do you.'

'Do you want to drive?'

'No. You drive.' Stephanie liked to drive the big powerful car but she was not in the mood this afternoon.

Venetia opened the boot for the porter who had arrived with the luggage from the plane while Stephanie climbed into the passenger seat. The car was warm and it needed to be. The autumn weather had more than a hint of winter, especially to Stephanie's sun-warmed body.

They drove into London in near silence though not an uncomfortable one. The truth was that the silence was one of anticipation. Both women knew what was going to happen when they got to the house, or to be more accurate Stephanie knew and Venetia hoped.

Venetia's position in Devlin's life was ambiguous. She acted as his roving personal assistant and an expert in computers but, though she had her freedom, she was in the end like any of the other slaves in the

26

castle. She had been caught embezzling from one of Devlin's companies, extracting a large sum of money by virtue of her skill with a computer. The risk of prosecution still hung over her head though now she had become so invaluble to him it was unlikely it would ever be invoked. Nevertheless her position was very different from Stephanie's. And Venetia knew perfectly well it was not her place to make assumptions about what Stephanie might want to do. Devlin had delegated his authority to Stephanie. And it was absolute. There were no exceptions or exclusions.

Venetia drove the big powerful car skilfully. Stephanie watched her long slim legs; the right moved quickly from accelerator to brake while the left remained passive, resting against the transmission tunnel. The skirt of the red dress was too short for Venetia to wear stockings so her legs were encased in tights, their nylon woven with Lycra to give their black colouring a slippery sheen, as though they were wet. Most of her thighs were on view, the skirt only veiling the two inches below the plane of her sex.

'You're a beautiful woman,' Stephanie said, almost to herself.

'So are you.' Venetia's eyes did not leave the road.

'I've missed your body.' It was true. Stephanie only realised how much now she was seeing Venetia again. There was an electricity between them, a tension that was entirely sexual. Stephanie's whole body seemed to be melting with desire. She could hardly control her feelings. And, she reminded herself, she had no need to. She put her hand on Venetia's thigh and squeezed it hard. Venetia moaned. Stephanie moved her hand down between her legs, up to where the nylon covered Venetia's sex. It felt damp. Venetia wore no knickers.

They had come off the motorway and the car was threading its way along suburban streets. At a traffic-light Venetia took the opportunity to steal a look at Stephanie. Their eyes met but neither smiled.

They arrived at the house, a large double-fronted Georgian building, impeccably restored with a circular gravel drive behind a bank of mature cedar trees. It was just beginning to get dark as Venetia brought the car to a halt, its big tyres crunching on the gravel of the driveway.

Stephanie's hand was still resting between her legs. She made no attempt to get out of the car. For a moment the two women sat completely still. Stephanie thought she felt Venetia's labia pulse under her fingers.

'Come on,' Stephanie said, pulling her hand away reluctantly and opening the car door. She strode to the little columned portico where the front door was already being opened by one of the three servants who kept the house permanently available for visitors. He hurried to collect the luggage from the boot.

The heating in the house was on and it felt warm. Stephanie walked straight up to the main bedroom, Devlin's bedroom, the bedroom where the picture of the woman with the extraordinary crimson vulva hung, its colour so vivid it seemed to throb with life. At one time Devlin had only been able to get an erection if he were looking at the picture. Stephanie had changed all that. As her cases were brought into the adjoining dressing-room, Stephanie took a bottle of champagne from the fridge that was set in the wall, carefully concealed by painted panelling, and two crystal champagne flutes which immediately frosted with condensation on contact with the warm air.

Venetia stood in the doorway of the bedroom as

28

Stephanie put the glasses down. She looked uncertain, as though not sure what was expected of her, despite Stephanie's advances in the car.

'Do you want me?' She would like to have put it more subtly but couldn't think of the words.

'Open this,' Stephanie said, handing her the bottle.

While Venetia unwrapped the foil and wound the cage off the cork Stephanie went over to the beautifully made chest of drawers that was the only item of furniture in the room beside the large bed, bedside tables and the black television mounted on the wall opposite the bed. The chest was made of yew inlaid with satinwood. Each of its seventy or so small drawers was fitted with an inset brass pull ring.

'Did you know about this?' Stephanie said, indicating the chest.

'Yes,' Venetia said as she eased the cork out of the bottle with hardly a sound. 'I arranged it.'

'Oh, I wondered who had. He could hardly have got his secretary to do it.'

'Do you know how it works?'

'I found out last time by trial and error.'

Stephanie pulled out one of the drawers at random. It was arranged like a miniature filing cabinet with divisions marked with alphabetically arranged capital letters. The drawer she had opened was divided from SA to TR. Between each card division was a series of envelopes in heavy vellum. Each envelope contained a white index card on which was typed a name and a four-figure number; behind this card was a set of photographs. Stephanie picked out four envelopes, again at random. She threw the envelopes on the bed and picked up the champagne flute which Venetia had filled with wine.

'Cheers,' she said, sipping the Louis Roederer Cristal champagne. She sat on the edge of the bed and flicked open each of the envelopes in turn. Then she chose one and took out the white card and the top photograph. It was of a rather young blonde. The white card identified her as Patsy Francis. Stephanie flicked through the rest of the pictures, first the enlargements of her facial features, nose, eyes, ears, followed by a series of enlargements of her breasts and labia. After these were twelve photographs of her in various sexual positions. Stephanie moved to the second envelope. The white card was neatly typed with the name Katherine Connors who the photographs revealed to be a thirty-five-year-old woman with rather large features and sagging breasts. The third envelope contained Doreen Palmer, a woman whose face was so stunning she could easily have been a professional model and who had a slim willowy body to match. The last envelope was of a woman called Maureen Daniels. She was a black girl, no more than twenty, Stephanie guessed, with a rather podgy overweight body but a very high and proud bust.

Venetia stood watching nervously as Stephanie searched through the envelopes. She was not sure what Stephanie's attitude was to all this. Devlin had ordered her to arrange all the envelopes, get all the enlargements developed and see that the cameras that took the pictures were maintained, though she had had nothing to do with installing them. They had been installed long before she had joined Devlin's household. Some of the photographs went back years. Others were more recent although none had been taken, as far as she knew, since Stephanie had arrived on the scene. Some were women Devlin had had here in the house. Some were slaves from the castle. Still others had been guests at the castle. Not all the photographs involved Devlin; there were couples – carefully cross-indexed – who had stayed at the house or castle, heterosexual and, rarely, homosexual women. All had been photographed – without their knowledge – for Devlin's entertainment and perverse pleasure. Before Stephanie had arrived Devlin had, Venetia knew, spent hours alone in this room, which she had heard Stephanie call his wanking pit.

'Her,' Stephanie said. On the top right-hand corner of the envelope were the letters CD followed by the numbers 640. It was Doreen Palmer. 'Put her on,' Stephanie ordered as she stood up and unzipped the black wool skirt. She let it fall to the floor and then pulled the cream sweater over her head. The black satin bra pushed her breasts together and up into a full cleavage. The tiny matching black satin panties were no more than a frilly triangle of material covering the base of her navel at the front, and a similarly small triangular area at the back. The suspender belt, a wide band of material with very narrow suspenders, was black satin too.

Venetia pulled out the drawer of the right-hand bedside table where the controls for the system were housed. Stephanie had found all this for herself on the last visit to the house. As she unpinned her long black hair and brushed it out Venetia punched the code into the sophisticated computer and the CD-ROM player it controlled. The television flicked to life.

'Take your things off,' Stephanie ordered, her voice not at all friendly. For the moment the tenderness she had felt for Venetia in the car had gone and she was content to treat Venetia as she would any of the female slaves at the castle. She enjoyed Venetia's uncertainty, it amused her. She was playing the mistress

31

again, and it was a role that gave her more than a *frisson* of pleasure.

Without a word Venetia pulled the red jersey over her head. She wore a white underwired bra and the shiny black tights. She reached behind her back and unclipped the bra, leaning forward to shuck herself out of it, then straightening up again, her breasts quivering at their freedom. Stephanie was always amazed at her breasts. Though each was the size of a large round melon, almost three quarters of a sphere, they seemed to be suspended on her chest as if by some invisible support. Her nipples actually pointed upwards, so high and firm was her bust.

Under the tights Stephanie could see the outline of her sex, her sparse, wispy pubic hair hiding nothing. As she pulled the tights down over her long legs Stephanie watched the heaviness of her breasts bouncing against each other. She remembered now how they had felt pressed against her own, their nipples hard as stone . . . She stopped that train of thought. First things first.

Propping herself up comfortably on the left of the bed with the pillows against the wall, she faced the television.

'So let's see what Doreen got up to.' She nodded for the naked Venetia to press the controls.

The screen of the television jumped to life. At first it was only the picture of a bedroom, but not this bedroom. Nor was it anywhere in the castle. The room was sparsely furnished, a bed and not much else.

'Where is this?' Stephanie asked, indicating for Venetia to sit next to her on the bed, on the right where she could still reach the controls.

'It's a flat in Belgravia. Devlin sold it just before he met you.'

A naked man entered the shot. Stephanie had assumed she was going to see Devlin performing with the stunning Ms Palmer but this man had dark olive skin with curly black hair, a thick black moustache and pubic hair to match. His penis was large but flaccid and circumcised; his chest and body, apart from the fleece around his cock, were completely hairless. Though he had a big belly the muscles on his arms and legs were well developed. He sat on the foot of the bed, obviously watching someone out of camera range.

Doreen Palmer walked into the picture. She was just as beautiful as her photographs suggested. Her naked back was perfectly contoured with her scapulae distinctly outlined and her pert, tight but small arse rising abruptly from her long slim thighs. As she knelt in front of the olive-skinned man and looked up into his deep brown eyes she seemed, by contrast, incredibly fair of complexion, her skin almost white, her blonde hair adding to the impression.

'I want to please you,' she said in a rather light but pleasant voice.

'I fuck you.' His accent was Arabic, Stephanie thought.

'No,' the woman said, shaking her head but not smiling, 'that's not want you want is it?'

'I want.'

'Don't you understand? I said I'll do anything. Don't be shy darling. Anything . . .'

'I fuck you,' he repeated.

'Darling,' she said like a mother clucking at a small child. 'Leave it to me . . .'

It was quite obvious from their attitude that neither party was aware that they were being filmed. Doreen dropped her head into the Arab's lap and began to suck his cock into her mouth. She sucked it to erection, which took only a few seconds, then raised her head until all but the glans was out of her mouth. She immediately plunged down on it again, so far down that Stephanie could see her cheeks bulge. After three or four strokes the man caught her head in his hands.

'You make me come,' he said with a hint of anger in his voice.

'Ahmed . . .' she said, letting his cock slip from between her lips. 'You can come in my mouth. I love that. I love spunk. I love tasting spunk. I just want to please you.' Her tone was not something Stephanie understood. It was definitely not that of a lover trying to find ways of pleasing the object of her affections. It was more desperate, as though pleasing this Arab was a matter of some importance.

'I fuck you then.'

'If that's what you want,' she said, but for some reason she did not sound convinced.

Doreen got to her feet. As she turned to get on to the bed Stephanie saw her breasts for the first time. They were beautifully shaped, not large but perfectly round with disproportionately large nipples that were hard and erect with a dark brown areola. She stooped to kiss the man but he turned away.

'No kiss,' he said, brusquely standing up, his erect cock at right-angles to his body.

'Fuck me then,' Doreen said provocatively and with a certain amount of anger. She lay on the bed and opened her legs. Her pubic hair was as blonde as the hair on her head and as thick. She combed it apart with the fingers of both hands, then inserted two fingers deep into her cunt right up to the knuckle. She moaned.

The Arab watched. 'I like this,' he said, standing over her.

'Do you know what I like, Ahmed?'

'No.'

Doreen's fingers plunged in and out of her cunt. The Arab knelt on the bed between her legs so he could get a better view of her masturbation.

'Do you want to know?'

'You like this,' he said as he gazed into her crotch.

'But what I really like. Do you know what I really like?' She seemed more confident now as if she had found the key, as if she knew how to get whatever it was she wanted from this man.

'No.'

'I arranged it before. Look at the top of the bed . . .'

'Bed?'

'At the top in the middle, under the pillow.'

He crawled up the bed on his knees and pulled the pillow away. Lying on the sheet Stephanie could see a pair of handcuffs attached to a short white nylon rope that was obviously, in turn, secured either to the bed or the wall behind it.

'This . . .' The Arab picked up the cuffs and worked them between his fingers as if trying to see how they locked.

'I like to be bound, Ahmed. Helpless. I love the feeling of being helpless.' The rate at which her fingers were pummelling in and out of her sex was now so fast it was virtually a blur on the television screen. But for some reason Stephanie felt this was all a performance, a show staged for the Arab's benefit, to turn him on.

It was clearly working too. The Arab suddenly snaked out a hand, caught the woman by the wrist and pulled her fingers out from between her legs and up over her head, snapping the steel cuff into place in

35

a seemingly effortless manoeuvre. With equal speed he had grabbed and secured the other hand.

'You want . . .' he said gruffly. It was not a question. His erection was much bigger now and a tear of fluid had formed at its tip. Doreen writhed against her bonds, twisting her long slender body on the bed.

'Yes, I want,' she said.

'You want . . .' he repeated, taking his cock in his hand and wanking it hard. With his other hand he leant over her body and pulled her hip, turning her on her stomach. She did not resist, but twisted her head round so she could look back at him. The look in her eyes was full of excitement.

Almost unconsciously Stephanie had cupped one hand over her left breast while the other stroked the black satin that covered the crease of her sex. For a moment she tore her eyes from the television screen to look at Venetia's naked body. There was little to choose between Venetia and Doreen. Both were long-limbed and sensuous. Both had bodies that seemed to purr with sex. But their needs were very different. Stephanie could see Venetia's need. She was not turned on by what was on the screen: Venetia had no interest in heterosexual sex. Her body was throbbing, aching, keening because of Stephanie's proximity, because she hoped and prayed that Stephanie would turn to her soon and use her or ask to be used. Venetia's eyes were on Stephanie's long stockinged legs, flicking up to the satin-covered breasts and the triangle of her belly, when she dared.

Stephanie returned to the television, ignoring Venetia's need for the time being. She was teasing Venetia, she knew, and doing it deliberately.

Doreen's need was for cock. As the Arab moved down the bed she thrust her bum high into the air. In response he slapped it hard with the palm of his hand. Obviously this amused him. He wrapped one arm around her waist and used his other hand to slap each of her buttocks in turn three or four times. Then he got between Doreen's long legs and was pulling her up on to her knees by taking hold of her hips. Her arse was reddened by the spanking he had given her.

'You want . . .' he grunted again.

'Yes,' she said. 'Do it.' She twisted around again to try and look into his eyes but it was impossible with her hands bound and stretched out in front of her. He had pulled her back so far the steel cuffs bit into her wrists.

He pushed his rampant cock forward but not into her labia. His target was higher and smaller.

'You want . . .' It was his litany. With a massive thrust he jammed the head of his cock into the corrugated bud of her anus. Doreen groaned. With his hands on her hips he used all his considerable strength to pull her back onto him. The movement tightened the short nylon rope, Doreen's arms pulled to their limit. She opened the fingers of both hands like the petals of some strange flower, her bound wrists its stem, and screamed as the Arab's penis sunk all the way down into the rear passage of her body. But she recovered instantly and ground her buttocks against his navel, moaning 'yes' every time he thrust forward.

'Who are they?' Stephanie asked Venetia.

'I think the Arab was a customer of Devlin's.'

Doreen was coming, screaming at the top of her voice, her whole body thrashing around on the cock impaled inside her.

'And Doreen?'

'Don't know.'

The Arab slapped his hand down on Doreen's writhing buttock and the thwack of skin on skin filled the air. It only served to redouble Doreen's efforts, thrusting herself against him with new vigour.

'A slave?' Stephanie asked.

'Probably someone he had on the hook.'

'And she's working very hard to get off it.'

The Arab groaned, his big muscles locked and he held himself completely still, letting Doreen's movements bring him off, his cock spunking in her arse.

'She's very beautiful.'

'Yes she is,' Venetia said quietly.

'Turn it off.'

There were the words Venetia most wanted to hear. She pressed the buttons on the bedside console and the screen went black.

'Do you want one of the others?' Venetia asked, hoping the answer would be no.

'It's still early, isn't it? I want to go out and eat something.' Stephanie enjoyed the expression of disappointment she saw on Venetia's face, still in the mood to tease. 'But not yet.'

Venetia didn't know what to do. She didn't like being played with like this but she knew she had no choice.

Stephanie leant forward. 'Undo my bra,' she said deliberately coldly as though issuing an order to one of the slaves.

Venetia knelt up on the bed and reached behind Stephanie's back to unfasten the clips of the bra.

'Take it off,' Stephanie ordered in the same tone. A *frisson* of pleasure ran through her nerves at the sound of her own voice, so controlled, so calculating. The castle had taught her how to please herself, how to get what she wanted. She moved her body not at all as Venetia's hands pulled the satin bra straps from her shoulders, allowing her to work them down over her arms until the cups of the bra fell away from her breasts. Only then did she lift her arms to allow the bra to fall away. Her breasts trembled, their nipples prominent.

She looked straight into Venetia's eyes. She could see her uncertainty, and even a slight flare of resentment at the way she was being treated. Very slowly Stephanie reached up with her hand to touch Venetia's cheek, caressing it gently with the back of her hand. She had suddenly tired of the game she was playing. She didn't want them to be mistress and slave anymore. She wanted them to be two women, equal, together.

'Venetia,' she said, her voice soft and tender now, 'would you make love to me, darling? Do whatever you want to me. I want to feel you again. Like we were the first time.'

'It's different now.'

'It doesn't have to be. I'm sorry . . . it takes me some time to adjust from the castle. Let's just be together.'

Stephanie kissed both Venetia's cheeks and then centred on her mouth, kissing her hard, sucking up her tongue and her lower lip, feeling Venetia's breasts crushing into her, running her hands down Venetia's long spine and over the plump curves of her buttocks. Without breaking the kiss she murmured in Venetia's mouth, 'Do it to me, do it to me . . .'

Venetia's heart was pounding. She pushed Stephanie back on the bed until she was lying flat. Then she moved her mouth down her neck, planting it with little pecking kisses, all the way down her throat and up again, up the long prominent tendons of her neck and onto her ear. She nibbled the fat lobe between her teeth, then sent her hot wet tongue deep into its whorls, deep down as far as it would go. Stephanie moaned and arched her body off the bed as an unconscious reaction to this invasion, feeling the sap oozing out of her sex as she ground her thighs together.

Venetia's hand fell to Stephanie's firm breasts. As her tongue described circles in Stephanie's ear her long fingers teased at Stephanie's hard, puckered nipple. Using her perfectly manicured fingernails Venetia pinched the tender flesh between her thumb and forefinger. Stephanie moaned again.

Leaving her ear, Venetia's mouth kissed its way down the length of Stephanie's neck, down over the hollow of her collar-bone and up along the rise of her breast, replacing her fingers with her mouth at the nipple. Freed from this duty, while her tongue nudged and circled and prodded at the hard button of flesh, her hand smoothed its way down past Stephanie's iron-flat navel and over the silky frills of her satin panties.

Stephanie's legs were already open, one leg bent slightly at the knee, the other flat against the sheets. Using the softness of the satin, Venetia's hand stroked her lower belly, feeling the harsh pubic hair underneath. Then she allowed her hand lower, down over the precipitious curve of the pubic bone until she could feel the softness of Stephanie's labia under the shiny satin. There, down between her legs the material was damp. Venetia stroked gently at first, the whole length of the crease from anus to clitoris, using the satin to press into the delicate flesh. As her tongue worked Stephanie's nipple, moving now from one breast to the other, her hand gradually pressed harder, pushing the satin up into the folds of Stephanie's labia, pressing deeper then with just one finger until the material rode right up into the wet warmth of her sex itself, up until Venetia's finger, sheathed by satin like some strange contraceptive, was up to the knuckle in Stephanie's sex.

Stephanie writhed on it, arching off the bed again, rotating her hips from side to side, feeling the odd sensation of satin soaking up the juices of her body. She was very excited now. The image of Doreen, that slim beautiful body, being opened and buggered by the Arab played in her mind as it had on the screen. She could hear her scream, the unique noise of pain and exquisite pleasure inexorably mixed.

Venetia left the satin pressed into Stephanie's sex but extracted her finger. Releasing the nipple from her mouth she sat up and used both hands to pull at the waistband of the panties, easing them over Stephanie's hips. Stephanie co-operated, lifting her buttocks off the bed. The panties rolled down her thighs until the satin in her sex formed the apex of a triangle of black fabric. Slowly Venetia pulled down, watching the material slip from between Stephanie's labia. Stephanie shuddered as it finally left the folds of her tender pink niche.

Throwing the wet panties aside, Venetia bent over Stephanie's body. She unclipped the four suspenders from the welts of the stockings and rolled the black nylon down Stephanie's legs. She unclipped the suspender belt too and pulled it away. Stephanie was naked.

Venetia looked down at Stephanie's body, allowing the feeling of desire it provoked to rush through her like a drug. She dipped her head until she was kissing Stephanie's navel, inserted her tongue into her belly-

41

button, then licked and kissed her way down until she could feel pubic hair brushing her lips. But she did not delve lower. She had other ideas. Her mouth trailed down the slope of Stephanie's thigh, her lips and tongue working continuously on the inner flesh until it had reached her knee. Here she paused, sucking on the kneecap while her hands, both hands, caressed and kneaded the top of Stephanie's thigh, grazing her labia but no more than that.

As she moved her mouth lower, down over Stephanie's calf, she straightened her legs from her kneeling position so she was lying alongside Stephanie on her stomach. Her mouth reached Stephanie's feet. She licked her toes and sucked on them.

Stephanie's body throbbed. Venetia was a wonderful lover. Her touch, her mouth, the things she did were perfect. Deep in her sex Stephanie felt her excitement gathering like storm clouds, thick and dark and ready to erupt.

Venetia was parting Stephanie's thighs with her hands, spreading them wide apart. As she did she slid further down the bed until Stephanie felt her heavy breasts at her feet. What was she doing? Venetia rolled on to her side and slid the foot of her bottom leg, the one on the sheets, under Stephanie's knee. Stephanie was still not sure what she intended. Venetia's leg pushed up under Stephanie's thigh. Groping around she found both Stephanie's hands and locked her fingers into them tightly. Then suddenly she pulled hard and rolled Stephanie onto her side so their two bodies slid towards each other and the V of their thighs, the melting centres of their sex, were forced together. With their heads at opposite ends of the bed, their legs open, their cunts were crushed against each other, joined.

It was an incredible sensation. Stephanie felt her body pulsing as she held Venetia's hands tightly, using them to lever herself down onto Venetia's cunt. She could feel Venetia's labia, her heat, her wetness, just as well as she could feel her own. They ground against each other, rocking from side to side, their bodies like a modern sculpture of entangled limbs, Venetia's calf at Stephanie's throat, Stephanie's foot curled under Venetia's neck. All that mattered was their cunts, all that mattered was the rhythm of their bodies and the strange but wonderful sucking sensation that their wet labia produced. It felt like two mouths kissing.

As they moved the contact got deeper. It was as though they were melting together. But then, quite suddenly, Venetia changed the angle of their bodies slightly and Stephanie gasped as she felt the bud of her clitoris right up against the bloated, pulsing lozenge of Venetia's. It felt like a cock, a tiny miniature cock, probing against her. She had never felt anything quite like it. Stephanie knew it was going to make her come, the remorseless rhythm as Venetia rubbed their clitorises together was impossible to resist.

'Oh yes, yes . . .' Stephanie moaned. 'Darling . . . yes . . .' They writhed on the bed, rocking, rolling, undulating against each other, like two snakes coiled together.

And then her body gave way and she was falling back down into billowing clouds of sensation, down until she could feel nothing but the incredible sensitivity of her own sex pressing against another cunt, another clitoris, like a mirror reflecting and defining and amplifying every feeling. She knew Venetia had come at almost the same moment. Somewhere in her mind she could just distinguish the pulsing of her own

43

orgasm from the throbbing labia and juicy wetness of Venetia's own climax.

Slowly Venetia unwound herself from Stephanie's body and came to lie beside her, shoulder to shoulder.

'Wonderful,' Stephanie whispered.

'You want more, don't you?'

'Yes, I do . . . You're very sensitive aren't you?'

'What do you want?'

'Godemiché.' It was the word the beautiful black French girl Jasmina had taught her.

'Godemiché?' Venetia looked puzzled.

'It's French for dildo,' Stephanie said, smiling.

Without another word Venetia got up off the bed and walked into the dressing-room. Experimentally Stephanie opened her legs and stroked her labia. They felt tender but deliciously alive, still humming with pleasure. She was not finished. Venetia was right, her body yearned for more. She heard Venetia opening a drawer but could not see her. Her fingers pressed into her clitoris and she closed her eyes as a wave of pleasure shot through her nerves, joining up with the aftermath of the orgasm that still lingered in her body. With her eyes closed she rubbed a little imaginary circle on the tiny bud at the centre of her sex and was overwhelmed again by a rush of exquisite sensation, instantly reminding her of how Venetia's sex had felt pressed so intimately against her own.

When she opened her eyes again Venetia stood by the bed. She had strapped herself into a tight harness of thick black leather. A belt encircled her waist. From each side of her hip and from the middle three leather straps ran down to the junction of her thighs, where they joined to become one, ran up and over her sex and between the cleft of her buttocks. High on her buttocks the strap was then buckled tightly again to the leather at her waist. Where the three straps met, directly over her pubic triangle, a large black plastic dildo had been pushed through a hole in the leather, its base flared out in a shape that neatly covered her pubis and was held firm by the straps. At the apex of the triangle the black plastic was extended, curving down between her legs.

'Is this what you wanted?'

'Where did you get that?'

'There's a whole chest of stuff in the dressing room. Didn't you find it when you were here last?'

Venetia was squeezing a thick sticky cream from a tube over the head of the dildo. She smeared it over the whole length, making it glisten.

'Fuck me, Venetia,' Stephanie said, her excitement increasing as she watched Venetia's fingers working on the dildo. 'I need it.'

It was time. Stephanie scissored her legs apart. There was something extraordinarily sexy about watching Venetia standing there, her gorgeous body strapped with leather, a dildo jutting from her loins, her hand playing with it as though it were a cock.

Venetia knelt on the bed between Stephanie's legs. Then she lent down until her breasts rested against Stephanie's, her rock-hard nipples pressing into Stephanie's chest. With her hand she guided the head of the dildo to the opening of Stephanie's cunt. Immediately Stephanie wrapped her arms around Venetia's back, and pulled herself down onto the black shaft. She was in no mood for subtlety. The shaft filled her, took her breath away with its size. A dildo was not like a cock. It was cold and hard, not warm and alive. Venetia started moving like a man, fucking her like a man would with a cock, bucking her hips up and down, pushing the dildo forward with her pubis.

45

Stephanie's cunt was awash with juices and the lubricant Venetia had applied to the dildo. She could feel its unyielding hardness churning inside her, right up against the neck of her womb, but best of all was the thick black leather that held it in place, crushed into her clitoris. Almost from the moment it had entered her she had started to come again, twisting and wriggling under Venetia's soft feminine body, enjoying the contrast, feeling her spongy tits against her own, her soft arse under her hands, and yet feeling the rigid shaft she was propelling into her like a man. Waves of sensation rolled over her as Venetia's buttocks propelled the dildo back and forth. Waves of sensation joined with emotion and with memory, a thousand sexual images ran through her head. Somewhere at the back of her mind the thought occurred to her that perhaps that was the reason her orgasms were so much more intense and shattering than they had been before she'd started her sexual adventure. Perhaps sex was cumulative, perhaps images from all the orgasms she'd had in the last months joined together each time, conspired each time to bring her off harder, deeper, longer. Like now. Like the orgasm that rushed through her body now, wiping out all conscious thought, destroying everything but sensation, breaking over the head of the dildo and out to touch and excite every nerve in her body and lock every muscle, as her eyes rolled back in her head to envelope her in a blackness so total it was as though she'd passed out.

She felt the dildo slide out of her sex and Venetia's body roll to one side. For a moment she could not move. The aftermath was too involving, demanding all her mind and senses. But as her mind slowly regained precedence over her emotions again, she turned her head to look at Venetia who was lying on her side in a foetal position, her knees drawn up against her large breasts, the big black dildo nestling against her belly.

Stephanie got to her knees. She unbuckled the strap in the small of Venetia's back. Venetia opened her legs and Stephanie pulled the strap away. She unbuckled the waist belt too and threw the harness to one side.

Moving down the bed, Stephanie kissed Venetia's hip. There was no need to return the favour, of course. Venetia was a slave, a thief, she could be used like all the other slaves, used and discarded. But Venetia was special. It was only six months ago that Venetia had been the first woman Stephanie had ever had sex with. That wasn't quite true. There had been a woman before, with Martin, but Stephanie – though the experience had thrilled her – had always thought of that as Martin's fantasy, not her own. With Venetia, for the first time, it had been one on one. She could not delude herself that it was to give a man pleasure. The pleasure had been all her own. Of course then she had known nothing of the castle and all its secrets, and little about her own proclivities.

But whatever she had learnt subsequently had not changed her basic affection for Venetia and she knew it never would. She would play with her, tease her, use her but she could never leave her, as she was now, excited yet unfulfilled.

With pressure from her hand Stephanie indicated that Venetia should turn onto her back. Almost before she had done so Stephanie leant forward, her mouth lapping at Venetia's flat navel. Venetia opened her legs and Stephanie immediately moved her head down to her sparsely haired pubis. She could see where the straps of the harness had chafed her inner thighs and she kissed the red marks tenderly, making Venetia moan.

Venetia's labia were the most symmetrical Stephanie had ever seen, an almost perfect oval neatly contained by fleshy outer lips. Her fair pubic hair, nowhere longer than half an inch but not shaved or cut, only covered the triangle of her belly and there was nothing to conceal the detail of her sex. The labia glistened. Wrapping her arms around the underside of both her thighs, Stephanie used the tips of her fingers on either side to prise the labia apart. The aroma of sex filled the air as they opened with an audible squelch. Stephanie stared into the irregular dark entrance to her cunt. All this was calculated and controlled. What followed next was not. Suddenly something snapped in Stephanie. Her desire to feel and taste and suck on Venetia's hot wet sex overwhelmed her. Still holding the labia with the tips of her fingers, she plunged her head down between Venetia's thighs and centred her tongue on the opening she had made, thrusting her tongue into Venetia's cunt as far as it would go. Venetia's cunt felt tight and wet: she tasted sweet. Stephanie reamed her with her tongue and heard her moan with pleasure. She sucked her labia into her mouth too, greedy to taste every part of her.

Venetia's body was throbbing. She closed her eyes for a moment and in the darkness felt Stephanie's mouth working frantically on her sex. Then she opened them again to watch Stephanie's head bobbing between her thighs, her long black hair draped over her lap.

Venetia was coming. Her body began to sing as

Stephanie's mouth moved up from her cunt to her hard, engorged clitoris. The very tip of Stephanie's tongue teased it at first, just the faintest of touches. But the teasing didn't last long. Soon Stephanie couldn't resist the temptation to take up a rhythm, circle the little bud of nerves with the full weight of her tongue.

Venetia responded instantly. Her body began to heave, her breathing shallow and erratic. Her big breasts were trembling so much she had to steady them with her hands, pinching at her own nipples at the same time. The sensations in her body began to coalesce.

Stephanie sensed her mounting excitement, feeling the thrills of Venetia's body as they coursed through her nerves. Her clitoris was alive, dancing under Stephanie's tongue. Venetia was at the brink, her muscles stretched and taut, her body arched off the bed. At that moment Stephanie drove two fingers straight into the depths of Venetia's cunt, up into the flood of juices that ran down the silky walls. Venetia groaned with sheer unadulterated pleasure. Stephanie added a third finger and pushed all three as deep as her knuckles would allow. Her little finger found the opening of Venetia's anus and slipped into it with ease: the juices from her cunt had lubricated it copiously.

That was the last straw for Venetia. Stephanie's hand, virtually her whole hand, lunging into the two openings of her body, front and rear, took her over the edge. Every nerve, every muscle, everything that was capable of feeling sensation spasmed and locked. She arched off the bed one last time and then collapsed, melted, fell backward into pitch blackness and endless exploding pleasure, her mind completely overloaded with feeling.

But her collapse did not last long. On the back of her orgasm was born a new desire. Stephanie was kneeling at her side, her buttocks raised in the air. Venetia let go of her breasts and reached over to pull at Stephanie's leg. Stephanie knew immediately what she wanted. And Stephanie wanted it too. She swung her legs open, without moving her mouth from Venetia's sex, and planted her thighs either side of Venetia's head, her sex, its thick pubic hair plastered down with its own wetness, inches from Venetia's mouth.

Stephanie's tongue redoubled its efforts. Having felt Venetia's orgasm she worked it harder, not making circles now but long sweeps up and down the whole plane of her sex from clitoris to anus, like a child licking an ice-cream, lapping up all the juices that ran from her body. Then she went back to her clitoris again, tonguing it delicately while her fingers reinserted themselves in cunt and anus and drove home with no gentleness.

Venetia tried to concentrate, fighting the feelings that threatened to overwhelm her again. She looped her arms around Stephanie's thighs and levered her head off the bed. Her tongue found Stephanie's clit, her fingers on her labia. Stephanie could not suppress a moan – though it was gagged on Venetia's sex – as she felt Venetia's hot mouth hard up against her already sensitised clitoris.

Venetia sucked, sucked the lozenge of flesh, sucked it up into her mouth like a limpet clinging to a rock. Stephanie moaned again, feeling herself tempted again, feeling that first tell-tale tingle that told her she would not be satisfied until yet another orgasm was wrung from her senses.

Everything was so exciting; every touch, every taste, everything she saw. What Venetia did to her was perfectly matched to what she did to Venetia. It was a harmony like music and both women knew it would end only one way. They felt each other's excitement, felt the waves of pleasure pounding through their bodies, the peaks getting higher and the troughs deeper until there was nothing but feeling, their clitorises and cunts raw with so much sensation, begging to be released from the tension that filled them.

There was so little time between Venetia's orgasm and Stephanie's that it was like one massive coming. So close were they, so perfectly tuned to each other's body, so able to feel exactly what the other one felt, each nuance of feeling, each wave of sensation, that it was as if their orgasm was doubled, echoing from one body to another like sound in a canyon, bouncing back and forth.

They clung to each other as though they were drowning, their bodies sinking together into the sea of absolute pleasure.

Stephanie was the first to move. She got to her feet and picked up the black leather harness from the floor. The dildo was still wet and glistened.

She strapped the leather around her waist and stooped to pull the harness between her legs.

'Buckle it for me, Venetia,' she said, a tone of hardness creeping into her voice again.

Chapter Three

The black stretched Cadillac limousine was not the ideal car to drive into the centre of London but its chauffeur was used to manoeuvring its length through the sometimes narrow streets and for Stephanie the cavernous and luxurious interior was something she particularly enjoyed. She had not been in it since it had taken her to the airfield for her first flight to Lake Trasimeno and the island castle. That seemed a long time ago now, though it was in fact no more than a few months.

Stephanie had breakfasted lightly and alone. Venetia had gone to the office early to deal with queries from Devlin in Moscow that had come in overnight. As Stephanie intended to spend the whole morning shopping she wore a cream wool dress that buttoned down the front: it would be easy to get into and out of while she was trying on clothes. Her fur coat was beside her on the black leather bench seat of the Cadillac against the possibility of an autumn chill.

She was tempted by the champagne that rested in a silver wine-cooler in a custom-made bar built from walnut, with receptacles for glasses as well as the wine. But she decided she would wait until later; she would probably be glad of a glass around mid-morning.

The Cadillac glided to a halt outside Yves Saint Laurent in Bond Street, the chauffeur quickly getting out and running round to open the rear passenger door for Stephanie. She didn't need the coat. The heavy cloud of yesterday had been replaced by a clear sky and the sun had already taken the morning chill from the air. The chauffeur also opened the plate-glass door to the shop.

Inside, Stephanie browsed happily with an assistant in attendance, obviously impressed by the waiting limousine. For the next three hours Stephanie was in and out of the changing rooms of most of the couture houses in Bond Street: Versace, Ferre, Gucci, Valentino and Lagerfeld. She chose shoes from Rossetti and le Perla underwear from Courtney, the Cadillac following her, her purchases loaded into its vast boot.

By twelve-thirty she was tired and hungry, and decided to forego the champagne in the car for a glass of champagne over lunch. As it was so near she got the Cadillac to take her to the Ritz where she was ushered through the revolving doors in Arlington Street by a uniformed commissionaire and escorted to a table in the bar by a morning-suited under-manager. Almost immediately a smart white linen-jacketed waiter – not so different from the uniform of the castle servants – appeared to take her order.

'Good morning madam, what may I get you?'

'A glass of champagne. And would you ask the restaurant for a table for lunch? Just for one.'

'Certainly, madam.'

The waiter disappeared. It was only a minute before he set a glass of champagne down on the table in front of her. She sipped it gratefully.

'The table's booked, madam,' he said.

'Thank you,' Stephanie nodded, the champagne instantly restoring her energy level. She looked around her as the waiter walked away again. Most of the tables were occupied by businessmen, all wearing suits and talking earnestly. There were two floridly dressed women in one corner, both looking as though they had come up from the country for the day. But apart from them and one woman, a young blonde, sitting at a table with four men, there were no other women to be seen.

'Did you want to see a menu, madam?' A waiter was standing in front of her, holding out a large restaurant menu bound in leather.

'No. I know what I want. Do you have any oysters?'

'Yes, madam.'

'I'll have a dozen please. And then a roast partridge.'

'With a selection of vegetables?'

'Yes. And a good claret. A half-bottle.'

The waiter looked quizzical. 'The good clarets only come in bottles, madam.'

'I suppose you're right. Then bring me a bottle of Haut Brion. A good year. And what I don't drink you can have.'

The remark did not bring a smile to his face. 'Certainly madam.' He bowed slightly and went away.

The one thing the kitchens at the castle could not cater for was English game and the idea of having a partridge had taken Stephanie's fancy. She found herself salivating at the prospect. It was hardly a light lunch but she would compensate by having little to eat tonight.

'Excuse . . .' The voice came from her left. She turned to identify its owner. A middle-aged Japanese man sat at the table next to hers. He was immaculately dressed in a navy blue suit, a white shirt and a navy silk tie. His black hair was thick and wavy, beginning to grey over his ears. His face was rugged and strong, his chin square and his hooded epicanthic eyes a very dark brown. 'Excuse . . .' he repeated, his voice a velvet thickness with only a hint of a Japanese accent, 'I heard you order partridge. What is, please?'

'Ah . . . it's a bird, game bird.'

'Bird, like chicken?'

'Yes. Well no, not really, it's wild. Quite a gamey taste.'

'I try, I think. I have been in England six months but I never heard of this.'

'Oh, the season's only just started. You can only get them in the autumn.'

'I see. I see. Thank you. Please excuse the interruption.'

Apart from his eyes, there was very little Japanese about the man. The way he sat, relaxed and at ease, suggested a strong physical presence. He looked fit. He was, Stephanie thought, a very attractive man.

'Why don't you join me?' she said.

'No. I interrupt. Please forgive this.'

'Not at all. I'd like it, please. Would you like a glass of champagne?'

'In Japan, for a woman to offer man champagne, would be considered . . . odd.'

'We're not in Japan.'

He smiled broadly at that, showing his very white and regular teeth. 'Then I accept.'

The man got up. He was taller than most Japanese men and broad in the chest. His suit fitted perfectly. Stephanie glimpsed a gold Rolex on his wrist and gold cuff-links. He stood in front of her.

'Kakuta Kanjii,' he said, bowing, then extended his hand.

'Stephanie Curtis.' She shook his hand.

He sat in the chair opposite her, his eyes glancing over her body, pausing to enjoy the view of her crossed legs the knee-length of the skirt of the dress provided. Stephanie caught the waiter's eye and ordered another glass of champagne with sign language.

'I do not usually drink at lunchtime,' Kanjii said.

'So what are you doing in London?'

'I come to sell my equipment. I have company that makes machines. Robots. For factories. I work in London six months and in Tokyo six months.'

'Your English is very good.'

'I try. I think it will be better. You have ever been to Japan?'

'No.'

'It is very crowded. But also beautiful. Mount Fuji, and at the sea.'

'I'd love to go there.'

Kanjii talked easily, his body relaxed, occasionally using his hands for emphasis. He had long fingers with his nails professionally manicured; the backs of his fingers and hands were lightly covered with long black hairs. He was more than passingly attractive, Stephanie decided. It was something in those dark eyes, the way they looked at her, his eyelids giving the impression of intensity. Even after the excesses of last night Stephanie felt her body stirring, imagining those hands on her body, and those eyes.

They talked constantly and had lunch together, Kanjii ordering the same meal as Stephanie and enthusing over the roast partridge and the 1971 Haut Brion the wine waiter had selected. He seemed fascinated with every word she said, looking steadily at her across the lunch table in the restaurant overlooking Green Park, the leaves on the trees browned and yellowed by the season, though still mostly clinging precariously to the branches.

'So you live in Italy now?' he asked.

'Yes. In a castle on an island in Lake Trasimeno.'

'It is beautiful, yes?'

'Very.'

'And may I please be personal?'

'You may.'

'You do not wear a wedding band. You are not married?'

'No.'

'But you are with a man nevertheless?'

'Yes . . .' She saw his face fall slightly as she said it, '. . . and no.'

'No?' He brightened at this.

'The castle belongs to a man, yes, but I am a free agent. I do what I please. We have an arrangement.'

'It is what you called civilised?'

'Yes, I suppose so.'

'And he allows you to do whatever . . .'

'It is not a question of him allowing anything,' she said quickly. It came out more sternly than she intended. Of course she could hardly tell Kanjii the truth, that it was not a question of what Devlin allowed her but what she allowed him.

'He must be a . . . an unusual man I think.'

'Yes, that would be a fair description,' she smiled.

They both ordered espresso coffee. It came in tiny white cups. Kanjii talked about Japan and his business and how he tried to adapt himself to European ways. It was, he told her, very confusing especially when it came to women.

'In Japan the women, they now become more liberated, like the West. But still there are old traditions.'

'Which do you prefer?'

He smiled to himself. 'I like of course, you sophisticated Western women. So confident. So stylish.'

'But?'

'If I am honest, of course I prefer the old ways. It is natural. Japanese men were privileged. They were honoured. They were fêted. Women were servants to men, even wives were servants. I would be hypocrite if I say I did not like this. I did. I do. But I know things will change. And I like also the Western way. I find the women, women like you . . . interesting.'

'Tell me about geishas,' Stephanie said as the coffee arrived.

'That is a very complex question.'

'Is it? I thought they were a sort of prostitute.'

Kanjii laughed out loud. 'You are very direct.'

'Aren't they?'

'Oh yes. Yes, that is precisely what they are. But much more also. More honourable I think. And especially more trained. It takes some years to become a geisha, the system is very regulated.'

'And that still exists.'

'Oh yes. Not as much perhaps. And it is now very expensive. Now in Japan there are prostitutes like anywhere in the world. You pay only for sex, quick sex. In the geisha house it is not only sex. It is ritual and respect. The old ways . . .'

'Old ways?'

'Ways to please a man, ways to honour a man.'

'Sexual ways?'

'Yes of course. But in the old Japan sex was regarded as an art or perhaps a science. It was taken very seriously. Here in the West I think it is often regarded in the same way as you regard fast food, something to be dealt with quickly.'

'I don't like fast food,' Stephanie said, gazing into his eyes.

Kanjii returned her stare while he took a sip of his coffee. She noticed he had very long eyelashes.

'The arts of sex belong to the geisha. That is why they must study. If a man has been with the geishas it is something he will never forget.'

'And a woman?'

He looked her straight in the eye. There was a silence before he said, 'The arts of the geisha were designed for men. I see no reason why, in these modern times, they cannot be adapted to a woman.'

'Sounds fascinating.'

'You will excuse me for being a little slow. I still find you Western women very . . .'

'Direct?'

'Yes.' He paused. 'Perhaps you would like to judge for yourself?'

'How can I do that?' His dark eyes seemed to be making her heart beat faster.

'I invite you to my penthouse. The view is spectacular.'

'And?'

'I think you will be surprised. Pleasantly surprised.'

'When?' she said bluntly.

'Why not this afternoon?'

'Why not?' The prospect of spending the afternoon with Kanjii was a thousand times more interesting than more shopping. And she was intrigued.

Stephanie finished her second cup of espresso and made the universal sign for the bill – pretending to write with one hand on the palm of the other – to a distant waiter who nodded and disappeared through the kitchen entrance.

'I will buy the lunch please,' he said quietly.

'No, let me.'

'This is a new experience for me.'

'Then perhaps we are both in for new experiences this afternoon,' Stephanie said as she dropped a credit card onto the plate on which the bill was neatly folded.

They left the hotel together. Stephanie's chauffeur was waiting with the rear passenger door open. He must have spotted her walking down the corridor towards the revolving doors. Kanjii also had a chauffeur, who stood by a smart claret-red Bentley. He dismissed him with a wave of his hand and they both climbed into the Cadillac. Kanjii gave the chauffeur his address, an apartment building in Lowndes Square, and the big car headed off down Piccadilly.

The journey took no more than ten minutes and they both said very little, Stephanie wondering what on earth she had let herself in for and feeling a distinctly pleasant sensation in anticipation. Kanjii contented himself with looking at her knees, clad in ultra-sheer nylon, with a slightly creamy colouring to match the dress.

The doorman at the building opened the Cadillac door almost before the car had come to a standstill.

'Afternoon, sir,' he said, saluting with his other hand.

'Afternoon, George,' Kanjii said, leading the way up a short flight of steps and holding open a large panelled door for Stephanie to enter.

The entrance hall of the building was luxurious, suggesting the cost of the flats it contained. Speckled granite in an orangey black formed the floor with the walls lined in a light peachy silk. A modern stainless steel lift stood opposite the entrance doors. Between the two a fake gas fire burnt brightly in a fire-surround made from another and contrasting slab of granite.

They took the lift to the top floor. The lift doors opened to reveal a short passageway with only one door.

'You have the whole floor?'

'I need the space,' Kanjii said, punching numbers into a combination lock on the doorjamb. The door sprang open.

Kanjii led the way down a long wide hall decorated with small framed Japanese tapestries, into the living room. One side of the room was made entirely of glass and beyond it was, as promised, a spectacular view over the rooftops of London. Stephanie went to the window and stared. On the street below she could see the black Cadillac parked outside the building, the chauffeur leaning against the bonnet talking to the doorman. She suspected he was going to have a long wait.

'So here we are,' she said. 'You were right about the view.'

It was a spectacular apartment too, with absolutely no expense spared. The furnishings were sparse but every item, from the huge white silk sofas to the modern black lacquered cabinets, were superb examples of craftsmanship. Not all the paintings, as with the decorations in the hall, were Japanese or even oriental. But all the Western art was post-impressionist. Stephanie recognised a Rothko and a Miro.

'Would you like another drink?' he asked.

'No, I don't think I would.'

'That is good.'

'So what happens now?' She sat on one of the white sofas and crossed her legs. She watched Kanjii's eyes follow the movement with interest.

'That is up to you.'

'Is it?'

'You are interested in the geisha experience?'

'Yes, but we're a long way from Japan.'

'I adopt many European ways. But I also like to have something of my country always with me. I am a rich man. I can afford what for some men, certainly men in Japan, would be only a dream.'

'Geishas?'

'Precisely so.'

'Here? In your penthouse?'

'If you wish, please come with me.' He indicated a door at the far end of the room. 'You do wish, I think.'

Stephanie got to her feet with no hesitation. Kanjii led her to the door, then opened it and stood aside for her to enter. For a moment she was disorientated. She had been expecting the door to lead to another room; instead it lead directly onto a huge roof garden, a Japanese water garden with a wooden bridge over a quite deep pond stocked with ornamental carp, and full of large white water-lilies. At one edge of the pond a waterfall led down to another pond, only slightly smaller than the first, equally well stocked with fish and flora.

All around the edges of the pond were miniature trees, their branches carefully pruned to encourage artful growth. In the lower pool a series of rocks were assembled in a strict pattern and a bamboo water-clock clunked regularly as its water level rose and fell. A miniature pagoda stood on one shore. Wind chimes hung down from the trees.

Kanjii led the way across the bridge and down a series of wooden steps made from logs to the lower level. To one side, actually set in the side of a grassy bank, was a wooden door, fronted with the bark from some exotic tree.

'This way,' he said.

'It's beautiful,' Stephanie commented.

'I come here for peace. Gardens in Japan are like art too.'

'I can see that.'

He opened the door for her and she stepped through into a small narrow hallway. This was totally Japanese, white paper walls framed in thin black lacquered wood.

'I leave you here for a moment. I must make an arrangement. It is not usual for women to be entertained by geishas.'

'I suppose not.'

'In Japan we have a saying: "Take only what you are given and give only what you cannot take". You wait here please.' With that Kanjii slid one of the white panels aside, slipped through it and drew it back into place.

Stephanie looked around the hall but there was nothing to see. The carpeting was black, and there were no decorations or pictures other than the white paper walls. She could hear her own heart beat. It was more rapid than usual. Then one of the panels slid open and a petite Japanese girl came out into the passageway. She was dressed in white cotton knickers of an old-fashioned design, the cut so low on the leg and high on the waist they looked almost like shorts. Apart from the knickers the girl was naked. Her breasts were virtually non-existent, no more than slight inclines on her chest, and even her nipples were tiny, the size of cherry stones and just as hard. They were an extremely strange colour too, a red so dark it was almost black. Her jet-black hair was cut short and parted in the middle. It was absolutely straight without a hint of a curl and she had a fringe below the parting that covered most of her forehead.

She put her hands together in an attitude of prayer and bowed deeply to Stephanie. Stephanie bowed back but only slightly. The girl said something in Japanese. Stephanie looked puzzled. The girl gestured, obviously meaning for Stephanie to follow her as she turned and set off through the sliding paper panels.

Stephanie found herself in another small hallway, at the end of which the Japanese girl slid open another panel and gestured for Stephanie to step through. The room beyond was an authentic version – at least Stephanie took it to be authentic – of a Japanese bathhouse. The walls were faced in stone and the floor tiled in foot-square slabs of slate. These same slabs had been made to form a rectangular bath sunken into the middle of the floor. Water was pouring into the bath from a large split bamboo pipe, the flow controlled by taps mounted at the side in the floor itself. Onc side of this rectangular bath was inlaid with steps, also made of slate and leading right down into it. Everywhere the room was draped with plants, ivy and palms and eucalyptus. The scent of the eucalyptus filled the air.

Standing waiting for her was not Kanjii but three more girls, all dressed like the first, in white cotton knickers, all with the same short jet-black hair, and all virtually the same height. But though one of the girls had the same flat breasts as the first, the other two had a much fuller shape and, though not large, they were firm and round and topped by ample nipples.

In unison all three girls greeted Stephanie, bowing with their hands together. The first girl spoke in Japanese again. Then one of the other girls came forward, one of those with the more rounded breasts and, clearly from her face, a little older than the others.

'She says please to do nothing.'

'Nothing?'

'Is custom.'

The custom for men, Stephanie thought but did not say. She found herself surrounded by the four women. She felt hands pulling off her dress, taking down her tights and panties, unclipping her bra. In seconds she was completely naked. The four pairs of hands remained on her naked body, guiding her over to the steps of the bath. All four women descended into the water with her, the white cotton knickers immediately soaking up the water and becoming transparent.

The water was well over waist-deep. Each woman took a large bar of soap and began to work on different parts of Stephanie's body; one on her back, one on her chest, one on her left leg and one on the right. To her astonishment two of the women dived below the surface of the water, scrubbing at her legs seemingly without coming up for air.

It may have been her imagination but the geishas – because she knew, of course, that was what these girls were – seemed to be concentrating their attention on her erogenous zones. The hands that washed her back moved to her breasts, the others worked at her buttocks, between her thighs, and over her belly, soaping and rinsing her flesh over and over again. There seemed to be hands everywhere, skilful, sensitive hands, knowing how to make her nerves alternate between being soothed and being excited.

Stephanie felt herself swooning with pleasure. But they had anticipated that and two girls stood behind her to support her weight as she swayed backwards, losing her balance under the dextrous assault. Fingers delved into her pubic hair now. Stephanie knew her cunt was wet but the water sealed her labia. No fingers ventured to break the seal but instead caressed her clitoris while other fingers pummelled and nipped and pulled at her nipples, and lips kissed her neck on either side of her shoulders. There was no pretence of washing now, this was manipulation with only one purpose.

Slowly, almost carrying her bodily out of the water and up the steps, they led Stephanie from the bath. To one side of the room was a small cubicle, its door made from split bamboo. As one of the girls opened the door Stephanie felt a blast of heat, almost like a sauna, and an even stronger smell of eucalyptus. Inside was a low wooden frame like a long rectangular box which had been completely filled with natural sponges to form a springy, soft mattress.

Without her knowing exactly how they did it, the girls seemed to lift Stephanie off her feet. They laid her on the sponges, which were wet but not with water. They had been soaked in some sort of oil. It was an extraordinary sensation, like floating on a sea of silky thick oil, the sponges so soft they felt as though they were not supporting her at all. The oil had been warmed, it was sensuous against her naked flesh.

Three geishas knelt at Stephanie's side while the fourth stood over her with a small earthenware Japanese bowl. Slowly she tipped the bowl to one side and a trickle of warmed oil ran down onto Stephanie's naked body, down first over her neck, then her collar-bone, then the valley of her breasts, then up over her breasts as the geisha moved the bowl. The geisha directed the thin stream right onto one nipple and then onto the other. The warm heavy oil hitting her corrugated flesh made Stephanie shudder with pleasure. The geisha eventually moved the bowl so the thin stream trickled down over her belly, the oil pooling in her belly-button. The stream moved on, down into the triangle of her pubis and along the top of her thighs, right down her legs until it was trickling into her toes.

Stephanie squirmed. She could think of nothing but the physical sensation. She had never experienced anything like this.

The stream of oil finished. The fourth girl put the bowl down and joined the others kneeling at Stephanie's side, two on each side of the wooden frame. She said something in Japanese and immediately the girls' hands descended on Stephanie's oil-smeared body, rubbing the oil into and over her flesh.

She was going to come. There was no way she could stop herself with this sort of attention. Eight hands caressing her, the warm oil making the contact frictionless. The hands stroked and kneaded and massaged her expertly. The hands were powerful, practised, the fingers strong. There was a hand on each of her breasts, and on each of her thighs, and hands reached down through the sponge and out again to knead each of her buttocks. There were hands at her neck and belly and clitoris. She lost track. There were hands everywhere; everywhere that is, but inside her. She was not penetrated either in her cunt or anus.

Not that it mattered. It didn't inhibit her climax. Her body was trembling from top to toe. She was moaning. Not one distinct sound but a continuous noise almost like a whimper.

The geisha who had poured the oil lent forward and whispered in her ear three or four words of Japanese, perhaps forgetting she needed to speak English. Then she remembered.

'For the man he comes now. You too must come. It is expected I think.'

And Stephanie came. But it was not like any orgasm she had experienced before. Instead of a sharp explosion of feeling, her body seemed to open, like the petals of a flower, open up to a steadily rising tide of sensation that completely engulfed her just as much as a normal orgasm. But this did not abate. It kept on and on and on until Stephanie was writhing on the sponges, wriggling against the hands on her body, tossing her head from side to side. The orgasm was not centred on her sex like it usually was: it seemed to be coming from everywhere all at the same time, every inch of her flesh under the probing fingers as sensitive as a clitoris, as open and vulnerable.

On and on and on. Stephanie stilled her body, let it float and felt the heat of the room, and her sweat and the oil that now covered every inch of her body. She lay completely motionless, the hands working unceasingly, knowingly, as she felt herself reach another plateau of feeling: she was totally open, unprotected, the hands touching nerves she never knew she had.

Eventually, after how long she had no way of knowing, the hands left her, one after another, until she was floating on the sponges on her own and her body began to come down from its high. She must have fallen asleep because when she woke up only one of the geishas – the eldest who spoke English – remained. She was sitting on a small wooden three-legged stool by the door.

'You good now?' she asked quietly.

'Oh yes . . .' Stephanie replied. She sat up with difficulty. The geisha helped her to stand. She was not at all sure how she felt.

The geisha led her out of the cubicle. In the corner

of the stone-clad room was a powerful modern shower, with runnels cut into the slate tiling to drain its water away.

'Shower please,' the geisha said. 'You feel better.'

And it was true. As the warm jets of water pummelled her body and washed away the oil, Stephanie felt a sudden flood of health and well-being. This time she was clearly meant to soap herself, which she did vigorously until the last trace of oil had disappeared. By the time she had finished her whole body appeared to glow. She felt alive and alert.

The geisha returned with one of the others and, using two big white towels, they quickly dried Stephanie's body. But this time their touch was strictly practical. Even though they dried her breasts and between her thighs Stephanie felt not a hint of sexual arousal.

As soon as she was dry the geisha indicated an arch at the far end of the bath-house. 'Please . . .' she said. As Stephanie walked over to the arch, another geisha appeared carrying a heavy silk kimono in a very pale yellow.

'Please . . .' the geisha said, now indicating the kimono. Stephanie slipped it over her shoulders with their help.

The geisha who had brought the kimono had changed out of the white cotton knickers and wore a Kheong-Sam in dark red satin, split to the very top of her thigh. Another of the geishas stood by the archway in the same outfit. They both wore make-up, their faces a chalky white, their eyes heavy with black mascara. Their shoes were Western-style white leather court shoes, though with low heels, not the traditional wooden sandals. In fact, apart from the make-up they were not dressed at all how Stephanie had imagined they would be.

While the two geishas who had dried her disappeared, presumably to change, the two in red led Stephanie down another white-paper-panelled hallway, opening yet another sliding panel into a small room. In the centre of the room was a raised dais about a foot from the floor, and on the dais was a simple white mattress. To one side of the mattress was a lamp, a pyramid of white paper under which a lightbulb burned, lighting the room in a dim glow. On one of the white paper walls was a black lacquered table and on the table a single orchid on a long stem was buried in a solid and very tall narrow pyramid of glass.

The two geishas took the kimono from Stephanie's shoulders and while one of the girls folded it neatly the other indicated that Stephanie should lie on the mattress. Stephanie obeyed, feeling again the excitement of anticipation. The room was obviously specially prepared for some ritual: the dais and bed had the feel of an altar. As if to confirm that impression the two geishas knelt on either side of the mattress at the top end. One spoke to the other in Japanese. Whatever the remark meant, Stephanie had the feeling it referred to her body. Almost immediately the other two geishas arrived. They were dressed identically to the first two, the same clothes, the same make-up and the same rather incongruous shoes. Without a word they knelt on the dais on either side of the mattress at the bottom end. All four girls knelt with their heads bowed, their hands folded together on their knees.

As if by a pre-arranged signal each stretched out both hands at exactly the same moment and grasped Stephanie either by the wrist or the ankle. Slowly they pulled her limbs apart until she was spread-eagled on the bed. Almost at the same time Stephanie heard the sound of Japanese music, strange dissonant chords plucked on a lyre-like instrument.

Kanjii entered through the sliding panel. He closed it behind him. In his hand he carried a small black box, its surface a grainy matt finish. All the way round the bottom of the box were louvred bars like ventilation ducts. He mounted the dais and stood looking down at Stephanie's body held open by his geishas. She saw his eyes settle on her sex, its pubic hair newly fluffed up by the shower.

'You are a very beautiful woman,' he said quietly.

She did not reply. She felt her body stirring under his gaze. She had been through some strange sexual experiences in the last month, but this had to be one of the strangest. Two hours ago she had been sitting having lunch with this total stranger. Now she was lying naked in front of him with four women holding her down, women who had already explored her body intimately.

Kanjii wore a light black kimono under which his legs were bare.

'Seven centuries of the art of sex. That is what the geishas are taught,' he said. The geisha holding her left hand lent forward and put her finger to Stephanie's lips. 'It is a custom that you say nothing. It is expected. You are treated as a man so you behave, please, like a man.'

Kanjii did not smile. He walked around the mattress and set the black box down on the dais just behind Stephanie's head. It seemed to be humming slightly. 'We Japanese allow technology to help us even with the most ancient of our rituals. This is the ritual of five-pointed star.' He indicated her wrists and ankles held tightly by the geishas and then

71

Stephanie's open vulva. He returned to the foot of the bed.

Slipping the kimono off, he let it fall to the floor. Stephanie looked at his body. It was hard, muscled and hairless but his cock was small. He knelt on the mattress between her legs. The eldest geisha handed him a strange object made from what looked like ivory. It was in the shape of the thumb and forefinger of a hand except the thumb was double the thickness of a normal thumb and the forefinger twice as long.

Stephanie was aware of a sweet-flowered aroma. It seemed to be coming from the black box behind her head. But it was more than just a perfume. She breathed it in deeply and felt a surge of pleasure akin to sudden intoxication.

Kanjii said a single word in Japanese. The four geishas tightened their grip on Stephanie's body, stretching her limbs further apart, rocking back on their heels. Kanjii took the ivory object and moved forward on his knees until he was between her thighs. He used the finger of the ivory to caress between Stephanie's labia and up under the little hood of flesh to her clitoris.

Stephanie felt her body shiver with excitement. The ivory felt cold and hard. Kanjii used it to circle the little nodule of nerves. He could sense her arousal. Her labia were wet, her body trembling.

Very slowly he pushed the ivory lower, using the tip of its finger to nudge gently into her cunt.

Something odd was happening to Stephanie. She was excited out of all proportion to the stimulation she was receiving. She could feel her whole body pounding as though her pulse was racing. As the ivory nosed into the wet walls of her cunt, no more than an inch, as she felt her body stretched taut, she knew she was going to come and she knew why. Whatever the little black box was producing, the aroma was enhancing her sexual feelings, heating her blood. It made her feel that there was nothing but sex, that she was drunk, drunk on sex. As she felt the curved finger of ivory probe her body she came, sharply, almost painfully, her nerves sending shock-waves of sensation spiralling through her.

Kanjii rode the long finger of ivory up into her cunt on the tide of orgasm. Now the thick thumb was nudging her anus. He pushed on, the bud of her anus parting to admit the intruder.

Stephanie took a deep breath, wanting to inhale the intoxicating scent. As the fumes worked into her body she felt her mind react, another surge of passion. As the thick, cold ivory penetrated her anus Stephanie came again as sharply as the first time, her body quivering with excitement. She wanted to move but the geishas held her tight. She knew the pressure on her wrists and ankles, the tautness in the tendons of her elbows and knees, was increasing her pleasure. She could feel her orgasm acutely there, where she was stretched apart. But it was not only the constriction that was making her come so forcefully, nor the stupefying aroma. The ivory itself seemed to be reaching into places in her sex she had never felt before, places where new nerves delivered new sensations.

Kanjii pushed the dildo home, right up her, the thumb in her arse, the long thin finger deep in her cunt. He could feel what was happening to her. It was beginning to happen to him too. He was not immune to the fumes from the black box, he could feel his blood racing and his excitement increasing. His cock was rock-hard and throbbing. The perfume from the box coloured every sense, intensified every sensation.

Stephanie strained her head up off the mattress, wanting to see what Kanjii was doing. His hand was working the dildo between her legs, pulling it in and out of her body. She looked at each of the geishas. They were all watching Kanjii work, watching the ivory slide in and out of her sex. The idea wrung another orgasm out of nowhere. She bucked her body against its force, the strong hands of the geishas holding her tight.

Kanjii pulled the ivory from her body and briefly caressed her clitoris with the tip of his finger. In contrast to the dildo his finger felt so warm Stephanie almost came again. She knew the powerful flowery aroma was responsible for her vivid reactions. She breathed deeply again, wanting to embrace its effects.

'Now it is time for the ritual of the single flower.' As Kanjii said the words the geishas released Stephanie's body, her tortured limbs reacting with a flood of pleasure which almost sent her over the edge again. He leant forward and carefully positioned himself so he was lying on her body, his cock where the dildo had been at the entrance to her cunt. She could feel her juices leaking out over it.

The geishas were pulling the single sheet that covered the mattress out and wrapping it over Kanjii's back, encasing them both in the white cotton. Under the sheet Stephanie saw a series of wide satin ribbons laid out one against the other, all the way down the bed. Kanjii suddenly thrust his cock forward, up into Stephanie's cunt. Stephanie shuddered with delight. Whereas the dildo had been thin and cold, Kanjii's cock by contrast was thick and hot. It did not fill her. But the nerves the dildo had awakened seemed to be ultra-active and sung their pleasure at this new invasion.

The geishas were picking up one ribbon at a time, wrapping them around Kanjii's back, first over Stephanie's shoulders, then down his spine, one after another until even his buttocks were encased. They tied them tightly, forcing Kanjii's body against Stephanie's. Once their torsos were bound they turned their attention to their limbs. Closing both Stephanie's and Kanjii's legs, they bound ribbons around them until they too were completely enclosed and held tightly together. As their arms were bound to their sides by the ribbon around their backs, in minutes they were totally enveloped in white satin ribbon. Only their heads were free. That did not last long. Kanjii's mouth moved over Stephanie's, his tongue immediately penetrating her lips, as she felt ribbon being wound around her head, not as tightly as the bindings on their bodies but tightly enough to hold them together. Now darkness descended and she could only feel.

Kanjii did not move. His cock and his tongue were deep inside her but he did not move. He could not move. Neither of them could. All Stephanie could do was feel. She could feel her nipples, hard as rock, pressed flat into Kanjii's muscular chest. She could feel the whole length of her body, the body that had been washed and oiled and pampered by the geishas and now felt so sensitive it was almost as if it had never felt anything before. She could feel, most of all, her cunt, clinging tightly to the hard bone of Kanjii's cock, her juices running down him, her clitoris bound against him, the very mouth of her womb seeming to kiss the tip of his glans.

Stephanie was more aware of her own body than she had ever been. She could hear her pulse drumming in her ear. She could feel her heart beating. The aroma that she had inhaled still lingered in her mind, enhancing every feeling.

Still Kanjii did not move. She wondered if he could. They were bound so tightly together he probably couldn't. But he didn't try. His cock was throbbing, though, and it seemed to be getting hotter and hotter, like a red-hot poker inside her.

Things began to change. She felt herself losing sensation, her body going numb. But the more she lost from her outer limbs the more she gained in her sex. She didn't think she had ever felt a cock so clearly. She seemed to be able to feel every detail of it, the ridge of the glans, the long swollen tube of the urethra on the underside. It was as though her cunt had become articulate, as though it was a hand clutching and holding and sensing every inch of his cock.

She sucked on his tongue. She sucked hard and felt his cock's reaction, twitching inside her. The pulse of his body seemed to increase. She could feel his excitement building. Of course he was feeling exactly what she was feeling; he would be able to feel her cunt just as graphically, and her tits, and the long contours of her thighs.

Kanjii's cock swelled inside her, filling her more, throbbing harder. She knew he was going to come. And what was more astonishing was that she knew she was going to come with him. She knew she would feel his spunk better than she'd ever felt spunk before. She gloried in her good fortune, in all the wonderful sexual feelings the geishas had given her. And now this . . .

Kanjii's cock swelled again. So sensitive was her cunt now that Stephanie could feel his spunk rising from his balls. He had not moved. He didn't need to.

His cock began to spasm, bucking against the confines of its delicious wet prison. He moaned, the sound echoing in her open mouth, and his cock jerked wildly inside her, spitting spunk, hot white gobs of spunk, right out into the depths of her cunt. She had never felt anything like it. She could feel every jet, she felt it hitting her womb, the very top of her cunt. She could feel every bit, each separate, distinct, each cranking up the engine of her own orgasm, already primed and ready, until the biggest eruption of all, the final spasm, splashed spunk deepest of all and sent Stephanie crashing down into an orgasm like nothing she had had before. Her body fought to express its pleasure in movement but the ribbon held her tight. Her nerves reacted against the constriction seemingly by doubling their feeling, action and counter-action becoming the same.

Inside her, almost at once, she felt the spunk trickling down the already soaking wet walls of her cunt, down over Kanjii's balls. Another orgasm, not as intense but just as pleasurable, rocked her into complete submission.

He handed her the small cup of sake served at body temperature. She drunk the sticky, strong liquid gratefully. She needed it, needed it badly.

'I've never experienced anything like that,' she said honestly.

'The geishas adapted well, I think. They are not used to dealing with women.'

They were back in the main living room. It was dark now and the panoramic windows provided an amazing vista of London's lights from the Telecom Tower to the hotels of Park Lane. The sake was served in a special china bottle. The cups were tiny and Stephanie had downed hers in one gulp. Kanjii refilled the cup.

'What you have experienced is only the beginning. There are many rituals. The art is in the ritual and in knowing which ritual is best for which person. That is what a geisha is trained for. And I know too, I think.'

'Know what?'

He sipped his sake before continuing. 'I know what would be the ritual you would most enjoy.'

'Well I certainly enjoyed the . . . what did you call it?'

'First the five-pointed star. Then the single flower.'

'Actually I don't think "enjoy" was the right word.'

'But for you I think the Seven Samurai . . .'

Stephanie felt a little thrill of excitement. 'What does that involve?'

'I cannot tell you. It is for a man of course. It would have to be adapted to a woman. But that would be no problem. I would show you but you will be returning to Italy . . .'

'No, not for a few days.' Stephanie was intrigued again, which she was clearly meant to be.

'Tomorrow I have to go to Paris. But the following evening . . . Thursday?'

'Thursday is fine.'

Stephanie felt a shiver of anticipation run down her spine. It was a delicious feeling. Her whole body was still recovering from the sensations it had experienced. The geishas had slowly and gently unwrapped the ribbons that had bound their bodies so tightly together. They had taken Stephanie back into the bath-house, where they had helped her shower and left her alone to put on her clothes, which were brought to her neatly folded. The eldest had then escorted her through the Japanese garden and back into the living room where Kanjii was waiting in slacks and a clean white shirt.

'I expected the geishas to wear a more traditional costume,' Stephanie said.

'In Japan they do, of course. But here it seems right to adapt a little. For myself too I find it more ... sexy.' For the first time since she had met him, Kanjii's face was grinning broadly.

'And did you find me sexy?'

'You, my dear lady, were perfection. For a Western woman.'

'Of course.' Stephanie was not at all offended by the reservation. 'After what I've been through I can hardly imagine anything more ...'

'Interesting?' he suggested.

'Fulfilling,' she said.

He insisted on showing her down to her car. The chauffeur was asleep at the wheel, a newspaper covering his face. He started awake and ran round to open the passenger door.

'Till Thursday then,' Kanjii said, kissing her hand lightly and then bowing.

'Eight-thirty?' Stephanie asked.

'Fine,' he said.

'I can't wait.'

She got into the big back seat of the Cadillac and realised it was perfectly true. She couldn't wait.

Chapter Four

Having more or less completed her trawl of the Bond Street and South Molton Street shops on Tuesday, Stephanie decided that on Wednesday she would investigate Knightsbridge and Sloane Street. She got the Cadillac to drop her off at Harrods where she browsed happily for an hour before walking down to Harvey Nichols, telling the chauffeur to wait at Montepeliano where she intended to have a light lunch.

As she walked through Knightsbridge, looking in shop windows but not bothering to go into any of the shops, she had a strange, unaccountable feeling: that she was being followed. Standing in one of the shop doorways she pretended to be looking at the clothes but glanced instead behind her. There was no one who looked remotely interested in her. A burly ginger-haired man in a suede blouson walked past her and up the street without giving her a glance and a small sprightly woman in her sixties, carrying a miniature poodle, did the same. No one dived into a shop to hide, or turned and walked in the opposite direction. No one appeared in the least interested in her. She looked both ways. The ginger-haired man had disappeared.

It was a bout of paranoia, Stephanie decided, though what had caused it she couldn't imagine. She walked on, glancing back over her shoulder from time to time but never once caught anyone who could properly arouse her suspicions.

In Sloane Street she wandered into one or two shops and tried on various items: skirts, blouses, a suit. But whether it was because she could find nothing to her taste, or just not being in the mood for shopping, she bought nothing. She felt an odd sense of foreboding and whatever she did she couldn't shake it off. The entirely irrational prospect of being followed had raised a spectre in her mind that she had never been able completely to lay to rest. After all she had been drugged and kidnapped from the castle only months ago, held in a cellar, naked and cold, for days. Though she had managed to free herself and get her revenge on the perpetrator, the experience, not surprisingly, had left its mental scars on her. If it hadn't been for her own guile she could have been there still. The thought chilled her, and for a second she stood in front of a row of clothes and shivered.

'Are you all right, madam?' A rather matronly assistant asked, seeing the colour drain from Stephanie's face.

'I'm fine,' she replied. 'Thanks.'

She walked past the concerned woman, out of the shop and strode purposefully towards Montepeliano. What she needed was a drink and something to eat, then she would feel better.

And she did. Seated in the bustling Italian restaurant with a stiff vodka martini in front of her and her chauffeur seated outside in the car, she felt her confidence return. She damned Gianni, her kidnapper, and was able to smile to herself at the thought of what she had done to him by way of revenge.

She ate some grilled prawns and a green salad and drank most of the bottle of vintage Barolo, which didn't go with the fish at all but which she ordered because she wanted something warm and full-bodied.

It was the cold in the cellars in which she had been trapped that had left the deepest mark on her psyche and whenever she recalled the experience it took her some time to make herself feel warm again. A large double espresso helped too.

Feeling better, she got the Cadillac to take her to the top end of the Fulham Road where she had read of a clothes shop she particularly wanted to see. The chauffeur indicated where he would wait for her and she ventured into the highly decorated shop, its exterior hand-painted in a marble effect of black and green. The interior continued the same colour scheme, the centre of the shop very dark but the clothes arrayed on rails that were bathed in pools of light from overhead spots.

The clothes were certainly unusual but so outrageously expensive that, even on Devlin's budget, Stephanie blanched. It was not only the money. The styles were so outré it was difficult to imagine a single occasion she could wear them on. They were definitely not clothes that would turn Devlin, or any of Devlin's guests, on.

Disappointed, she wandered out and was thinking about going home when she noticed a small shop window opposite and a few doors down from the pretentiously marbled emporium. The absolutely plain but beautifully cut black dress in the window was in such contrast to the over-elaboration of the clothes she had just seen that Stephanie liked it immediately.

The old-fashioned bell above the door tinkled as Stephanie entered the shop. It was small with only two rows of clothes, one on each side of a narrow space. There was a small counter at the back and a curtain behind which was what Stephanie took to be the changing room. As she browsed through the first rail of clothes a woman appeared from behind the counter.

'Can I help you?' she said, smiling and coming round into the centre of the shop. She was an extraordinarily striking woman. Her hair was long and very blonde, her strong face beautifully balanced by high cheek-bones and a long but slender nose. Her eyes, edged with eye-liner and shadow, the lashes thick with black mascara, were very large and very blue. Her mouth was big too, her fleshy lips in a shade of lipstick that could accurately be called jungle red. It matched the nail varnish painted on her long, manicured finger-nails.

'I'd like to try on the dress in the window,' Stephanie said.

'Of course.' The woman went to the rack of clothes opposite and extracted a black dress. She held it up. 'This is your size, I should think.'

She took the dress and went to the curtain at the back of the shop. Stephanie followed her. The woman wore very high-heeled black court shoes and a black skirt that hugged the curves of her large but shapely buttocks. Above the skirt she wore a white silk blouse through which Stephanie could see the lace of a white teddy. Her long legs were sheathed in black nylon with a fully fashioned heel and seams running up the dead centre of her slim calves. Though her body was attractive it didn't quite match her face. There was something angular and a little awkward about it. Even her breasts, which were not large, appeared to jut out rather than flow from her chest.

She held the curtain aside and hung the dress on a hook just inside the entrance. The changing room was not the usual cubicle size. It was more like a small room with a re-upholstered Victorian *chaise longue* and a large full-length mirror on one wall. The ceiling had been tented with a rich red material which had also been used in panels on the walls. The thick carpeting was in a light pink.

'This is pretty,' Stephanie said.

'I always hated those little telephone-box changing rooms. Can't relax in those. If you need anything I'll be outside.'

The woman let the curtain drop and Stephanie unzipped the light grey jersey dress she was wearing and tried on the black. As she had suspected, it was sexy and flattering, its cinched waist emphasising her full breasts and the curves of her hips. She whirled in the mirror, then went out into the shop.

'Oh, that really suits you,' the woman said.

'I think so.' Stephanie looked at herself in the mirror at the front of the shop in natural daylight.

'What's this material?'

'Unusual, isn't it? Moiré taffeta.'

The material made patterns of shade in the clinging black.

'It's beautiful. I'll take it.'

'It's my own design.'

'Really?'

'Everything in here.'

'Well, congratulations. It's great.'

For the next hour Stephanie tried on almost everything in the shop and ended up buying three dresses and a yellow suit, all beautifully tailored and cut. She had looked at the lapels which all read: VIVIENNE ELSON. Vivienne Elson, Stephanie decided, was a clever woman. She was definitely going to make this shop a regular stop whenever she came to London.

Stephanie had watched Vivienne through the gap in the curtains as she'd changed into the various outfits. Vivienne had a pose and grace about her as she walked around the shop straightening clothes here, rearranging the flowers there, generally fussing over detail. There was something unusual about her and it was an unusualness that Stephanie found very attractive.

She supposed it was natural, considering the life she now led, but to Stephanie a sexual agenda always seemed to be very close to the surface. Even the chill she had experienced this morning had not apparently cooled it. Of course what had happened with Kanjii still burned in her body and mind vividly – if she cared to think about it she could still feel his spunk shooting into her – so, she supposed, it was not surprising that her response to this obviously very talented woman should be, at least in part, a sexual one.

'Could you help me?' she called. The zip on the last dress she had tried seemed to be stuck. Or was that just an excuse? She could have worked it free on her own.

'Of course.'

Vivienne pulled the curtain aside and entered the changing room.

'The zip . . .' Stephanie turned her back so Vivienne could see for herself.

Cool fingers freed the obstacle and pulled the tongue of the zip down into the small of Stephanie's back, making the zip sing.

Stephanie stepped out of the dress and replaced it on its hanger. 'I think you're very clever,' she said, then turned to face Vivienne. 'And very attractive.'

'Thank you,' Vivienne said, blushing slightly. But she did not move. 'So are you.' She took the hanger from Stephanie and their hands touched. Immediately Stephanie kissed Vivienne on the cheek, feeling a sudden rush of excitement as she did so. Seducing women was not something she'd done often.

'What was that for?' Vivienne asked, her eyes looking at the rich contours of Stephanie's body, covered now only by a deep blue three-quarter cup bra, matching tanga panties and grey hold-up stockings whose welt was so high they practically grazed Stephanie's crotch.

Stephanie paused before she said, 'I find you very attractive.'

'You mean sexually?'

'Yes. And let's say I don't believe in repressing my feelings any more. I've learnt not to. If you find the idea unacceptable then we'll forget I ever said it.'

'Are you a lesbian?' Vivienne made the word sound like some sort of medical disorder.

Stephanie laughed. 'I like sex. I enjoy it. Men and women. As far as I'm concerned it all comes down to the same thing.'

'I like it too,' the woman said with a wistful tone that Stephanie didn't understand.

'What does that mean?' Stephanie asked.

'Nothing.'

Stephanie took a step forward, wrapped her arms around the white blouse and pulled Vivienne into a full-blooded kiss, pressing her tongue into her mouth. Vivienne did not resist. She kissed back tentatively at first and then more firmly, wrapping her arms around Stephanie in turn.

'Can you close the shop?' Stephanie said when their mouths parted.

'Now?'

'It's nearly five.'

'Look, I think there's something I should tell you . . .'

'Just lock the door.'

Stephanie sat on the *chaise longue*, putting one foot up on the seat and leaving the other on the floor so her legs were apart and the flat plane of her sex, covered by the tight-fitting blue panties, was exposed. Her thick pubic hair under the material made her crotch look as though it had been padded.

Vivienne hesitated, then walked into the shop. She returned seconds later and this time, with no hesitation, knelt on the thick carpet in front of Stephanie's open legs. She bent her head and kissed the knee of the leg that rested on the floor, then worked her mouth up the stocking to the welt that held it in place. It was as though she had made a decision and wanted to carry it through quickly before she could think to change her mind.

Her mouth slipped onto the open crotch of Stephanie's panties, sucking on them, sucking through them to Stephanie's sex. Her mouth felt incredibly hot. Stephanie moaned. Again with no hesitation, Vivienne's fingers delved under the leg of the panties until they were pressed into Stephanie's labia, and then, straight up with no impediment, into her cunt.

'Is that what you wanted?' Vivienne asked as though proud she had proved something to herself. Her voice was much lower in tone.

'Yes . . .'

Stephanie had got what she wanted again. She had aroused Vivienne's interest. She had no idea if Vivienne had ever done this with a woman before and didn't want to ask. Of course, she should never have started this. It was crazy. The last thing in the world she needed was another sexual experience, not after Venetia and Kanjii and everything else. What was wrong with her? Was it like a drug, the more she got the more she wanted? Or was it just that her sexual temperature was so high at the moment it was simply irresistible?

She should have apologised to the woman, told her it was a mistake and gone home. Or arranged to meet at another time when she was next in London. But though that was what she should have done, it was not what she had any intention of doing.

Instead Stephanie wriggled herself down onto the two thick fingers that probed her cunt, feeling herself juicing around them.

'Is this what you wanted?' Vivienne repeated, pushing a third finger up alongside the other two while her other hand went into the high-cut leg of the panties and searched Stephanie's pubic thatch until she found her clitoris.

'Yes . . .' Stephanie moaned.

With no delicacy or finesse, the tip of Vivienne's finger started to wank the clit from side to side, vigorously pressing down on it at the same time.

'And this . . .'

The finger worked harder in time to the thrusts of the others in Stephanie's cunt. Stephanie wanted to reach out and hold her back, stop her being so fierce, but at the same time she was enjoying – if enjoyment was the right word – the lack of subtlety. There was something basic about what Vivienne was doing to her, like someone who had not done something before or at least had not practised it for a long time. Either way the energy was exciting and Stephanie didn't want to spoil her enthusiasm.

Besides, it was only seconds before Stephanie lost the ability to do anything consciously. For some reason she suddenly smelled the strange aroma from Kanjii's black box and it kicked her body into a higher gear, making her juice copiously, opening her body like a flower, allowing Vivienne's fingers deeper on their inward thrust.

Vivienne could feel her response. Remorselessly she wanked at the hard knot of her clit while her fingers imitated the action of a cock. It had been a long time since she'd done this. She shouldn't have been doing it now. She should have ignored this woman's provocation and done nothing. But she couldn't. There was something about her, something too profound to ignore. It was beginning to hurt her, as she knew it would, and hurt her a lot, but she was determined she would finish what she had began.

Stephanie felt her body climbing to the brink. She looked at the woman kneeling between her legs, a stranger, a stranger minutes before, now doing the most intimate things to her. It was a power she seemed to have, a directness and honesty. It would never have occurred to her before but now it was a trait people responded to. It was power.

Her nerves sung, the different chords came together and became one harmony, her body vibrating in unison and pitching her over into the black abyss where there was only absolute pleasure.

Vivienne sensed that the climax had passed. She pulled away gently, but remained on her knees. She looked awkward and embarrassed.

'I'm sorry. I didn't ... I mean it was too hard to ...' she said, not finding the right words to express her confused feelings.

'Shh ...' Stephanie said.

'I just haven't ...'

Stephanie slipped down beside her on to the soft carpet, putting her arm around Vivienne's shoulder. 'Now it's my turn,' she said, caressing her arm.

'No,' the woman said in alarm.

'Why not?' Stephanie said, moving her hand to Vivienne's breast. Strangely it felt cold.

'You can't.'

'I can.'

Stephanie kissed her on the mouth. At first Vivienne resisted. But she was weak. She allowed Stephanie to push her back onto the floor until she was lying on her back with Stephanie beside her. She allowed Stephanie's tongue between her lips, though even then she was mouthing the words 'no, no, no,' as Stephanie's hand unzipped her skirt at the side and delved beneath the waistband. But Vivienne did not make any attempt to stop her: she had accepted the inevitable.

Stephanie's hand felt a suspender belt holding up the seamed stockings but there was something else under the white teddy. It was a pantie girdle, a very tight pantie girdle. She wormed her hand under the teddy and on to the elasticated girdle, down to Vivienne's crotch, at which point Vivienne broke the kiss.

'I tried to tell you,' she said as she felt Stephanie's fingers feeling around the shape and weight of her cock and balls, heavily strapped up under the unyielding crotch of the pantie girdle but obvious nevertheless.

'You're a man?'

'Yes. I'm sorry. I should never have ...'

'Then fuck me.' Stephanie said simply.

'What?' Vivienne looked astonished. She had expected distaste and disdain, but not this reaction.

'You heard.' Stephanie was looking down into Vivienne's big, heavily made-up eyes, and feeling tantalised by what she saw. The idea that this beautiful woman, as feminine and lovely as any she'd seen, also had a cock was exciting, wonderfully exciting.

Vivienne could see she was serious that she meant what she said.

'Give me a minute.'

She got to her feet, walked through the curtain and out into the small office that was tucked behind the shop counter.

Stephanie watched her through the gap in the curtains. She pulled off her blouse and the skirt. A tight white bra held spongy, flesh-coloured artificial tits in place under the white teddy. Vivienne unhooked the crotch of the teddy and pulled the heavy pantie girdle down her hips. Quickly she unstrapped the cock from the tiny belts that held it down. It erected immediately, pushing up inside the lace of the teddy, framed by the long fingers of the white suspender belt.

Vivienne's hands were trembling. She adjusted her hair in a little mirror on the office wall and adjusted her stockings. The crotch of the teddy hung down between her legs like a tail. She debated taking the teddy off altogether but the bra that held her tits in place was so ugly on its own. Taking a deep breath, she walked back into the changing room.

Stephanie had taken off the deep blue panties. She was fingering her labia through the thick pubic hair, feeling her own excitement. She wanted to be fucked by the strange vision that stood in front of her.

'You've made me very hot, Vivienne.'

'No one's ever seen me like this.'

'You're beautiful. You're a beautiful woman with a cock. It's the best of both worlds. All the softness and femininity of a woman, all the hardness of a man.' It was true. In an odd way the cock seemed not to belong to Vivienne. It was a thing apart, an afterthought, an appendage.

91

'Shall I keep the teddy on? It looks strange undone like this.'

'Just come down here and fuck me, Vivienne,' Stephanie said, emphasising her name.

Vivienne knelt in front of Stephanie, the cock still entangled in the white lace. The fluid it had produced made a wet mark on the front of the teddy. Stephanie pulled the material away and circled the phallus with her hand.

'Fuck me,' she said.

Vivienne slid down on top of her. The cock slipped between her legs and up into her labia, as nylon stockings rasped together at the top of their thighs. Stephanie bucked her hips to position it at the opening of her sex and immediately skewered herself down on it. Vivienne moaned. The cock felt big and hard and hot. Stephanie wanted it badly. The whole image of this 'woman' had turned her on. Her hands caressed Vivienne's thighs deliberately feeling the welts of the stockings and the long white suspenders. She brought her hand up to Vivienne's chest to squeeze at her bra. The strange rubbery filling underneath felt sticky and gelatinous but Vivienne moaned as though Stephanie had squeezed a real breast.

'You're so wet,' Vivienne whispered in her ear.

'It's you, you're turning me on, all this ...' she fingered the bra to indicate what she meant.

Vivienne began to move her cock in and out of Stephanie's liquid cunt. It felt so good, so welcoming. She was turned on too, turned on by this woman's acceptance of her, of what she was. She pummelled faster and harder.

Stephanie raised her head to look down over Vivienne's shoulder and watched her buttocks plunging in and out between Stephanie's thighs. She could see the white suspenders and stockings pulled taut, she could feel the silky teddy against her, she could smell the perfume Vivienne was wearing. She was being fucked by a woman, not with a cold plastic dildo but by a hot hard cock.

She could feel Vivienne coming, the cock swelling, the rhythm increasing. She wanted Vivienne to come because she was coming too, her body trembling, a long slow build-up as the cock moved in her cunt and she felt the familiarity of a woman's body against hers and, at the same time, the unfamiliarity of the woman fucking her like a man. Her hands caressed the white teddy, the suspenders, the stockings, their feel turning her on more, emphasising the oddity of it all.

'I'm coming . . .' she moaned, wanting Vivienne to know, wanting her to be free to spunk too. But it was not before Stephanie's body had bucked and trembled and locked, not until her orgasm had flooded every nerve, not until she had felt herself falling into a pit of absolute pleasure, her eyes rolled back, her body transported to another plane and then relaxed, that Vivienne's cock slowed then spasmed, jetting spunk out into the place it had found in Stephanie's willing sex.

The dinner was served in a Western-style dining room sitting at a table, not kneeling, as Stephanie had expected, on the floor. But the food was Japanese and served with elaborate ceremony by two of the geishas dressed, this time, in the traditional heavily embroided brocade kimonos and traditional wooden sandals, their waists bound in the wide white silk 'obis', the padded cushion worn, as Kanjii explained, at the front by girls in training, and at the back by those geishas who had learned all the secrets of their profession.

Stephanie wore a tight black strapless dress, its bodice wired to hold her breasts in a deep cleavage, the rest of its length clinging to her body almost as though it had been painted on. Its skirt was very short, revealing most of her thighs. Apart from sheer Lycra tights and dark blue high heels Stephanie wore nothing else. She had put her dark hair up into a chignon and her neck was bare too: it was long and shapely, its tendons prominent, the hollows of her throat deeply defined.

Each Japanese dish was a painting, arranged on various coloured plates, all shaped differently – squares and rectangles as well as round – as if a still-life composition for some oil painting. Even the soup arrived in delicate bowls with little lids on square plates, all colour-coordinated to make an impression of a carefully constructed work of art. But as well as the visual aspect the food was delicious, the soup a lightly flavoured consommé, the sashimi with green mustard, fresh and light and the beef teriyaki – cooked in front of them by one of the geishas – a wonderful combination of tastes unlike anything Stephanie had eaten before.

They drunk warm sake and Kanjii talked about Japan. But it was Stephanie who brought up the subject of the Seven Samurai.

'So tell me about tonight's ritual?' she asked when the meal was over and the geishas served green tea in large earthenware mugs with no handles.

Kanjii smiled. 'I will show you but I will not tell you,' he said.

'It is a ritual, like the ones you showed me before?' Stephanie's body shivered slightly as she remembered the single flower.

94

'Oh yes. All these things are passed down from generation to generation in the geisha houses.'

'They are like brothels?'

'Yes and no. Yes, men pay for the attention of women. But it is not always with money. A man may help a geisha house in many ways, according to his ability. And once he is associated with a particular house it becomes a tradition of the family. I took my son. He will take his son. It is passed on in this way.'

'And it's not dying out with Western influences?'

'Oh yes, it is. Now it is mostly for rich men like me. In the old days all Japanese men went to geisha.'

'And their wives?'

'The wives would come to geisha house too. It was not a secret for men to go there. It was honourable.'

'But your geishas don't belong to a geisha house?'

'No. The house my family used was going out of business. I took it over. For my exclusive use. I will pass it on to my sons. All the old traditions will die eventually.' He looked sad. 'Not yet but soon. It will no longer be honourable profession for women.'

They walked through into the living room and Kanjii offered more sake. Considering what lay ahead, Stephanie asked if she could have a brandy instead. Kanjii poured a good measure from a bottle of Janneau Armagnac into a crystal brandy balloon. He poured one for himself too. Stephanie did not sit down. She sipped the liquor as she looked out at the view, the lights of the city sparkling against a very black and starless sky.

'One Western custom I find totally acceptable,' he said, touching his glass against the side of hers.

The golden liquid was wonderfully smooth and Stephanie felt a buzz of excitement that the time she had so eagerly awaited had almost come. Her imagination had run riot in the last two days in trying to picture what the ritual of the Seven Samurai might involve. If she cared to think about it, she could still feel the way she had been laid open on the futon and stretched by the geishas before she had been closed and bound around Kanjii's cock: it was the combination of having the nerves in her shoulders and hips so tortured by being pulled taut while her clitoris was laid open and exposed and then being bound into a tight neat package, unable to move, unable to do anything but feel. It was like going from cold to hot. It was not something she could ever have imagined but being held like that, stretched on a human rack, then forcibly held down on Kanjii's cock had made her feel ten times more sensitive. She shivered again as she remembered how distinctly she had felt Kanjii spunking inside her. If the Seven Samurai was another ritual of this sort, it was definitely something to look forward to.

'It is time I think,' Kanjii said, finishing his brandy.

Stephanie did not finish hers. She set the glass down and followed Kanjii to the garden door.

They crossed the wooden bridge. It was a beautiful clear night and the sound of the waterfall and the chill of the autumn air made Stephanie shiver slightly in the very scanty dress. The garden was illuminated at night by carefully placed floodlights and the water splashing up from the fountain glistened like diamonds as the drops created tiny rainbows of light.

Kanjii opened the door set in the grass bank and Stephanie stepped inside, her heart beating faster. In the white paper hall two of the geishas, the eldest one who spoke English and another one Stephanie had not seen before, stood waiting, both dressed only in the white cotton knickers they had worn before. At

Kanjii's arrival they put their hands together, finger to finger in an attitude of prayer and bowed deeply. He bowed too.

The eldest geisha opened the sliding panel and the geishas led the way into the bath-house. Their pert bottoms looked alluring in the tight white cotton that fitted snugly over the cheeks of their arses as they walked ahead.

Four geishas waited in the stone-clad bath-house, all in just the white cotton knickers. Three of the girls gathered around Kanjii – after an exchange of bows – and three around Stephanie. She felt the zip of her dress being undone and the black silk peeled from her body. Her tights were pulled down her legs and her shoes levered off her feet. Kanjii too was being stripped.

After the chill outside, the bath-house was warm. The six geishas led Kanjii and Stephanie over to the sunken bath and down the steps into the waist-high water. Hands covered their bodies with soap and rinsed it away. As Stephanie felt her sex being rubbed with soap she saw Kanjii's cock, already starting to erect, being lathered by two hands under water. Fingers delved into the cleft of her arse and the crease of her labia, washing every crevice.

The washing done, Kanjii led Stephanie up out of the bath and they stood together while the geishas dried them with small white towels, each geisha holding one towel. Kanjii's cock was fully erect now but other than drying it thoroughly – an enterprise undertaken by the eldest geisha – they made no attempt to touch it.

As soon as they were dry their bodies were powdered with a sweet talcum applied with the softest of brushes, the powder dusted up between Stephanie's legs and over her breasts. Next one of the geishas dripped a strong musky perfume from a bottle all over Kanjii's body, repeating the performance with Stephanie's. The aroma reminded her slightly of the scent the black box had produced, though it did not have the same intoxicating effect.

Kanjii said something in Japanese and the girls disappeared, filing through one of the sliding panels one by one.

'They go to prepare. Now I must prepare you.' Kanjii said, looking straight into her eyes. He took her hand and led her across the bath-house to a small alcove she had not noticed before, set back from the main room but stone-clad like the rest of the room. The alcove contained a large, rather low black table about the size of a small double bed. But it was no ordinary table. In the bottom third a large oval had been cut from its surface, the edges of the oval padded and bound in leather. The rest of the surface of the table was covered with a thin futon mattress into which had also been cut an oval hole to match exactly the one underneath.

'Intriguing,' Stephanie said.

'Lie here please,' Kanjii said, but as Stephanie began to mount the table he corrected her. 'Your head the other way.'

She swung round and lay back on the table until her head rested comfortably on the mattress. With her legs open the hole was positioned between her thighs. As Stephanie gazed up to the ceiling she saw the starless sky. The alcove's ceiling was made from glass. As she looked, one or two stars came into view, the heavy cloud of earlier beginning to clear slightly.

The eldest geisha returned first. She wore a red silk Kheong-Sam split so high on the thigh that it was obvious she was wearing nothing other than the shiny white tights that sheathed her legs and the white court shoes. Immediately she came to the top of the mattress and began unpinning Stephanie's hair, which they had been careful not to get wet as they bathed her. With a small brush she had brought with her she combed the hair out, draping it over the edge of the table. Then she pressed her finger to Stephanie's lips, as she had done before, to indicate the need for silence.

The other five geishas returned together, each in different-coloured Kheong-Sams, each wearing only tights and shoes. One joined the eldest at the top of the table by Stephanie's head, two stood at the foot of the table and two on either side in the middle. Kanjii stepped back to the wall and pressed a small switch, and Stephanie heard the whirr of electric motors. Suddenly the night sky and the few stars disappeared and a startling image replaced them: the glass ceiling had been turned into a mirror and Stephanie stared back at the image of herself lying on the futon surrounded by the geishas, their jet-black hair shining in the light. The sight sent a shudder through her body, a pulse of pure pleasure centred on her sex.

Kanjii spoke in Japanese. The two geishas at her feet each took an ankle and spread her legs apart until her feet were at the corners of the table. Each then began massaging her foot, the arch of her foot, the instep, her toes and ankles, kneading them with strong powerful fingers. Most of all they seemed to press their knuckles into the balls of her feet which produced a sensation Stephanie had never experienced before. It was as though her feet had suddenly become not just sensitive but sexually sensitive, sending waves of sensual pleasure up her legs to her already-throbbing cunt.

Kanjii issued another command. The two geishas half-way up the table reached forward with both hands to grasp Stephanie's breasts, kneading and moulding them, pinching and pulling at her nipples with just the right degree of pressure, treading a careful line between pain and pleasure. What was extraordinary was that their action was perfectly synchronised; each movement, each caress, each pinch exactly mirrored on the other breast. And so was the action on her feet. The pleasure seemed to be rising up her body, the sensations from her feet amplified by the pleasure in her breasts. Stephanie moaned.

For the third time Kanjii issued instructions. The two geishas at the top of the table began stroking Stephanie's neck on either side. That alone, in combination with the other hands, made Stephanie tremble helplessly with pleasure. Then the geishas moved to her ears. Again with perfectly synchronised movements their fingers circled the outer surfaces, around the back, around the edge, then plunged a little finger deep into the delicate inner whorls. Stephanie had known her ears were sensitive but nothing like this.

The six pairs of hands working on her body seemed to add up to more. Even though they never left her feet or breasts or ears, Stephanie had the curious sensation that they were everywhere, all over her, that the feelings they were provoking somehow joined up to make her whole body feel like it was sensuously alive. She looked up at herself in the mirror, watching the hands moving on her breasts and ears and feet. She moaned loudly, wanting to see her mouth move in the mirror.

She had lost sight of Kanjii. She looked for him in the mirror but she daren't move her head for fear of disturbing the exquisite rhythm the geishas used. She could see it all in the mirror, in unison, a harmony of movement, each stroke, each circle, translated in different movements but feeling nevertheless the same, as though all six hands belonged to the same body.

In the mirror she suddenly saw Kanjii's head, his dark hair, appear between her thighs. He had knelt under the table and pushed his head through the oval aperture.

'The Seventh Samurai,' he said proudly.

The geishas moved as one again. In exactly the same second Stephanie felt a hot wet mouth descend on her toes, her nipples and into her ears. In exactly the same second she felt tongues licking at her flesh. In exactly the same second she felt Kanjii's tongue plunging down on to her clitoris.

It was as though she was suspended, as though she were floating, her only contact with the surface the seven mouths that touched her body. But that was not the most extraordinary feeling. Kanjii's tongue manipulated her clitoris but it was as though she had seven clitorises. She could not distinguish between the feelings from her ear or nipple or toes. They were all the same, the same intensity, the same sensitivity, the same aching sexual pleasure, the same throbbing pulsing sensation. She could not concentrate on one. They all demanded her attention.

To say she was coming was an understatement. She was exploding, her whole body on fire and her mind, because if she could hold her eyes open – and it was hard not to let them roll back with pleasure – she could see in the mirror the most exotic sight she had ever seen, her prostrate body ministered to by six women and one man – the Seven Samurai.

'Oh God . . .' she screamed as loud as she could, wanting to hear the vibration of the sound. It matched the whole vibration of her body, trembling out of control. The seven clitorises they had created produced seven times the intensity of feeling. As her orgasm broke over her she could not tell from where it came, from her breast or toe or clitoris or in her head where two tongues artfully probed so deep in her ears she thought they would touch her brain. If it broke anywhere it was there in her head, there over the two hot tongues that seemed to go deeper than she would ever have believed possible, there in her fevered mind. But then she felt new waves gathering from her nipples and toes and clitoris and new orgasms erupted over and over again until, after a very long time, she was capable of feeling no more.

Slowly the geishas left her, not all together this time, but slowly one by one. Each departure felt as shattering as if a cock were slipping from her body after intercourse. Each produced a little aftermath of shock. Kanjii was the last to take his mouth away.

She must have slept, exhausted by the intensity of emotion, because when she opened her eyes the geishas had gone and only Kanjii remained in the alcove, sitting in a small wooden chair and watching her. Above, the ceiling had turned back to glass and more stars had appeared in the sky.

'Are you all right?' he asked, seeing her awaken.

'I think so,' she said, sitting up on one elbow.

'It is a new experience, I think.'

'Very. This has been going on in Japan for centuries?'

'Oh yes. Of course not for the women. It was designed for men. In Japan a man's wealth was measured by the number of geishas he could afford to keep. For most men the Seven Samurai would represent exceptional wealth. But it is not the ultimate.'

Stephanie swung her legs onto the side of the table and got up a little unsteadily. There was a small jug of water and two bright yellow beakers on a little side-table.

'Is this water?'

'Yes.'

She poured herself a glass and drank it thirstily.

'What is the ultimate, then?'

'The Thirteen Samurai,' Kanjii replied.

'Thirteen?'

'Two geishas for the toes, the nipples, ears, knees, fingers of both hands, and one mouth for each of the balls. Naturally enough the Thirteenth Samurai is for the cock.'

'My God . . .' Stephanie tried to imagine it. They sometimes had twelve slaves at the castle so it was something she could try on Devlin. Kanjii had taught her a lot of lessons she intended to apply at the castle.

'So now you have experienced the Japanese way.'

'Where are the geishas?'

Stephanie stood in front of Kanjii, her naked body inches from his face.

'Why?'

'Don't you think you'd better get them back in here?' She pressed her navel into his face.

'For what reason?' he said, pulling back to look up into her eyes.

'The Seven Samurai is for men.'

'I don't . . .'

'I'll be the Seventh Samurai this time.' She stroked Kanjii's face. 'Or don't you think I have enough experience?'

'I think it would be most exciting, but I . . .'

'Just get them back.'

It didn't take long for the geishas to file back into the alcove while Kanjii lay back on the low table. Stephanie found the switch which converted the ceiling glass into a mirror and watched as the image of Kanjii came into view.

Kanjii was not erect. But as soon as the two geishas began to manipulate his feet his cock unfurled rapidly. By the time the third and fourth geishas touched his nipples it was fully erect and throbbing visibly.

The same pattern they had followed with Stephanie, they used on Kanjii. Every detail was the same, a time-honoured ritual. The eldest geisha nodded to Stephanie when it was time to take her position. She slipped under the table and emerged with her head between Kanjii's thighs. As the geishas' mouths sucked and licked at his toes and ears and nipples, Stephanie sucked his big hard shaft into her mouth.

Kanjii's whole body was trembling just like Stephanie's had done. He was looking at himself in the mirror, watching his geishas and Stephanie's long black hair flowing over his thighs as she bobbed up and down on his cock. Her mouth was expert. Had she been a geisha she would have been trained to synchronise her rhythms with the others, but her lack of expertise in this direction was compensated for by her total expertise in the way she licked and sucked and drew his cock back and forth in her mouth.

Stephanie felt his spunk rising. Kneeling under the table, she felt her own sex pulsing again, reminded of how it had been made to feel. She pressed her legs together as she felt a gush of juices on her thighs. Her body was expressing its needs too. The Japanese arts of love were all very well but her body demanded something a little cruder and more direct.

Quickly she crawled out from under the table. The geishas, though not taking their mouths from their allotted tasks, looked astonished. Kanjii raised his head to see what was happening but the ritual forbade him to speak. Stephanie was climbing on the table. With no hesitation she straddled Kanjii's navel, groped with her hand behind her for his cock and held it tightly at the slippery nest of her cunt.

'You want it, don't you?' she said.

Kanjii nodded, making the geishas on his ears temporarily lose their stroke.

In one movement Stephanie dropped down onto Kanjii's cock, impaling herself on him. It took her breath away. It was hot and very hard. Kanjii lowered his head. This was not the tradition but it was exciting. The geishas found his ears again, their tongues inserted deep, taking up the rhythm of the mouths on his nipples and toes.

He moaned as Stephanie began to move up and down on him, her hands pressing down on his navel, bucking her hips up and down. She wanted her own pleasure and ground her clitoris against his hard pubic bone over and over again until her mind was filled with sex, until it replayed images of her stretched out on the table, of her in the other room drugged with scent and fucked, of her now, her whole body beginning to pulse with pleasure as she felt her orgasm break, as her cunt convulsed around the hard shaft deep inside it and she screamed with the sharp ravishing sensations that flooded every nerve.

It was only as she came down from her high that she realised Kanjii hadn't come. She felt his hard cock still inside her. She knew instinctively what he wanted. It was tradition, ritual. She had suggested it after all, she should be prepared to finish it. She had

105

succumbed to pure selfishness; now it was time to do her duty. Quickly she scrambled off the table and knelt under it again, thrusting her head up into the oval aperture. She took Kanjii's cock, sleek with her juices, and sucked it hard. Watching the eldest geisha she tried to match the motion of her head to her own motion, tried now to be the perfect geisha. She felt her own juices leaking from her sex and running down her thighs, and tasted them on Kanjii's cock. But she tried to concentrate. It was not easy. Her mind was still full of images, of everything that had happened to her in the penthouse, all the ways the geishas had washed her and fingered her and held her.

As she felt Kanjii's cock swelling in her mouth she remembered how it had felt as it had swollen inside her, bound tightly inside her so it could not move, how she had felt his spunk spraying from his body. She suddenly thought of what that would be like with Devlin, with Devlin's monstrous cock spasming inside her. She shuddered, trying to put such thoughts aside and think only of what she was doing.

Kanjii's cock twitched hard in her mouth as she timed her movement to coincide with the sweep of the tongues she could see at his ear. She knew what he was feeling. She knew how those tongues felt, hot and wet and so close to the brain they felt as though they were inside it.

It swelled up one more time, Kanjii moaned, a low animal moan, a sound produced deep in his body, and his cock began to spasm, jerking against her tongue and her lips as it spat spunk down into her throat, his moan continuous, his body rigid.

There was too much spunk for Stephanie to swallow. Some escaped from the corner of her mouth and dribbled down into Kanjii's pubic hair.

The geishas withdrew one by one until they were alone again. Stephanie finally released his cock from her mouth and came out from under the table.

'I spoiled it,' she said, standing looking down at him.

'No. No. It was wonderful. Wonderful. I think I make it part of the ritual for the next four hundred years.'

'Do I get to be an honorary geisha?'

'Of course. I will confer the honour myself.'

'And no doubt that involves another ritual.'

Kanjii laughed. 'Oh yes. A long and arduous one, I fear.'

'But not tonight.'

'Definitely not tonight.'

Chapter Five

Venetia supervised the luggage being loaded into the boot of the Cadillac. Stephanie's two cases had increased to four as the result of her purchases in Bond Street and at Vivienne Elson's boutique. With Devlin's return from Moscow, it had been decided that Venetia should go to the castle with Stephanie as Devlin had a considerable amount of work to catch up on from the various corners of his empire, which Venetia could help him sort out.

It was a beautiful autumn morning. The sun shone in a clear blue sky, the temperature a crisp chill, the scent of autumn as heavy as any perfume. The trees at the front of Devlin's house were mottled shades of brown and the driveway was already covered with a sprinkling of dried leaves that cracked underfoot.

The chauffeur stood with the rear door open as Stephanie came out of the house.

'All done,' Venetia said, closing the boot.

'We're off then.' Stephanie climbed into the car. She was wearing black high-heeled boots and a red wool dress with a knee-length skirt and full-length sleeves. She had combed her hair out and it tumbled onto her shoulders, clean and shining with health.

As soon as Venetia sat down beside her on the long leather bench seat, her slender body and big breasts well served by the black one-piece tailored suit she wore, the chauffeur closed the passenger door and got behind the wheel. Starting the engine, he headed the big car out of the driveway and into the road.

'Well, that was a very pleasant interlude,' Stephanie said, contemplating her five days in London. Kanjii and Vivienne, not to mention Venetia and Devlin's recording equipment, had made it a fascinating experience. Kanjii in particular had given her food for thought. What the geishas had done had not only thrilled her but provided her with a fund of ideas for ways of entertaining the guests – and herself – at the castle. She looked forward to enacting the ritual she had been taught, especially as Kanjii had promised he would send her one of the aroma boxes he had used on her first visit.

The Cadillac glided effortlessly through the traffic and Stephanie relaxed. Though she had enjoyed her time in London, it would be good to get back to the castle and particularly good to see Devlin again. She realised she had missed him. He'd called her once from Moscow but the line was so bad she had had little opportunity to say much to him other than to confirm their plans. He had decided it would be easier to charter a plane from Moscow rather than get the Learjet to pick him up. It would be quicker, he'd told her, and he was anxious to get back to the castle as soon as possible.

Venetia said nothing, sitting quietly, her long legs crossed.

'I think I'd like a drink,' Stephanie said.

'Champagne?' There was a bottle of champagne in the silver wine-cooler recessed in the walnut cabinet, as ever.

'Why not? I didn't indulge last night, after all.' The excitements of the geishas had left Stephanie drained. She had spent yesterday quietly recovering. After a visit to a health club where she had done an hour's aerobics and had a long swim, she had gone out to dinner with Venetia but had drunk only mineral water. She had slept alone, her sexual appetite for once satiated.

Venetia opened the bottle and expertly poured the fizzing wine into a flute.

'Aren't you going to join me?' Stephanie prompted.

Venetia poured herself a glass too.

'Here's to our return. It's been nice to see London again but the cold's beginning to get to me.'

They clinked their glasses together and sipped the wine. It was then, as she had turned to face Venetia, that Stephanie noticed the car through the back window. It was a dirty brown Ford Sierra. For some reason she had seen it before. The odd sensation she had had in Sloane Street returned: she had the feeling she was being followed.

'What's the matter?' Venetia asked, seeing the colour drain from her face.

'That car . . . have you seen it before?'

Venetia looked out of the window. 'No, I don't think so. It might have been parked outside the house. No. No, I think it was another one . . .'

'Are you sure?'

'Not positive.'

'I've had this funny feeling I've been followed.'

'Really?'

'It's just paranoia, I suppose.'

As she said it, the brown Sierra took an opportunity of a gap in the traffic and surged passed the Cadillac, instantly calming Stephanie's fears.

They were on a dual carriageway to the west of London now, and the morning traffic was light. The Sierra had gone completely and by the time they pulled through the gates of the private airfield, the sudden fear that had gripped her had evaporated, helped no doubt by another glass of champagne. The chauffeur drew the Cadillac up right outside the landing ramp of the Learjet, which stood ready on a taxiway, and ran round to open the passenger door. As Stephanie and Venetia mounted the steps of the plane he began unloading the luggage.

Susie stood at the top of the ramp, her Kheong-Sam reminding Stephanie of recent pleasures.

'Morning, madam,' she said with her usual lack of enthusiasm.

'Good morning Susie,' Stephanie said, sitting in one of the large leather armchairs in the main cabin, while Venetia sat opposite her. From the window she saw the chauffeur taking her cases to the rear of the plane and the ramp that led directly to the cargo hold.

'Would you like anything to drink?' Susie asked.

'No thank you, we had champagne in the car. Later perhaps.'

'Yes, madam. Don't forget to fasten your seat-belt. We'll be taking off in five minutes. We have radar clearance from air traffic control.'

'That was quick.'

'Yes, sometimes we are lucky.'

Susie walked back to the forward cabin, the split in the Kheong-Sam revealing her shapely thigh. She closed the door in the bulkhead behind her.

'I thought we'd have a longer wait,' Stephanie said.

'I told the car to be there at twelve, just in case,' Venetia said.

'Good. We'll lunch on the terrace.'

'They said the sun was out.'

'That's definitely what I need.'

111

The twin jets set either side of the tail began to whine and the plane nosed forward down the taxiway. Stephanie noticed, rather strangely she thought, that the Cadillac had not driven away. The driver was sitting at the wheel. It looked as if he had fallen asleep. Must have had a late night, Stephanie thought to herself, smiling.

The plane turned onto the runway.

'Good morning ladies.' It was the captain's voice over the tannoy. 'We have permission to take off in one minute. Estimated time of arrival at the lake will be twelve-ten. We'll be cruising at 29,000 feet at a speed of 590 mph. I hope you have a pleasant flight.'

Almost immediately the engine noise rose to a crescendo and the plane shot forward. In seconds they were airborne. As Stephanie gazed out of the window at the ground below she saw a sight that filled her with horror. Parked well out of sight behind one of the Portakabins was a brown Sierra.

Just as Stephanie was about to tell Venetia to look down, the rear cabin door was flung open. Three men and a woman burst into the main cabin. Two of the men carried knives, big wicked-looking hunting knives, their edges serrated, their blades glinting. Before either Stephanie or Venetia had time to react, before they could even flick the clips of the seat-belts, and with the plane still climbing steeply, the men had jumped astride their bodies and held the knives to their throats.

'Don't make a sound,' the man on Stephanie hissed, his face covered, like all four of them, by a woolly ski-mask that had been sewn up to leave just the opening for the eyes.

The third man and the woman had positioned themselves besides the door to the forward cabin.

'Does this call the stewardess?' he asked, indicating the call button located on the side of the bulkhead by the window. Stephanie nodded. There was something familiar about his voice but she could not place it.

The man pressed the call button. They waited. After a minute Susie swung through the cabin door. 'Yes, mad . . .?' Before she could finish the question the man behind the door clamped his big hand over the Malaysian woman's mouth as his arm held her firmly around the waist. She struggled but made no impression on his hard muscular body. The woman closed the door and locked it.

'Well, that's better,' the man kneeling on Stephanie said.

'What the hell do you want?' Stephanie said, fearing she knew the answer.

'I think it's time for introductions.' Without taking the knife from her throat the man used his free hand to reach to the top of the ski-mask and pull it off his head. Stephanie recognised him immediately. During her time at the castle one or two of the slaves had been uncooperative and difficult. Despite the continual threat of being returned to England to face prosecution for their crimes, they continually railed against the life at the castle and were constantly having to be punished for insolence and misbehaviour. The face that grinned into hers now was one of the worst offenders. 'So now the boot's on the other foot, eh mistress?' he sneered.

'Andrew,' Stephanie said quietly.

He took the knife from her throat. 'And I'm sure you haven't forgotten my friend.'

The woman pulled her mask off. Again Stephanie recognised her immediately. Amanda had been one of the most difficult of all the slaves: like Andrew she had been punished countless times.

113

'Oh, I'm sure she remembers me,' Amanda said. 'I certainly remember her.'

'What do you want?' Stephanie repeated.

Amanda went back into the rear cabin and came back with a nylon hold-all which she unzipped.

'Well now,' Andrew said, 'that's a good question, isn't it Amanda?'

'Certainly is,' she replied.

Stephanie looked into Andrew's face. He had short, very curly blond hair with a sallow complexion and light blue eyes. He was not tall and, she remembered, his body was far from athletic, but he was slim and could definitely be described as attractive. Amanda on the other hand was a brunette, her hair cut short, her eyes an unusual light brown colour. She was not tall either and her body gave the impression of being plump, though Stephanie knew this was misleading. Under the dark slacks and shirt she wore – in common with the other three – her body was hard with muscle, her breasts full and firm, her buttocks long and meaty, her waist particularly narrow.

'First,' Andrew said, 'I think we want revenge for the way we were treated at your hands. After that, well I think we'll have to decide that when the time comes, won't we?' He turned his attention to Susie. 'Can you speak to the cockpit from in here?'

'Yes sir,' she replied.

'Tell them the mistress here doesn't want to be disturbed. And don't be tempted to say anything else.'

Susie picked up an intercom phone mounted on the dividing wall and relayed the message. She knew the captain would not be surprised. Since he had been flying the Learjet for Devlin nothing surprised him, especially when Stephanie was aboard.

'Well now, I don't want to be rude. I'd better introduce my two friends, hadn't I mistress?' He said the word "mistress" with special emphasis. The man who had held Susie removed the ski-mask. He was balding, with irregular teeth and a crooked nose that made him look as if he had once been a boxer. His shirt bulged with a considerable paunch. 'This is Mick.'

The man kneeling over Venetia pulled his mask off too. His face was tanned, his hair a curly ginger and his appearance swarthy. His chin was shaded with what was obviously a rough beard. His eyes were a dark green. Stephanie recognised him too: it was the man in the suede blouson who she had seen in Knightsbridge.

'And this is Paul.'

'She's seen me before.' Paul could see the recognition in Stephanie's eyes.

Stephanie gazed up at Andrew with contempt. His blond hair made him look younger than he was. His mouth, still spread in a grin, showed his regular capped teeth.

'How did you find us?' Stephanie asked. The precautions Devlin took against just this eventuality Stephanie had always regarded as paranoia, but they were extremely thorough. The slaves were never even allowed to see the interior of the plane, let alone the direction they were travelling. From the temperature they might have guessed the castle was in the Mediterranean but there was nothing to suggest it was in Italy, let alone where in Italy. But somehow Andrew had beaten the system.

He was too proud of his own cleverness not to want to tell her the details. 'I have a mate in air traffic control. There aren't many of these babies in the air, darling.' He pronounced the word 'darling' in his distinct Cockney accent. 'It wasn't difficult to find one with regular flights south. It had to be south didn't it? France, Spain, Italy. So it turns out there's a lot of flights to Lake Trasimeno. I bought a guidebook. There's a medieval castle in the middle of the lake. Bingo. That's where we're going. My mate tipped me off when he got the flight plan for the next arrival and we've been following you ever since. Couldn't have been simpler, darling. Course I needed a bit of extra help. But my friends here were only too glad to come along when I told them about all the facilities at the castle, all the extras they could enjoy . . .' He laughed. 'All the team sports.'

Amanda had taken two sets of handcuffs from the hold-all. Andrew climbed off Stephanie and got to his feet.

'Get up. Slowly. Put your hands behind your back. And don't try anything.' He emphasised the point by holding the knife up again.

Stephanie flicked open the seat-belt and did as she was told. She saw absolutely no alternative. She felt the cold steel cuffs snapped over her wrists by Amanda.

'Now you,' Paul said, getting up off Venetia and keeping his knife in evidence as she obeyed. Quickly Amanda applied the cuffs to Venetia's wrists as the two men returned the big hunting knives to leather sheaths strapped to their waists.

'What about her?' Mick said, indicating Susie who had stood stock-still as though hoping they wouldn't notice her. 'She's just my type.'

'No,' Andrew said sharply. 'She's just an employee. Aren't you?'

'Yes, sir. I just work for the company.'

'And you're going to be good, aren't you darling?'

Andrew said, coming over to stare into Susie's eyes menacingly.

'Yes sir. I don't want to have any trouble.'

'See. Good as gold. She probably hates this bitch as much as I do. Why don't you get us all a drink? Vodka, lots of ice. You've got ice, haven't you?'

'Yes sir.'

The bar was towards the rear of the plane. Susie pushed past the two captive women to get the drinks.

'Come here,' Andrew said, looking at Stephanie.

'What for?' she replied defiantly.

'Oh dear, that's not the right attitude at all is it? Don't you remember your little rules: obey everything you are told without question?'

'I'm not your slave,' Stephanie snapped.

'Really? Well, we'll see about that. When we get to the castle we're going to have a trial. A fair trial, with a judge and a jury. Of course if you're found guilty then it'll be up to me to decide what to do with you. And I have a very vivid imagination.'

'What am I supposed to have done?'

'Oh, come on darling . . .'

'You had a choice. You didn't have to come to the castle. It was your punishment. If you'd rather we'd gone to the police . . .'

'Shut up,' Andrew shouted, his anger getting on top of him. Then he said more quietly. 'You'll get your chance to defend yourself.'

The plane began to bank slightly, changing to a more southerly direction. Andrew slumped into one of the leather armchairs as Susie handed him a large tumbler of vodka on the rocks. She handed the others drinks too, then returned to the bar where she hoped she would remain inconspicuous.

'Well, cheers everybody. It seems we've accomplished our mission. Now we have the queen bee here I'm sure the rest of the workers will be no problem.'

'Can't wait,' Mick said, slumping down on to the sofa. He stretched out his hand and caught Venetia by the wrist, pulling her onto his lap as Paul sat down beside him.

'She's beautiful,' Paul said.

'Don't worry, there's plenty more where that came from. The rest of the slaves will be so glad to see us you'll have wall to wall women.'

Amanda walked back into the cargo hold. In a few minutes she emerged with one of Stephanie's cases. It was not locked. She pulled the case open to reveal Stephanie's new clothes mixed in with the ones she had brought from the castle. She tore open the various packages and held up the clothes in front of her body.

'Look at this. Must have cost a fortune.' She was holding up a camiknicker Stephanie had bought in Bond Street.

'Suits you, darling,' Andrew said.

Paul reached forward and fingered the material obscenely. 'Feels like silk,' he said, bringing the material to his face and letting it brush his lips. 'As we've got some time on our hands, why don't we have a look at our little prize?' He nodded towards Stephanie.

'Yes,' Mick agreed. 'Come on love, give us a little in-flight entertainment.' His hand squeezed Venetia's breast as he said it. She winced and tried to wriggle away from him, a look of horror on her face that perhaps only Stephanie understood.

'Well, mistress,' Andrew sneered. 'I think you'd better do as you're told, don't you?'

Stephanie said nothing, looking Andrew straight in the eyes. He had been cocky and stubborn at the

118

castle and she was not at all surprised he had organised this plot. Even when he had finally bent to
her will she had suspected there was still defiance
lurking beneath the surface. Equally she knew that
unless she did exactly what she was told he was capable of making her life a living hell.

'We're waiting,' Amanda said, sitting on the floor
among discarded wrappings and new clothes.

'Take my handcuffs off and I'll give you a show,'
Stephanie said steadily.

'No way darling. You'll manage.' Andrew took a
swig of his vodka. The ice clinked against the side of
the glass. 'Come on, we're getting impatient. You've
got a treat boys, she's a real looker I can tell you.'
Andrew got up from his seat suddenly and walked
right up to Stephanie. He squeezed her cheeks together between his thumb and fingers. 'I know, don't
I mistress? The way you used me to rub suntan oil all
over your body while I had that blasted pouch
chained round my cock. You do remember making
me do that, don't you?'

'Yes,' she said knowing instinctively that she
shouldn't show him the fear she felt.

'Good. So let my friends see what you've got.'

Andrew went to the bar and slammed his glass
down on its small wooden counter. Susie quickly
poured him another drink.

How she was expected to get her dress off with her
hands cuffed behind her back she did not know. She
knelt on the floor and managed to catch the hem in
her left hand, wriggling it up over her thighs and
waist but she could not pull it any higher.

'She's stuck,' Mick said, stating the obvious.

'Give her a hand,' Paul said.

'Leave her,' Andrew ordered.

Stephanie managed to hook the dress on the arm of one of the chairs. By dipping her body below the level of the arm she pulled the dress up over her bra and around her neck, though of course it was still trapped behind her shoulders. That was as far as she could get. She stood up. Under the dress she was wearing creamy beige-coloured French knickers, with matching suspender belt and soft cup bra. The knickers had V-shaped inserts of lace over her navel and at the side of her hips. Her stockings were beige too, their broad welts pulled into peaks by the taut suspenders.

'Well, just look at that,' Paul said, studying her body closely.

'Come on,' Andrew said irritably.

'I can't do any more,' Stephanie said, stretching her wrists against the cuffs to demonstrate her inability.

'Help her.' Andrew's eyes fell on Susie.

'Me, sir?' Susie's voice trembled with fear.

'Yes, you. Get her dress off.' Susie didn't move. 'Now.'

Quickly Susie came round the bar to stand in front of Stephanie. Their eyes met. For the first time since she had known her, Stephanie saw a look of sympathy in Susie's eyes: she actually cared.

'Sorry . . .' Susie whispered.

'It's all right. Just do it.'

Susie's hands were trembling as her fingers pulled the dress up over Stephanie's head and down over her arms until it was hanging by its sleeves from the cuffed wrists. Seeing the problem Andrew stepped forward, unsheathed his knife and sliced the wool away. The dress fell to the floor. While the knife was out he slipped it into the strap of the bra between Stephanie's shoulder-blades and sliced it in two. He cut both the shoulder straps with equal ease and the bra fell away from Stephanie's breasts.

'Pretty good,' Mick said as Andrew gave Susie a shove to indicate she should get back behind the bar. 'But not as good as these.' His hands wrapped round both Venetia's breasts, weighing them as if they were some sort of fruit. Again there was panic on Venetia's face.

'She's gorgeous,' Paul said, staring. 'Gorgeous.'

'There's lots more where that came from,' Amanda said, beginning to pack things back into the suitcase.

'Well, this is definitely the only way to travel,' Paul said, stretching back on the sofa.

Andrew came back towards Stephanie, the vodka glass in his hand. 'So now,' he said, looking into her eyes, 'the boot is on the other foot.'

'It appears so,' she said calmly, looking back at him unflinchingly. 'And what do you think you're going to do now?' Her tone was icy.

'I told you.' He touched the glass against her nipple. She did not move. The nipple hardened. 'How long before we land?' he asked Susie.

'Thirty minutes,' she replied, looking at her watch.

'Good. Now I want you to tell the captain that he is to take off again the moment we are out of the plane.' He was still looking at Susie.

'That's the plan anyway,' Stephanie said.

'How convenient.'

'What about me?' Susie asked, fearing they were going to take her with them to the castle. 'Am I to leave with the plane?'

'Would you prefer to stay?'

'No sir.'

'You're free to go. What are you going to do? Call the police? I don't think so, do you? I don't think the mistress here wants the police crawling all over the castle, do you darling?'

It had never occurred to Stephanie before. What Devlin had organised at the castle was not illegal but if it became public knowledge by being splashed all over the tabloid press, as it undoubtedly would be if the police became involved, it would seriously embarrass him and his business empire. Andrew was absolutely right about that.

'Say nothing, Susie,' Stephanie said.

'But . . .'

'Tell the pilot he's to return to London and wait for instructions. You go with him. Nothing else. Understood?'

Susie nodded.

'That's a good girl,' Andrew declared.

What Stephanie really wanted to tell Susie was how to contact Devlin in Moscow. But even if she could have said something she had no idea where he was. There was a chance he would ring the main office in London but it was unlikely. He was due back tomorrow and would leave everything until then. Devlin would be walking into a trap and there was no way to warn him.

Susie walked towards the front cabin.

'And don't get any ideas about telling him to go back to London. If this plane changes direction you'll be the first to suffer. Do you understand? Don't make the mistake of thinking I won't do it.'

'Do as he says, Susie,' Stephanie said firmly.

Susie nodded again, unlocked the front cabin door and went inside.

'Still giving orders, aren't you?' Amanda said, standing up. 'Well, it's going to be our turn to give orders now, bitch. I'm looking forward to giving you some orders after what you did to me.'

122

'I didn't do anything you didn't ask for. Either of you.'

'We didn't have any choice, did we?' Amanda replied, her eyes blazing with anger.

'Calm down, Mandy. There's plenty of time for that later.'

'I'd like some time for this now,' Micky said, pawing Venetia's body more aggressively.

'Take her in the back then,' Paul suggested.

'Don't be so coy. Do it here.' Amanda said.

'No,' Venetia cried. 'Please, no . . . Not with a man . . . please.'

'There's time,' Andrew looked at his watch. 'Plenty of time.'

Mick started to unbutton the front of the black one-piece that Venetia wore. She twisted her body, pulling the buttons out of his grasp.

'No, no, no, no. Please.' Venetia managed to free herself altogether and scrambled to her feet, running over to Andrew. She dropped on her knees in front of him. 'I'm not like her,' she said, looking at Stephanie standing alone in the high-heel boots, stockings and French knickers, her breasts naked and proud. 'I'm a slave just like you were. Devlin caught me embezzling. He used me just like he used you.'

'What are you talking about?' Andrew asked.

'They've got files on me just like they have on you. I stole from Devlin. I'm just like all the other slaves. Just because I'm good with computers he needs me in London. Otherwise I'd be in the cellars with the other slaves.'

'Is this true?' Andrew asked Stephanie.

'Yes,' she said quietly. It was perfectly true and Stephanie didn't blame Venetia for trying to save herself. If anyone had to be punished, if anyone was to be put on trial or whatever else Andrew's mind had thought up, it was her, not Venetia. Venetia was not bisexual. She was a lesbian through and through and being fucked by a man was a violation for her. It had happened once, Devlin had been forced to allow it to happen once, but otherwise because of her special place in the system he had respected her sexual proclivities. At the castle she had only been used by the female guests. Stephanie knew the terror Mick's fondling had already instilled in her.

'Well . . . let me think . . .' Andrew said nothing for a moment.

'It's a set-up, Andy. Come on.' Mick was stroking himself to erection through his trousers.

'No, no. If it's true she could be very helpful to us, Mick. Very helpful. You know all the computer codes?'

'Yes.'

'You can get it to wipe our files?'

'Yes. Easily.'

'Is everything stored on the computer?'

'Yes. But there are hard copies too.'

'You see, Mick. She didn't have to tell us that.'

'We can order them to destroy the files on us.' Amanda said. 'They'll believe her.'

'Exactly.'

'I'll do anything you want. Except sleep with a man . . . I just can't . . .'

'OK. You've got a deal.'

'I won't let you down.'

'You better not.'

Venetia strained at her wrists as if asking for the handcuffs to be removed. Andrew took a set of keys from his shirt pocket, twisted her round and unlocked the cuffs. Venetia rubbed her sore wrists as soon as she was free.

'I don't trust her,' Mick said grudgingly.

'I'm on your side,' Venetia said with conviction. 'I've had to work like a dog for years because he had that bloody file on me. You think I liked it. Especially when this bitch turned up.' She indicated Stephanie with a dismissive wave of her hand. 'She's got Devlin eating out of her hand. He'll do anything for her. He's besotted by her. If you're going to have a trial you can count me in. I'll give evidence against her, lots of it. The way the bitch has treated me.'

Andrew started to laugh. 'Well, that's great. And you know all Devlin's little secrets?'

'All of them.'

'Well, we're really in business then.' Andrew went to the bar and reached over it to find the vodka bottle. He poured more into everyone's glass and gave Venetia a glass too. She drunk a silent toast with the rest of them.

They strapped Stephanie, still naked from the waist up, into one of the leather armchairs as the plane banked to come in to land. She could see the whole of Lake Trasimeno laid out under the plane as it descended, the castle on the island with its extensive orchards and walled garden and vineyard revealed in every detail. She had never been less glad to see the place.

Curiously, she was not frightened at the prospect of what Andrew planned. If you live by the sword you will, inevitably and metaphorically, die by it sooner or later. She had played a dangerous game. And now it was her turn to pay for it. She had ruled the castle and enjoyed every minute of it. But the tables had turned . . .

She cursed herself for not trusting her own intuition. She had realised she was being followed, at least her subconscious had, but she had done nothing about it. She had dismissed the feeling as paranoia. If she had not, if she had taken precautions, she would not be in the situation she found herself now.

Tomorrow Devlin would walk into the trap too. There was no way to warn him. Even if she managed to get away, run off when they landed – which was a slim chance – she wouldn't be able to get to him in time. And realistically, with her hands cuffed behind her back and wearing high-heeled boots, she'd hardly be able to outrun Andrew or Amanda, who was probably the fittest of the two.

Susie reappeared as soon as the plane had landed. She looked anxiously at Stephanie as though wanting to know what to do. But there was nothing Stephanie could say. There was no point shouting for her to call Devlin. She couldn't get him in Moscow. He was moving from place to place and even his main office didn't have a number. Stephanie hoped Susie or the pilot would have the sense to call the headquarters just in case Devlin phoned in but she knew that was a slim chance.

As the plane came to a halt Stephanie saw the black Mercedes that Devlin used to ferry them to and from the jetty, parked on the grass at the end of the concrete landing strip. As soon as the plane was stationary, Susie operated the exterior cabin door and extended the hydraulically operated landing ramp.

Without a word, as this had obviously been careful-ly planned, Mick and Paul descended the steps. Stephanie watched from the window as the driver got out of the car. There was a short scuffle and then Mick pushed the driver away. He began running faster and faster away from the plane. Mick was laughing.

Andrew had thought of everything. He was right not to be worried about the driver. There was no need to keep him prisoner, just as there was no need to hold the flight crew. The driver would be too scared to go to the police. He was only a local peasant hired by Devlin to drive for short trips and look after the car. He wouldn't want to get involved with the law. He probably didn't even have an official driving license. He had also seen enough to know that things went on at the castle that were better not talked about.

As the driver fled, Amanda unbuckled Stephanie's seat-belt and pulled her to her feet using her considerable strength. Her eyes looked at Stephanie with positive hatred and Stephanie knew why. Amanda had been wilful at the castle and had had to be punished several times. She had taken her punishment badly, never accepting that it was a condition of her service. She could always have chosen to return to England and face the consequences of prosecution. But clearly she didn't see it that way, as she led Stephanie to the door, her hand biting into Stephanie's upper arm.

'Tell her again,' Andrew said as they were about to leave the plane.

Susie stood looking bewildered.

'Do nothing Susie, you understand?' As though by telepathy she tried to tell her with her eyes to make every effort, however hopeless it might be, to try and contact Devlin.

'So good,' Andrew said, patting her bottom and leading her down the steps of the plane.

Stephanie's high heels clattered on the metal ramp. Whether the pilot was watching the strange sight of her being led to the car wearing only French knickers, stockings and boots, she could not see. She was pushed unceremoniously onto the back seat. Venetia got in beside her with Paul while Amanda and Andrew sat in the front. They didn't bother with the luggage. Amanda had decided there would be plenty of clothes for her to play with at the castle.

The noise of the jet engines rose immediately they were in the car, and it moved forward to the end of the runway, the pilot clearly taking his instructions literally. As the car pulled away the engines roared, the plane quivered for a moment, held by its brakes, and then, the brakes released, shot forward in a haze of noise and exhaust heat. In a minute it was soaring into the sky, banking away to the left and with it another slim hope that perhaps the pilot would have been able to do something to rescue Stephanie from her predicament.

It was a five-minute drive to the jetty where the speedboat would be waiting, sent out from the castle the moment the plane was heard overhead.

'If he sees her like this, the boatman may take off,' Amanda said, looking at Stephanie's naked breasts.

'Right. Cover her up,' Andrew ordered, looking at Venetia.

'What can I use?' Venetia said.

'Put this over her shoulders.' Amanda had brought a sweater from Stephanie's luggage which she'd tied around her waist. She pulled it off and handed it to Venetia, who fitted it over Stephanie's long hair and down over her breasts.

'He won't see her legs, that'll do.' They had come to a fork in the road. Andrew applied the brakes. 'Which way?'

'Left,' Stephanie said. There was no point in lying. They could drive all the way around the lake and find the jetty in the end.

A few minutes later the Mercedes drew up along-side the wooden jetty where the gleaming, spotlessly polished speedboat was moored, the boatman catnapping on the transom. He woke with a start as the car came to a halt.

'Call him over,' Andrew ordered.

The boatman was an old man. He had been plying the lake for thirty years in one boat or another. He saw Stephanie beckoning him to come to the car and obeyed immediately. As he got off the boat Mick got out of the car, smiling at him broadly.

'Nice boat,' Mick said.

'Si, si . . .' he replied.

There was no problem now. He was off the boat and Mick was between him and it. There was no way he could wrest Mick out of the way and untie the boat. It was all so simple. Mick jumped aboard and the old man stared helplessly as he watched Stephanie being pulled roughly from the car.

'Don't . . .' Stephanie said when it looked as though the boatman was going to take a swing at Andrew. 'Just go home.'

They all piled into the boat, leaving the old man on the shore. Mick worked the controls and soon had the boat heading out into the lake, however inexpertly. Across the vast expanse of water Stephanie could see the turrets of the castle on the island, like a setting for a fairy-tale, as a flock of grebes took fright at the noise of the engines.

As usual, two white-jacketed servants waited by the jetty, ready to take the luggage ashore. They looked puzzled as the boat approached. They were expecting only Stephanie and Venetia. Andrew started to laugh. As he suspected, there was no defence plan for the castle. The servants wouldn't run in and bolt the doors at the first sign of trouble. They would do nothing. The castle was open. The castle was theirs.

Docking the boat proved a difficult exercise with Mick's inexperience. Eventually Andrew threw one of the servants a line and they hauled the boat in alongside the rubber tyres that hung from the jetty. As soon as the forward and aft lines were secured they all stepped ashore. The servants looked at Stephanie with amazement – the sweater back around Amanda's waist, Stephanie's breasts bare, her nipples hardened by the cool of the air on the water – but said and did nothing. They had seen many strange sights at the castle and their mistress cuffed and semi-naked was not the strangest. They were paid well over the going rate for their discretion and did not intend to let this new development fash them. This was probably just some elaborate new game, a test of some sort the mistress had devised. Seeing there were no cases to carry, they stood passively as the little party walked in single file up the worn stone steps, under the arch of foliage and into the castle.

Stephanie had contemplated screaming for help but what could they have done? Even if all six servants had come out at the same time it would be unlikely that they could overpower the three men and Amanda. Certainly these two would have been thrown in the lake with no trouble. It was hopeless.

In the main hall, in front of the tapestry that hung from the largest wall and the sweeping marble staircase, they all stopped. The servants disappeared. Andrew looked around like a man surveying his new property.

'Some place,' Paul said.

'Oh, you haven't seen nothing yet. Amanda, why don't you take Paul and Mick down to the cellars?

130

You know what to do. I'm sure Bruno won't be much trouble. I'm going upstairs to enjoy myself.

'Oh, Bruno's no problem,' Amanda said.

It was probably true, Stephanie thought with increasing depression. Bruno, the keeper of the keys in the cellars, was no match for Paul and Mick, especially as they had the element of surprise.

'I'll be down in an hour or so,' Andrew said.

'Take your time,' Mick said.

'Yeah, if everything you've told us is true we'll be in no rush to enjoy the facilities.'

Amanda led them to the little door behind the tapestry.

'Shall I go to the office and get started on the files?' Venetia asked.

'Oh, I don't think so. Not yet. I think I'd prefer it if you came with me.'

'You can trust me, I told you . . .'

'Oh, I'm sure I can. But let's just say I'd prefer you to come with me for the time being. I wouldn't want you being tempted to make a little secret telephone call to Devlin or anybody else. Once I've disconnected all the phones you can roam around to your heart's content.'

'You think I'd do that?'

'Let's just go upstairs together. Then we can all relax.'

'Fine with me.'

'Take me to your room,' Andrew ordered, taking Stephanie's arm. He had only ever been to Stephanie's room the back way, through the stairs that led directly from the cellars, the metal pouch chained around his genitals, dreading what lay ahead of him.

As Stephanie mounted the marble ahead of him,

the little crescents of her buttocks visible under the legs of the French knickers, the tight suspenders pulling at the stockings, their welts somehow making the creamy flesh above them seem softer and more exposed, her thick pubic hair escaping the loose crotch as her thighs moved, it was definitely not dread Andrew felt now. It was an entirely different emotion.

Chapter Six

He sat on the double bed, his back propped up against the wall, and looked at the two women. Outside, through the terrace windows, he could see the lake spread out from the castle, its calm waters reflecting the scudding clouds that were now dominating the sky, big white clouds gathering from the west and darkening by the minute. But the weather did not concern him.

It was the moment Andrew Harlock had waited for, planned and calculated for, since his term at the castle had begun four months ago. Every day, every night, every minute of every hour, in the cellars or out in the gardens, being punished for his disobedience, or meekly obeying the orders he was given, he had thought of a way to get his revenge. He was that sort of man. He wasn't going to let the haughty, stuck-up, black-haired bitch get away with treating him like a piece of dirt. It was as simple as that. She was going to have to be made to pay for the humiliation she'd inflicted on him.

And his plan had worked perfectly, like clockwork. What Devlin and Stephanie did was outside the law. That was his trump card and he knew it. Devlin wouldn't call the police because the police would be followed by the press and that Devlin definitely didn't want.

It had been easy to recruit two friends to come

along for the ride. He'd promised them, with no exaggeration, sexual favours beyond their wildest dreams. Recruiting Amanda had been more difficult. She had served longer at the castle than he had but he knew she would relish the chance for revenge. Of all the slaves, she had always shown most spirit, and had been punished as regularly as he had. But he had no way of knowing when she would be released or how to contact her. One day in the gardens he had found himself working next to her. With a hoe he had scratched the word REVENGE in the soil at her feet. Quickly, before the overseers came past, she had scored a telephone number in the dirt. Every day after he had been sent back to England he had rung the number and after four weeks of trying she had finally answered. When he'd told her his plans she had jumped at the opportunity to return to the castle in more luxurious fashion.

And the rest had been easy. Easier than even he had imagined. He could not help grinning as he looked round the beautifully appointed bedroom with its silk-panelled walls and thick wool carpets, every item of furniture chosen with perfect taste, no expense spared. He was, he thought, the master of all he surveyed. Including the two women.

The room darkened as the sun disappeared finally behind a bank of cloud and rain began to drizzle on the terracotta paving outside.

'Come here,' he ordered, pointing at Stephanie. She obeyed, standing by the side of the bed. 'Very obedient,' he mocked. He ran his hand along her thigh, up over the welt of the beige stockings, onto the soft flesh of her thigh. Stephanie did not move. She saw his eyes looking hard at her body, at the way the knickers creased at the triangle of her belly, at the way her firm breasts jutted sharply from her chest. She knew what he was thinking, she had experienced the same reaction herself faced with an obedient slave: so many possibilities.

'You,' he said to Venetia, 'open a bottle of champagne.' He knew there was always champagne in the bedroom fridge recessed behind one of the silk panels. He'd seen it on more than one of his previous visits. Stephanie had sipped champagne while he'd been massaging her naked body, his cock straining against the confinement of the pouch. His anger rose again at the thought.

As Venetia went to the fridge Andrew swung himself off the bed. He started prowling around the room. At the far end where all the wardrobes and chests of drawers were kept, he started investigating their contents. He found Stephanie's lingerie and rifled through it. He found the drawers of equipment – straps and chains and leather harnesses, dildos and gags and silk or leather blindfolds – that Stephanie used on Devlin or the slaves.

'Well, what have we got here?' he said as he opened a specially constructed drawer within one of the wardrobes, a long drawer containing a selection of whips. He couldn't suppress a shudder as his body remembered what had been inflicted on him. He picked out a short riding crop and swished it experimentally through the air. He came back to the bed and used the leather loop on the end of the crop to caress Stephanie's cheek. 'Lie on the bed, mistress,' he said, his eyes sparkling with excitement. 'On your stomach.'

For a moment Stephanie hesitated.

'Do it,' Andrew barked angrily.

Awkwardly, with no hands for support, Stephanie

obeyed. She could feel Andrew's eyes on her arse. He followed them with the loop of the whip, tracing it along her thighs, over the welts of the stockings, up the suspenders, pushing it under the lace-edged leg of the knickers to reveal more of her buttocks. Stephanie expected to feel the cut of the whip at any moment.

Venetia had opened the champagne and handed Andrew a glass.

'Cheers,' she said, raising the glass she had poured for herself.

'Cheers, darling,' he said, swigging back the champagne and choking on the bubbles. He eyed Venetia's long legs in the tight trousers of the one-piece suit. 'I suppose I can't change your mind?'

Venetia did not need to ask what he meant. She could see it in his eyes. 'I told you I'd do anything but that.'

'What a waste.'

'What are you going to do to her?' Venetia asked.

He laughed, loudly and long. 'Everything. Everything she did to me and a great deal more.'

'I mean now.'

'Now. Now a little appetizer, I think. Lock the bedroom door and bring me the key. Get me one of those chains from the drawer, a small one.'

Venetia did both things at once. Andrew unbuttoned his shirt, slipped the doorkey onto the chain and hung it around his neck. Then he took the key of the handcuffs out of his pocket and unlocked them. Stephanie's wrists fell to her side.

'Take her boots and knickers off. Leave the stockings on. I like stockings.'

Venetia knelt on the bed and rolled Stephanie onto her back. She unzipped the boots and pulled them from Stephanie's calves, dropping them on the floor. Stephanie stared into her eyes, trying to see what was going on in her mind. She had treated Venetia badly occasionally but Venetia had always been special. They had always had a special relationship. Surely she hadn't forgotten that? But Venetia steadfastly refused to meet her gaze and her eyes were blank. Stephanie could see nothing there at all, no clue as to what she was thinking.

Taking the waistband of the French knickers in her hands, Venetia pulled them down Stephanie's hips, not waiting for her to raise her bottom off the bed.

'Oh yes, I remember that,' Andrew said, standing at the foot of the bed and looking up Stephanie's long stockinged legs. 'You come here,' he said to Venetia who got up off the bed immediately. 'Put your hand out,' he added.

Venetia held one hand up in front of Andrew who picked up the discarded handcuffs and snapped one cuff over her wrist. He pulled her over to the large radiator on the wall alongside the bed and clipped the other cuff around the pipe that led into it at skirting-board level.

'I thought I was on your side,' Venetia said, crouching on the floor.

'You are. It's just I don't want you getting any funny ideas while I'm otherwise engaged. I only like to have to think about one thing at a time.'

'I told you I'm a slave too.'

'I know what you said. Don't worry, you'll get plenty of chances to prove yourself . . .' Andrew picked up her glass of champagne and handed it to her with a broad smile. Then he walked back to the bed. 'Now . . .' he said, looking down at Stephanie, 'I can't tell you how much I've looked forward to this.'

Stephanie looked into his eyes. She could see his excitement. Quite calmly he stripped off his shoes and socks and pulled his trousers and pants down his legs. His cock was circumcised and semi-erect, surrounded by pubic hair as blond and curly as that on his head.

He knelt on the bed beside her and for a long moment did nothing but look at her magnificent body. He had seen it many times, naked and clothed, clad in lacy silk underwear, black satin basques, tight clinging Lycra, or hard leather corselettes. But always before he'd hardly dared to look for fear it would cause an erection to swell against the confines of the immovable metal pouch. This time his cock was free and it responded by coming to full erection, throbbing and hard, as his eyes roamed over her body.

'What do you want me to do?' Stephanie asked. There was no point in making things worse by not co-operating.

Andrew did not answer. Instead he swung his thigh across her chest so he was kneeling over her breasts, his rampant cock inches from her mouth. He grabbed her by the hair and pulled her onto him, as he'd dreamt of doing so many times since he'd left the castle.

Stephanie sucked his cock as best she could. She would have liked to have moved her head but his grip was too tight. She concentrated on tonguing the ridge under the glans, wanting to make him come as quickly as she could. Then it would be over, at least for the time being.

His grip slackened as the feelings in his cock intensified. He reached behind his back with one hand to feel for her cunt. With little finesse he found her labia and pushed two fingers inside. Her cunt was hot and wet. He pushed his fingers as deep as they would go and heard her moan against his cock.

Stephanie lunged her head forward. His cock filled her mouth. She could feel it beginning to swell with spunk. She worked faster, trying to make her mouth like her cunt, wet and tight, trying to suck out his spunk.

'Not so fast . . .' he said, pulling his cock out from between her lips. 'I know what you're trying to do.'

But she had largely succeeded. Andrew's excitement was intense. He knew he couldn't last long now. Quickly he swung off her and rolled her onto her stomach. In his mind he had imagined doing this so many times, he had wanked endlessly since he left the castle, thinking of this body and how it had tormented him, how he had endured the never-ending frustration. And now it was his. He knelt between her legs and pulled her hips up to meet him. He wanted to bugger her, to fuck her and bugger her, alternate between the two passages of her body, but now he knew he would only just manage to get his cock into that hot cunt, as its thick fleshy labia nudged at his balls.

He had dreamt of this moment. He pressed forward and felt his cock slide up the whole length of her tight wet cunt, right up until he could feel his balls resting against her arse. He thought he was going to come then, just on that one stroke, but he managed to control himself. He pulled back and lunged again, and that was it. His body took control, his cock began to spasm and he took his last glimpse of Stephanie's long back bisected by the suspender belt, and the tight suspenders stretching the welts of the stockings on her thighs, before his eyes rolled up and his spunk jetted into her body. He thought he felt her cunt contracting round his cock as though trying to milk every last drop of spunk from him, and as his orgasm finally ended he whimpered, for a reason he did not understand, one word.

'Mistress . . .'

It was a simple harness, but effective. A thick band of leather around the neck with a similar thick strap down between the shoulder-blades, to which were attached two leather cuffs, one on top of the other. Stephanie's wrists were buckled tightly into these cuffs, her elbows jutting out like chicken wings, her breasts thrust forward. She was completely naked now apart from a pair of black high heels Venetia had levered on to her feet. A chain, like a leash, was clipped to a D-ring in the front of the collar and it was by this that Andrew, wearing a white towelling robe from her bathroom, was leading her down the stone staircase that led directly to the cellars. Venetia, still in the tight black one-piece trouser-suit, brought up the rear.

As Andrew opened the thick wooden door at the bottom of the stairs they were greeted by a scene that looked like the orgies of ancient Rome. There were copulating couples everywhere. Mattresses had been dragged out of the individual cells on one side of the wide vaulted hallway and men and women ranged over them in a variety of positions. The slaves had all been freed and the males had quickly found the keys to the padlocks that held the metal pouches chained over their genitals. Without restriction for the first time in weeks, they were clearly giving vent to their frustrations. The female slaves showed no signs of being unwilling to help.

Stephanie glimpsed Paul lying on the floor while two women sucked and licked at his balls. Mick, on the other hand, was lying on his back on a mattress with one of the larger women slaves impaled on his cock. She, in turn, was sucking the cock of a male slave and wanking on the cock of another. A similar chain of bodies was formed at the far end of the corridor. A male had his head buried between the legs of one of the women who was sucking on the cock of a man who, in turn, was eagerly eating the labia of a second female whose mouth was clamped firmly over the cock of the first man. A complete circle of sex. In one corner Stephanie recognised Molly, the petite blonde with the large fleshy tits, who was busily engaged doing precisely what she had done to Stephanie while the Baron watched, but this time with another slave.

The wine cellars, just outside the slaves' quarters, had been liberally raided too. There were bottles of wine and fine brandy everywhere.

Only Amanda was missing. Stephanie could guess where she was. As if reading her mind, Andrew picked his way through the naked bodies, none of whom paid any attention, and led the way into the suite of rooms designed for the castle guests to entertain or be entertained by the slaves. Here there were two luxuriously appointed bedrooms with their own bathrooms and video equipment, together with another room; the punishment room, a large chamber formed from the original stone of the castle walls, with a flagstoned floor. Here every conceivable sexual whim could be satisfied, from bondage to rubber, leather, transvestism and the wishes of sadists and masochists. Chains, punishment frames, pulleys and racks filled the room and it was here, as Stephanie had suspected, they found Amanda.

She was naked but for a pair of skimpy black briefs and high heels. Her big muscular body was sweating and Stephanie could see why. Secured by his hands and feet with thick leather straps and lying face-down on one of the punishment frames was Bruno. It was Bruno who had administered most of the punishments awarded to the slaves and Stephanie guessed he would be the prime target for Amanda's revenge. The long whip she held in her hand and the welts that criss-crossed his heavy buttocks told their story.

She slashed the whip down on Bruno's buttocks again and he bucked against his bonds. Though he was mute he managed to produce a moan of pain. Amanda threw the whip aside.

'Having fun?' Andrew asked.

'Oh yes, I feel much better now I've given this bastard a taste of his own medicine.'

'I thought you might like to start on this,' Andrew said, pulling Stephanie forward by the leash.

'Not yet.' Amanda's eyes were blazing with excitement. She sidled up to Andrew and pulled the robe open, circling his cock with her hand. 'Why don't you come next door with me? I've got myself all worked up now, Andy. Wouldn't you like to take advantage of me?' She kissed him hard on the mouth and rubbed her breasts against his chest so he could feel the hardness of her nipples, at the same time pulling at his cock not at all gently. It begun to get hard.

'Come on then. Since everyone else seems to be having such a good time.'

'Bring her too,' Amanda said, looking at the naked Stephanie. 'She can watch.'

'And me?' Venetia said.

In the corridor outside the punishment room, Andrew saw that the outer door could be locked by a big old-fashioned mortice. He turned the key in the lock, then removed it.

'Now you can do what you like' he told Venetia as Amanda led Stephanie into one of the bedrooms.

So far the suite of rooms hadn't been touched by the chaos outside. Amanda slumped onto the big bed, her near-naked body glistening under the light. Skimming off her panties, she opened her legs wide and began to wank at her clitoris. Then she dipped a finger into her cunt, withdrew it, then sucked it into her mouth. She moaned at the taste like it was some great delicacy.

'Never knew revenge could taste so sweet,' she said.

Andrew took Stephanie's leash again and led her to the foot of the bed. The bed had short corner-posts projecting about a foot above the mattress, into each of which was set a solid brass ring. Andrew pushed Stephanie into a kneeling position facing the bed, and threaded the chain leash through the ring, tying it so tightly Stephanie's cheek was forced against the wooden post and she was unable to turn her head.

'Come on big boy, come and fuck me,' Amanda said.

But Andrew was looking around the room.

'What do you want?'

He saw what he was looking for. In a stand by the chest of drawers was a selection of three or four riding crops. He picked one up and tested it by swishing it through the air as he had done upstairs.

'You're not using that on me,' Amanda said at once.

'That's not what I had in mind,' Andrew said.

'On her is fine with me, as long as you hurry up and fuck me. Can't you see how much I need it?'

Andrew knelt on the bed, stripping off the robe and wanking his cock in his hand. As soon as it was completely hard he slid down onto the naked Amanda.

143

'Oh yes,' she moaned, feeling the tip of his shaft between her labia. Her body shuddered and she felt a great gush of her own juices flowing out of her sex. 'Give it to me,' she begged.

Andrew moved his hips up and back and his cock slipped into the opening of her cunt. He held it there, savouring the moment, feeling his glans almost sprayed with her copious juices, she was so wet.

'Give it to me Andy, I'm so hot.' Amanda squirmed her body underneath him.

'Is this what you want?' he said, bucking his hips forward, sinking his cock deep into the recesses of her body.

'Oh God . . .' she moaned. 'God, God, God . . .' she screamed with every inward stroke he made. 'God, God, God . . .' like air being forced out by a hammer-blow to the solar plexus.

As she started to come she looked down at Stephanie, helpless and naked at the foot of the bed. The image of her excited Amanda more. They had the power now, power to do anything. She felt her body trembling. Her sweat made the movement of their bodies slippery, slipping against each other, just as Andrew's cock was slippery inside her. As he plunged down into her she felt her nerves and muscles lock and her orgasm broke, smashing down on the head of his cock, so hard and so deep inside her.

He did not stop his rhythm. He had a different agenda. He knew what he wanted. He had felt it up-stairs with Stephanie. As he fucked her he'd yearned for the feeling. As soon as Amanda had recovered he slipped the whip into her hand.

'Beat me now,' he whispered. 'Beat my arse while I'm fucking you.'

'You want that?'

144

'I need it,' he said. In truth he would have liked Stephanie to whip him as she had in the past. In truth, he realised now, he had wanked himself over and over again not only on the idea of fucking his beautiful mistress but he had made himself hard and throbbing and spunking on the feelings he'd had from being whipped and from the hot red welts on his arse where the whip had left its mark. He needed that too.

'I'll do that.' The voice was calm and cool. Andrew looked over his shoulder. Venetia had changed into a black leather catsuit, its V-neck plunging to reveal the cleavage of her big round breasts, its leggings so tight they seemed to follow the crease of her sex itself. She took the whip from Amanda's hand and in one seemingly continuous movement raised it over her head and slashed it down on Andrew's buttocks before he could raise any objection.

A line of fire blazed across his white buttocks, making him plunge his cock into Amanda's sex and filling him instantly with the pulsing energy of a pain that turned quickly to breath-taking pleasure.

'Oh yes . . .' he groaned. He felt the red welt the whip had caused puckering his arse, burning hot.

Another stroke fell, and another. He wanted to look back at the amazon who was beating him so beautifully but couldn't concentrate on anything but the sensations boiling in his blood. His cock was on fire, driven forward harder and deeper by each stroke. This was what it was going to be like now. His every whim catered for in an instant. He could feel Stephanie's eyes on him, knew she could see the red welts appear on his buttocks, see his cock plunging into Amanda's sex and his balls banging against her arse, and that was all part of it, all part of the explosion that overtook him, his cock recoiling against the cavern of Amanda's soaking wet cunt to spit out hot white spunk for the second time that day.

It seemed a long time before his cock softened and was expelled from Amanda's sex, as though in slow motion. They both moaned involuntarily as the contact was lost. Andrew rolled over and looked up at Venetia.

'Well, maybe we can trust her.'

'Don't be so sure,' Amanda said more cynically. 'She's staying in the cells tonight. I won't sleep with her on the loose.'

'No, it's all right, she can spend the night with me. I'll handcuff her to the radiator.'

'As long as she's secure. Don't take any chances until Devlin turns up tomorrow.'

That remark startled Stephanie. How did they know Devlin was due tomorrow? She hadn't mentioned it and neither had Venetia.

Andy was untying the leash from the bed-post.

'Time for bed then, we've got a busy day tomorrow.'

He pulled Stephanie to her feet and out into the hall. He unlocked the outer door with the key and they were back in the main cellar. Some of the orgy had come to an end but other elements, Paul in particular, were still far from finished. He lay on one of the mattresses with his legs wide open and three girls taking it in turn to suck his cock. One had her finger inserted in his anus, the second held his balls in the palm of her hand, jiggling them up and down, while the third used her finger-nails to pinch his nipples with one hand, using the other to hold the shaft of his cock and share it out between their three hungry mouths. Saliva dripped from their chins. As Stephanie watched, Paul's body tensed, he stretched

146

out to his full length like someone waking from a deep sleep, and spunk oozed rather than jetted from his cock. Meticulously the three women shared it out between them, passing it from mouth to mouth, so they all had a taste.

The main cellar door was open as well as the smaller door to the back staircase, and many of the freed slaves had disappeared, no doubt to play and sleep in the comfort of the rooms upstairs. Stephanie could imagine the havoc they would cause. The cellars themselves were already littered with debris.

Andrew pulled Stephanie into one of the individual cells. Though the cellars of the castle were very old they had been rebuilt from stone quarried on the island to meet Devlin's particular requirements: twelve cells no more than eight feet by four, constructed under the vaulted ceiling. Each cell had a heavy wooden door with an observation port, a single overhead light and an iron ring set into the flagstone floor, to which a chain was attached by a metal link. At the end of the chain was a metal cuff.

Andrew had chosen the cell for Stephanie deliberately. It was the one he had been forced to use. Normally each cell had a mattress but the one for this cell had been dragged outside by the revellers.

'Sleep well,' Andrew said, snapping the metal cuff around Stephanie's ankle just as it had been secured every night around his.

'Don't leave me without . . .' Stephanie said, then stopped herself. She was about to beg him not to leave her like this, her arms tied into the small of her back, with nothing to sleep on, but she knew it was useless to plead with him. She had been hoisted on her own petard and she had just better get used to the idea.

The cell door slammed shut and the overhead light went out. Apart from the light that leaked under the door, the cell was completely black. Tentatively Stephanie sat on the floor. The chain leash from the collar hung down between her breasts, swinging against her nipples as she completed the difficult manoeuvre. She rested her arms against the wall which, with her wrists strapped up in the harness as they were, was not at all comfortable. She shifted around so that she rested her upper arm only against the stone but this was not much of an improvement in terms of comfort. It was going to be a long night.

Laughter and voices came from the corridor outside but finally died away and the cellars were quiet. The walls were too thick to hear any noise from the rooms above.

Stephanie closed her eyes, not because she thought she would sleep but because there was nothing to see. She suddenly felt a wave of exhaustion overcome her. There was no escape. It would be a miracle if Susie had managed to connect Devlin in Moscow. She might have tried the plane he was chartering but how would she know which company he was using? Even if the main office knew, there was no guarantee they could contact the crew, what with the difficulties of communications in Russia and the fact that they probably didn't know which city Devlin was in. If she did manage it then of course there would be a rescue. Devlin would find a way. But if she did not, when Devlin landed tomorrow, suspecting nothing, it would not be the usual driver who met him but Andrew and Amanda. He would be trapped, subjected like her to whatever wild plans Andrew had devised.

Stephanie's arms ached and the leather collar cuffed around her neck bit into the underside of her chin whenever she tried to lower her head a little. The strain on her elbows and arms forced into an awkward position by the harness made her want to cry. But that was one thing Andrew would never get the satisfaction of seeing. She found if she arched her head right back she could pull the leather strap between her shoulder-blades down slightly and ease the pressure in her arms but it was only temporary relief as the position soon made her neck ache instead.

For some time, since sleep was impossible, she allowed herself to wallow in despair. It could be a very long time before Andrew and Amanda and their friends tired of the delights of the castle. Clearly the female slaves were suitably grateful for their freedom. The impact of being released so unexpectedly from the extreme discomfort of the cellars had been immediate. The male slaves, deprived of their ability to have sex at all for so long, had reacted predictably and were still, no doubt, enjoying their new-found freedom in the bedrooms upstairs. Any promises Andrew had made his friends were being fulfilled in spades.

And in her despair Stephanie thought about Venetia. She remembered, with a chill that ran through her whole body, how badly she had treated her in London, how she had teased her and abused her. Was that why she had joined forces with Andrew so easily. Had she meant what she had said about being used like the other slaves? Stephanie had treated her like a slave in London, it was perfectly true, but she had also treated her like an equal. Well, almost. But was almost enough?

If Devlin walked into the trap that had been set for him tomorrow, Venetia was the only hope that something could be done to turn the tables on Andrew and Amanda. Perversely, though it was the middle of the night and cold, Stephanie felt a glimmer of hope.

Chapter Seven

In the cellars there was no way of telling day from night. Stephanie woke to find herself lying on her stomach on the stone floor without the slightest idea how long she had been asleep. She had no feeling in her arms until she sat up, when agonising pins and needles indicated the blood starting to flow again. Her optimism of the small hours had evaporated. She was dirty and cold and every muscle in her body ached. She was also hungry.

How long it was before the cell door was flung open and Amanda entered, Stephanie had no way of knowing. Her watch – the Patek Phillipe that Devlin had given her – was still on her wrist but her wrist was twisted up into the small of her back.

Clearly Amanda had been through Stephanie's wardrobes. She was wearing one of her wild silk dresses, belted at the waist. She had used Stephanie's scent liberally too, the rich aroma of Givenchy filling the cell.

'Get up,' she ordered.

Stephanie struggled to her feet. As soon as she was up Amanda grabbed the chain leash hanging down between her breasts. She had managed to extract her feet from the high heels during the night and Amanda saw them lying on the floor.

'Put those on again,' she ordered.

Stephanie did as she was told. As soon as she had

accomplished the task, so simple and yet impossibly hard with no hands to use for balance, Amanda tugged hard on the leash, almost making Stephanie stumble.

Out in the corridor the debris from last night lay everywhere: discarded clothes, bottles and the black leather-covered pouches littering the mattresses. At the end of the cellar, towards the main door, a block of toilets and showers had been installed. It was here that the slaves were made to scrub each other down every morning and evening after their day in the gardens. As Amanda marched her down to the showers Stephanie noticed that only one of the other cells was still bolted; there, she imagined, was where Bruno was being kept.

It was obvious that the cellars were completely deserted. When they reached the white tiled shower cubicles Amanda began unstrapping Stephanie's wrists. There was a chance here, Stephanie thought, a chance for escape. If she could overpower Amanda and release Bruno they might be able to get off the island. The speedboat might have been left at the jetty? But what if Andrew had taken its keys? Not only that, but her chances of overpowering Amanda were not good. Her arms were weakened by their constriction. As Amanda released them one at a time she could bearly move them at all, let alone use them to struggle against Amanda's considerable strength.

'Try it,' Amanda said. 'Just try it . . .' They were getting good at reading her mind.

With her arms freed, Amanda unbuckled the leather harness from around Stephanie's neck and threw it to the floor. She watched her like a hawk as first she allowed her into one of the toilet stalls and then made her shower, wash her hair and clean her teeth.

As soon as this was done, and without waiting for her to dry herself, Amanda produced a pair of leather cuffs joined together by a short stout chain.

'Hold out your hands,' she ordered.

As she was about to buckle the first cuff on Stephanie's wrist she noticed her Patek Phillipe watch.

'Well, this is very nice,' she said. She opened the bracelet that held the watch in place and slipped it off Stephanie's wrist and onto her own. 'Very nice,' she said, holding her wrist up to admire her new acquisition.

Amanda buckled the leather cuffs round Stephanie's wrists. Attached to the link which held the cuffs together was another chain, again like a leash, and by this Amanda tugged her forward.

'My shoes . . .' Stephanie protested.

Amanda thought about that for a moment, then allowed her to go back and wriggle her wet feet into them.

They progressed through the main door of the cellars, through the racks of vintage wine to the stone staircase that led to the main hall of the castle. Picking their way carefully up the worn steps they emerged into the daylight, Stephanie screwing up her eyes against its power after the gloom of the cell.

When she was able to see properly she was surprised at how little damage appeared to have been done. The hall looked perfectly normal with the exception of an empty brandy bottle in one of the huge terracotta pots that held the indoor palm trees.

Amanda headed down the long passage behind the main staircase that led to the office complex, the two women's high heels clacking on the marble floor. The small, ornately carved door at the end was open.

Beyond there was a large modern office, the hub of Devlin's business empire when he was staying at the castle. There were three secretary's desks, each with computer terminals, telephones, VDUs and fax machines. The walls were lined with white filing cabinets and shelves stacked with computer tapes and box files. But instead of the neatly arranged order the office usually displayed, there was now chaos. Every single filing cabinet had been ransacked and some had even toppled over onto the floor. There were files and paper everywhere.

On the far side of the room was Devlin's office. A long picture window had been cut into the side of the stone of the castle walls to reveal the gardens and orchards at the back of the castle. Here, in this office, there were no filing cabinets or computers, just a massive desk carved from a single piece of walnut, a low leather sofa, a leather high-backed swivel chair behind the desk and a single telephone. Stephanie could see that the swivel chair was occupied but as its back was turned towards her she could not tell by whom.

As Amanda pulled her into the room the desk chair swung round and Andrew put his feet up on the thick walnut of the desk.

'Sleep well?' he said, his eyes examining her naked body. 'Not very comfortable down there, is it?'

'She deserves it,' Venetia said. She was sitting on the leather sofa wearing a one-piece Lycra and nylon body suit like a leotard and a pair of tights combined in one garment. It was as transparent as tights, showing every line and curve of her body and her big spherical breasts, though most of these were already displayed by the plunging neckline of the Lycra that reached almost to her navel. The triangle of her belly was hidden under the body suit by a tiny black G-string matching the black shading of the one-piece. Her feet were clad in shiny black high-heeled ankle boots. She looked, whether at her own behest or Andrew's, like a whore in a brothel, a very expensive whore in a very expensive brothel.

Stephanie looked around. Devlin's private safe, set into the stone wall at floor level, was open and she could see the neat stacks of money inside: Swiss francs, pounds sterling and Italian lire.

Andrew had followed her eyes. 'Venetia has been most helpful,' he said.

Stephanie glanced at her but again she refused to meet her eyes. She knew Venetia had acted to protect herself but now it appeared she was prepared to go further. Stephanie had found it difficult to imagine that Venetia would betray her or Devlin but she was beginning to believe that was precisely what she was doing.

'However,' Andrew continued, 'we need your access code to the computer.'

'What are you going to do?' Stephanie asked.

'We're instructing the computer to destroy the files,' Venetia said, standing up. Her bizarre costume made her magnificent body look even more attractive; her big breasts trembled under the nylon, her breasts and buttocks stretching the weave of the material and therefore making the shading lighter, giving them an impression of whiteness in contrast to the less stressed areas where the denier was denser and blacker.

'Show her,' Andrew said, getting up from Devlin's chair. He was wearing jeans and one of Devlin's handmade white shirts.

The four filed into the outer office. Andrew was unable to resist the temptation to stroke Venetia's curvaceous arse. She greeted the touch with a shudder of distaste and slapped his hand away immediately.

'I thought we had an agreement,' she said.

'We do,' he replied. 'Doesn't stop me wanting.'

'As long as that's all you do.'

The nearest computer terminal was turned on and Stephanie read the instructions telling the mainframe to erase a whole list of files. At the bottom of the screen a message flashed in bright green capital letters: PLEASE TYPE SECURITY ACCESS CODE.

'Do it,' Andrew said, pushing Stephanie forward.

Stephanie did not hesitate. What was the point? She had no doubt what they would do to her if she tried to resist. She typed in four numbers and pressed the ENTER key. The screen went blank. One word, also flashing, appeared: SURE? Venetia moved Stephanie aside and typed in the word YES. The screen went blank again before, in micro-seconds, it read: FILES ERASED.

'Which leaves the hard copies . . .' Amanda said.

Venetia was already typing out instructions. 'This will go to Devlin's office in London. They will destroy the files.' She pressed the enter button.

Stephanie's heart missed a beat. She tried to remember what Venetia knew. The security arrangements had all been changed. Did Venetia know that no file would be destroyed without a security access code different from the one she had already given? They had made the change three months ago but had they told Venetia about it? Surely she must know, she knew everything about the computer system? If she did then she had not revealed it to Andrew and Amanda and knew perfectly well the files would not be destroyed. Which meant she was clearly still trying to act with Devlin's interests at heart. But what if she didn't? Then she was betraying them, totally prepared to do anything to save herself from Andrew, Mick and Paul or any of the male slaves. Perhaps she had not been told because it did not involve a computer program, just an instruction about files which had nothing to do with the computer. Stephanie tried to remember but couldn't.

'Are you sure they'll do it?' Andrew asked.

'Positive,' Venetia said, once again ignoring the look Stephanie was giving her. 'Look . . .'

The screen read: INSTRUCTIONS RECEIVED.

That seemed to satisfy Andrew. He turned to the wall and ripped out the sockets connecting the computer to the phone lines. He ripped out the telephones and the fax lines too. The main terminal for all the phones into the castle was a small grey box on the wall by the door. He kicked this hard until it fell apart, a tangle of coloured wires. 'Are there any other phones? Private lines?'

'No. They all come through here.'

'Good. Don't want to be disturbed, do we?'

'So now we just need to know when Devlin arrives?' Amanda said, staring at Venetia.

'I told you I don't know,' Venetia said quickly.

'We know it's today. We called his office. They were very helpful,' Andrew grinned. That was how they knew when he was coming back. 'But when?'

'I don't know. He didn't specify a time. We send the boat out when we hear the plane. The driver would do the same. That's normal.' Stephanie thought that sounded like a convincing lie. Devlin was expected at two. There was just a chance they might not get there in time if they waited until they heard the plane circling. There was normally time for the boat to get to the jetty by leaving when they heard

156

the plane, but they would also have to get into the car and find the landing strip. There was a slim chance that Devlin might be alerted if the car was late.

'I see.' Andrew was thinking. 'Well, I think we'll have to organise a little surprise party for Mr Devlin. There's no way he can be here before one. Then we'll sit and wait for him. Be prepared . . . isn't that right, mistress?' Once again he sneered at the word "mistress".

'If you say so.'

'But I do.' Andrew smiled broadly, coming right up to Stephanie, his face inches from hers. 'So let's go and see how our other preparations are getting on,' he said, catching the leash that hung from her wrists and jerking her forward.

Andrew led Stephanie out of the offices with Amanda and Venetia following. They walked down the long passage and out under the stairs into the main reception room. If Stephanie had any illusions that the slaves were not causing chaos in the castle, they soon disappeared. The living room and dining room were a total mess. Pictures had been ripped and torn from the walls, *objets d'art* smashed and red wine sprayed everywhere. All the bookcases had been ransacked, the books lying in heaps on the floor, and the priceless rugs cut into pieces.

In the dining room the massive glass table had been shattered into a thousand pieces and the glass display case containing English Georgian silver lay on its side, its contents gone.

In the living room a space had been cleared in front of the gothic fireplace, where a wooden table looted from one of the other rooms had been set up with two dining chairs behind it. To one side of the table and in front of it, two leather wing chairs had been placed side by side. Opposite these, on the other side, a smaller table and chair had been arranged. The rest of the space had been filled with a selection of chairs set in two rows.

'Excellent,' Andrew declared.

Mick and Paul had been supervising the work, each wearing nothing more than a pair of shorts – Devlin's shorts – belted with one of his silk Sulka ties. Three of the male slaves had been helping them, and one of the females. The males were clothed from Devlin's wardrobe too, Savile Row-tailored trousers and Jermyn Street shirts, their sleeves rolled up and their tails knotted at the navel. Stephanie recognised the black silk teddy the female was wearing as her own.

There had been five men and seven women in the cellars when they arrived but there was no sign of the others.

'Well we've got one defendant. Now we need the other,' Amanda said.

'Where are the others?' Andrew asked.

'Oh, they went to get the garden overseers. Seemed to think they had a score to settle . . .' Paul said.

'We do,' the female slave said eagerly. 'They're taking them down to the cellars . . .'

'Sounds like fun, I think I'll watch.' Mick grinned broadly.

'Well, it seems we've got a little time for a diversion,' Andrew said. 'Let me see. What shall we do now? Order some coffee while I'm thinking,' he said to Venetia.

'The servants have gone,' she replied.

'What!'

'They ran off this morning.'

'How could they? I locked the boat up in the boathouse myself. I've still got the keys.'

158

'There were two rowing-boats down by the orchard.'

'Did you know about this?' Amanda turned to Venetia menacingly.

'No, no, of course not. You can't expect them to stay with all this going on. Anyway, there's plenty of food in the kitchen. We can cook it ourselves.'

'True,' Andrew said.

'Can we go back to the cellars now? We don't want to miss the fun,' one of the male slaves asked.

'Sure. Do what you like until the trial starts. Give them one for me.' Andrew remembered how the over-seers had reacted to any hint of slackness in his work rate.

'I'm going too,' Amanda said as the slaves headed for the cellar door. 'I think this needs my personal attention.'

'Well, I've got an idea, since we've got time on our hands,' Andrew said as the slaves with Amanda and Mick headed for the cellars.

'I want to eat,' Paul said, his sexual appetite still satiated from the excesses of last night.

'Well, that just leaves me, doesn't it?' Andrew picked up the leash on Stephanie's cuffs and started to lead her out of the room. Venetia stayed where she was. 'Come on darling. You're going to play a part in what I've got in mind . . . And I don't want to leave you behind anyway, do I?'

Venetia caught up with him and slid her hand round his arm. 'Still don't trust me?' she said, her semi-nude body looking so sexy under its sheen of nylon Lycra.

'You're getting there,' he said, eyeing her body as they walked up the marble staircase.

Stephanie's bedroom was a mess too. All the wardrobe doors were open and all the drawers of the chests pulled out. There were clothes and lingerie and sexual equipment everywhere: panties, basques, whips, dildos, nipple clips, leather harnesses and gags strewn around the room as though a hurricane had torn through it. The bed had been slept in and the sheets were still ruffled.

Andrew looked at his watch.

'We've got two hours. So why don't you two girls give me a show? Apparently Venetia here is a lesbian. She's begged me not to put her with a man. Begged me. But I'm sure you knew all that, didn't you? You're quite intimate, I imagine. Difficult not to want a body like that, isn't it?' His eyes roamed Venetia's voluptuous curves, the body-stocking making them look obscenely ripe. 'So let's see what you get up to.'

For a moment neither woman did anything. Then Venetia turned to Stephanie and pulled her wrists up by the leash, with the intention of unbuckling the cuffs.

'You don't need to take those off. Just get on with it.'

Andrew pulled a chair up to the foot of the bed and sat down as Venetia gently put pressure on Stephanie's arms so she would sit on the bed. Strangely, considering the situation, Stephanie felt a flood of excitement course through her body. She knew what it was. After a cold sleepless night she was glad of any human contact, the warmth of another body against her.

She lay back on the bed without being told. Venetia lay down beside her and turned to kiss her mouth. Unavoidably their eyes met but Venetia's were blank, there was nothing there that Stephanie could see, no feeling, no secret conspiracy of silence, nothing to be read at all. What was she thinking?

160

Stephanie pressed herself against Venetia's body as far as she could with her hands cuffed in front of her. Venetia realised the problem, broke the kiss, picked up Stephanie's arms and looped them over her head, then immediately rolled on top of her and resumed the kiss. Their tongues vied for position, each wanting to explore the other's mouth. After the coldness of last night the softness and warmth of Venetia's body made Stephanie melt with emotion. She writhed her body against the slippery feel of the nylon, feeling Venetia's big breasts squeezing against her own, their legs intertwined. Venetia's thigh forcing its way between Stephanie's legs until she could feel her own wetness leaking out of her labia.

'I've always wanted to watch this,' Andrew said leaning forward in the chair, his elbows on his knees.

Stephanie closed her eyes. Venetia began to slide down her body. She didn't want to think about Andrew watching them, or about the castle or the trial or anything else. With her eyes closed she could just feel, feel Venetia's expert mouth sucking at the tendons of her neck, feel her tongue licking down to her breasts while her hands kneaded and squeezed them, presenting their nipples to be kissed and sucked and pinched with her teeth. Then Venetia's mouth worked lower down, out of the loop of Stephanie's bound arms, down to her belly where her tongue lapped at her thick black pubic hair.

Slowly, with both arms stretched up over her head so her hands could grip Stephanie's firm breasts, her tongue dipped onto her clitoris. The first contact was like an electric shock. Stephanie's body started at the impact. Then the tongue circled the foothills of the tiny mountain and the shockwave settled down into a regular pattern of exquisite sensation.

Occasionally her tongue would dip lower, down into Stephanie's fleshy, thick labia, wet with the sap from her body, and plunge up into the recesses of her cunt, as far up as it could go, circling again, touching the edges of the opening. But always it would return to the swollen clitoris, nudging it softly, then taking up a rhythm again, inevitable, remorseless, perfect.

It went on forever, or so it seemed. It was an escape, the only escape from her situation, the only way out. To let her body fly free.

Stephanie felt herself coming on Venetia's mouth as she had so many times before. But it was different this time. Instead of a big explosive climax, moaning, screaming almost, for her release, this was an implosion, smaller, quieter but no less profound. It was as if her subconscious was trying to keep it private, between Venetia – who she knew could feel each wave of come on her lips – and herself. A secret. Not wanting Andrew to see.

But Andrew had his own ideas. Stephanie felt the bed give beside her and she opened her eyes. Andrew was kneeling beside her head. He had stripped off his clothes and was naked, his smooth circumcised cock fully erect in his hand as he wanked it up and down.

'Lick them,' he said, swinging his thigh over Stephanie's face. 'Lick my balls.' He was facing her feet and positioning himself so that his scrotum was literally balanced on her mouth. It was loose and his balls heavy. 'Lick them,' he repeated, his voice hoarse with passion.

Stephanie opened her mouth and tongued his balls. She could feel his hand wanking the shaft of his cock up and down from top to bottom.

'Harder . . .'

Last night had been full of erotic spectacles. The

night had been spent in an orgy of sensual indulgence, so great he could hardly remember who he had fucked or sucked or wanked in what order. There was cunt and tit and arse everywhere but there had not been a greater erotic spectacle than the one in front of him now. Venetia's fair hair bobbed between Stephanie's thighs, her fine long back sheathed in sheer shiny nylon, Stephanie's breasts gripped tightly between her fingers. They were breasts and thighs he knew so well. He had oiled them, stroked them, massaged them not only in reality out on the terrace in the sun or here on this bed, but over and over in his dreams. He looked down at his cock and saw his balls being sucked down into her mouth. He wanked himself harder, increasing the pace of his hand. Both balls were between her lips now and she was flicking them with her tongue, pulling the skin of his cock tighter still, stretching his glans as his fingers passed over it, making it more sensitive, making him come. His cock jerked wildly and spunk sprayed out in a high arc into the air, landing over Stephanie's tits and Venetia's hands on them, and even splashing into Venetia's hair.

The plane circled the lake. The dark clouds of yesterday had not entirely cleared and the sun was continually being shaded by big fast-moving grey cirrus scudding across the sky. The Learjet, an identical model to Devlin's own plane, banked to the left, straightened up and descended smoothly, its airbrakes extended, perfectly lined up on the long concrete runway built especially for the purpose.

Amanda sat in the back of the Mercedes with Stephanie, the big hunting knife unsheathed on her lap. They had dressed her in a blue silk blouse, just

163

enough to make her look normal from the plane. But apart from the blouse she was naked, her hands cuffed behind her back, her ankles bound too by a thick rope in case she had thought to run and warn Devlin. Andrew and Paul sat in the front seats with Andrew at the wheel. Mick was outside, leaning against the bonnet. Devlin would assume his regular driver was sick. He wouldn't imagine anything was wrong with Stephanie sitting in the back.

It was hot in the car despite the fleeting clouds. Whenever the sun was out it beat down on the metal relentlessly and Stephanie could feel sweat running down her back and sides. As the noise of the plane increased overhead her heart beat faster. In minutes she would know if Devlin had come prepared or if, as she suspected, he was going to walk straight into a trap.

The plane landed in a squeal of tyres and the roar of jet engines thrown into reverse thrust. Braking at the far end of the runway the plane turned round and slowly – painfully slowly as far as Stephanie was concerned – taxied back towards the car. She saw Devlin's face at the window. He smiled. That meant nothing, she thought. The plane could be packed with men from his security company . . .

Amanda moved the knife from her lap to Stephanie's, the blade gleaming in a momentary shaft of sunlight. As the plane had approached, Andrew and Paul had ducked beneath the level of the doors.

'Smile,' Amanda said, twisting the knife slightly. She did not bother to duck. Another woman was no threat. She was just one of the slaves. Perhaps Stephanie had brought her along to amuse Devlin on the boat trip back to the castle: another of Stephanie's inventive little games.

The door of the plane opened and the landing ramp descended. Again its progress seemed impossibly slow. Stephanie had to force herself to breathe. She saw that Devlin's face had disappeared from the window but no one appeared at the open door. It remained empty, a black hole. It was impossible to see anything or anyone inside. Perhaps that was Devlin's plan, Stephanie thought, her pulse racing with hope, to lure them inside one by one and overpower them.

But then Devlin appeared, smiling broadly and carrying his briefcase. A tall, neatly uniformed stewardess appeared too, shaking his hand and, though the words could not be heard over the roar of the engines, obviously wishing him a 'nice day'. He walked down the steps as a steward emerged from the back of the plane with two leather cases.

Stephanie's heart fell. It had only been the slimmest chance that Susie or the pilot would manage to contact him, but it had been a chance. Now there was no hope. Devlin was blithely unaware of what awaited him. Mick took the two cases from the steward, who walked back to the plane.

'Smile,' Amanda repeated, twitching the knife against Stephanie's bare flesh.

If she cried out now, told him to run, he might just make it up the steps of the plane, but it was unlikely. Anyway, with the engines still running it would probably be impossible for him to hear her.

The steward was back in the plane and the landing ramp began retracting. Devlin walked towards the car with Mick behind him carrying the two cases. The plane door closed with a clunk that could be heard over the engine noise and the plane immediately began to roll forward, turning on its nose wheel to head to the take-off point. Now it was too late for anything. As the plane moved away the noise abated a little.

'Darling,' Devlin said as he got to the rear door of the Mercedes. He saw Stephanie's smile disappear at the same time he saw the nakedness of her thighs, the knife in her lap and Andrew and Paul bob up in the front seats.

'Don't do anything silly,' Mick said, dropping the cases and coming up right behind him.

The plane had reached its take-off position. As its engine roared to full throttle the tableau at the car was frozen. Stephanie glimpsed the pilot's face in the cockpit as the plane sped by. He wasn't looking at the car. In a mist of exhaust fumes and heat haze the small jet lifted into the air, the last chance gone.

'What is this?' Devlin said as soon as his voice could be heard.

'Shut up,' Andrew said, getting out of the car. Mick grabbed Devlin's arms and they marched around to the boot.

Two minutes later, Devlin's cases abandoned on the grass by the tarmac, the Mercedes pulled away with Devlin locked in the boot.

'You did well,' Andrew said, looking at Stephanie in the rear-view mirror as he drove.

'You bastard,' she spat.

'Not very nice,' he mocked. 'I think you're going to have to learn politeness.'

The rest was simple. They arrived at the jetty and Devlin was bundled out of the boot, handcuffed with his hands behind his back and marched onto the boat. Stephanie's ankles were freed and she too was put aboard, sitting next to Devlin on the long bench seat in the transom.

They put the Mercedes in the small lean-to that had been built alongside the jetty and locked it up. All four were in a festive mood.

'Mission accomplished,' Andrew said triumphantly as he gunned the engines inexpertly and headed the boat out across the lake.

Chapter Eight

'Bring the defendants into the dock.'

It was dark now and all the lights had been turned on in the reception rooms where the 'court' had been created. Mick and Paul sat behind the table that had been arranged to form the 'bench'. They had found two wigs, relatively short black wigs, and wore these balanced precariously on their heads, with black sheets draped around their shoulders to form robes.

Andrew sat behind the small table to one side of them and all the former slaves were arrayed in the various chairs set out in front. There were bottles of spirits and wine everywhere.

Stephanie had not seen Devlin since they had got back to the castle, nor been able to exchange a single word with him. She had been taken down to the cellars as soon as they'd got back and locked in her cell all afternoon. Devlin had been taken upstairs by Amanda, and it was Amanda, wearing a tight gold-sequinned leotard and matching leggings, who had come to collect her from the cell. Once again she had allowed her to shower and use the toilet under Amanda's eagle eye but this time she had been allowed to dry herself.

'Put this on,' Amanda commanded.

They had selected something deliberately lewd. It was a black leather leotard with full-length sleeves but with round cut-outs to expose the breasts and a similar arrangement for each cheek of her buttocks, seemingly spreading and separating them obscenely.

As soon as she had wriggled into the garment Amanda had produced a hood, also in black hide, which she pulled down over Stephanie's head. It laced tightly at the back, the soft leather stretching over the contours of Stephanie's face and taking their shape. There were small oval openings for her eyes but none for her mouth. As soon as she was satisfied the hood was in place Amanda used two straps to secure Stephanie's arms behind her back, one at the elbow, which forced Stephanie's exposed breasts forward, and one at the wrists.

After allowing her back into her shoes, she had led the way upstairs. In the main hall Devlin was waiting. He too had been laced into a tight leather hood and his arms strapped behind him but otherwise he was naked. There were red welts on his buttocks to testify to what Amanda had already subjected him to that afternoon. Venetia dressed again in the black leather she had worn last night in the cellars, stood beside him.

At the word from inside the 'court' they were pushed forward. A chorus of boos and hisses from the assembled company greeted their arrival. The slaves were all in various stages of undress, the men as well as the women decked out in lingerie from the castle's extensive collection. A couple of the men wore only tiny white lacy panties that hardly covered their cocks, while some of the females wore no panties at all and were dressed in red satin basques or leather corsets with stockings and ridiculously high-heeled shoes. Some wore bras but had turned the cups down to expose their breasts. Many carried whips and aimed blows at Stephanie's rudely exposed rump, or at Devlin's as they passed down the middle of the two rows of chairs.

At the front of the court they were pushed into the two wing chairs that stood side by side. A long leather strap was buckled around the back of each chair and across the top of their waists, effectively securing them in place.

'Order, order, order,' Paul shouted over the catcalls and shouted comments that filled the room. He banged the table with a poker from the fireplace. Silence eventually fell.

'That's better. Now we are gathered here today, members of the jury, to try a heinous crime. The two accused are charged with serious offences including robbery of personal freedom and obscene behaviour. Do you find them guilty or not guilty?'

'Guilty,' everyone cried at once.

'No, no, there's been no evidence yet,' Andrew said, standing up and looking exasperated.

'But everyone knows they're guilty,' Mick said.

'We're having a trial first. Call the first witness.'

'I want to be a witness,' one of the male slaves called out.

'You're on the jury,' Paul objected.

'Amanda's the first witness,' Andrew said.

'Call Amanda then.'

Amanda got up from the seat she had taken next to Venetia on the front row and came over to the small table where Andrew sat.

'Do you swear to tell the truth, the whole truth and nothing but the truth?'

'I do.'

'Will you please tell the court what happened to you on the night of the fifth of June,' Andrew said, getting to his feet.

170

'I was working for a company owned by this man
...' She pointed at the bound figure of Devlin.
'Yes?'
'I was told by my immediate superior to report im-
mediately to an office in the City of London.'
'And?'
'When I arrived I was shown into Devlin's office.
He told me he had documentary evidence that I had
been embezzling from his company and that unless I
agreed to be a slave, a sex slave ...' these words pro-
voked a bout of boos and hisses from the jury. '...
for the next three months he would go to the police
and have me prosecuted.'
'And what did you do?'
'I agreed, reluctantly.'
'And you can positively identify this man as being
in this court today?'
'I just did. Devlin, over there.'
'And now will you tell the court what happened at
the castle?'
'She happened.' Amanda pointed at Stephanie.
'Let the record show the witness has identified the
other defendant,' Andrew said solemnly.
'The bitch.'
'And what did she do to you?'
'She made my life a bloody misery, that's what.
Wouldn't leave me alone. Always on my back for the
slightest thing. Not putting my garden fatigues on
quickly enough, not calling her mistress.'
'And she had you punished for this?'
'Whipped by that maniac Bruno or used by the
guests, men and women.'
'Used in what way?'
'In any way they wanted. Sucking off the men and
women. Being fucked. Anything they wanted.'

171

'And did you complain?'

'All the time, and every time I complained I was punished again. Whipped or made to work for longer in the gardens. All by her.' She pointed at Stephanie again. There were cries of 'yes' from the other slaves.

'Now Amanda, remember you are under oath. We come to the crucial question. Did you embezzle money from Devlin's company?'

'Absolutely not. Not guilty.'

Other slaves leapt to their feet with cries of 'Right', 'Exactly', and 'Not guilty' and 'Me too'.

'You may step down,' Paul said.

'No,' Andrew objected again. 'She's got to be cross-examined.'

'There's no one to cross-examine her,' Paul said.

'Mick can do it,' Amanda suggested.

'I'm a judge.'

'I'll do it,' Venetia said, getting to her feet.

'Good idea,' Paul said, banging the poker on the table to restore order, as talking had broken out in the jury.

Venetia stood in front of the bench.

'Cross-examine, then,' Andrew prompted.

'Didn't you enjoy everything that was done to you?'

'Objection,' Andrew cried, jumping to his feet.

'Objection sustained,' Mick declared. 'It's irrelevant whether she enjoyed it or not.'

'Were you forced to do anything against your will?'

'Yes,' Amanda replied, 'everything.'

'No further questions,' Venetia said, sitting down.

Stephanie tried to say something but her voice was muffled in the leather hood. Devlin moved his knee against hers. He was right. There was no point in saying anything.

'You may stand down now, and the court would like to thank you for your evidence,' Paul said to Amanda.

'Thank you, your worship.'

'Next witness.'

'Venetia is the next witness,' Andrew said.

'But she's acting for the defence,' Mick said.

'I believe the defendants have waived their right to a defence, is that correct?' Andrew was grinning.

'Yes, your honour,' Venetia said.

'Oh well, that's all right then. You can be a witness,' Paul pronounced.

'Call Venetia,' Mick added.

Venetia got to her feet again and stood in front of Andrew at the small table. She repeated the oath.

'Well, perhaps you'd tell the court your sad story in your own words.' Andrew said.

Venetia was silent.

'Devlin abused you,' he prompted again.

'Yes. That's right. He found me embezzling like Amanda . . .'

Amanda jumped to her feet. 'I wasn't embezzling!'

'I mean . . .' Venetia corrected herself, 'I mean, he accused me of embezzling from one of his companies. I was offered the same chance as Amanda but because he needed my computer skills so he could make sure his computer programs couldn't be tampered with again, I was allowed freedom and not made to live at the castle.'

'But you were still a sex slave?'

'Yes, he let his girlfriend use me while he watched. She really hurt me.'

That much, Stephanie knew, was true. Venetia had told her about it when she and first described the history of her relationship with Devlin.

'That was the defendant?'

'No, before she came on the scene . . .'

'But she has used you too?'

'Oh yes. I had an agreement with Devlin that I would never be used by a man but they broke it. I tried to defend her, help her, stop her being beaten by a cruel and wicked man who Devlin desperately needed to save a major business deal. But she didn't help me in return. The bastard wanted to see me used by a man . . .' Venetia shuddered at the memory. 'She watched, they all watched.' Venetia spat the words out with real bile.

'Not a nice lady,' Andrew commented.

'And she's used me ever since.'

Stephanie felt her heart sink for the second time that day. She had hoped against hope that Venetia was still on their side, that she was pretending to co-operate to gain some advantage but from the bitterness in her tone she found that hard to believe any longer. What she said was all perfectly true. Gianni, the man Devlin had needed for business reasons, had insisted she was fucked in front of him, the first time she had ever had a man. And Stephanie had watched too and done nothing. It was obvious that Venetia had not forgotten or forgiven and that their supposed special relationship since had counted for less than Stephanie had imagined. It appeared that Venetia too wanted her revenge.

'No more questions,' Andrew said, sitting down.

'Cross-examine,' Mick said.

'Does the witness want to cross-examine herself?'

'The defendants have waived their right to a defence,' Andrew reminded them.

'Oh, right.'

'That concludes the case for the prosecution.'

'No,' came cries from the jury, 'I want to say some-thing'; 'Let me say something'; 'I want to give evi-dence'.

'Order, order . . .' Paul shouted, banging the poker.

'Let them speak,' Andrew said.

And they did. One after another the former slaves stood in front of the table and told stories of how they had been forced to come to the castle on trumped-up charges of fraud, theft and embezzlement, and had been used sexually by men and women. As their descriptions of what had been done to them became more and more graphic it was obvious that members of the jury were becoming aroused. In the front row of seats one of the men, who was wearing one of Stephanie's blacklace teddies, had got an enormous erection. Two women on either side of him had ex-tracted it from the silky material and while one sucked it enthusiastically, the other began kissing him on the mouth.

Paul banged the poker on the table to try and re-store order.

'Will the jury please consider their verdict?'

'Guilty,' everyone shouted at once.

The sight of the woman bending over kissing the man provoked another male to get up and begin stroking the tight curves of her buttocks. She was wearing a white lace basque and white stockings but no panties and his hands rapidly slipped between the cleft of her arse down to the folds of her cunt which was sparsely haired and very visible. She moaned as he pushed two fingers inside her.

'Order, order . . .' Paul tried to continue. 'And that is the verdict of you all?'

'Yes,' came the shouted reply.

The second man's cock had hardened. He pulled

down the white shorts – Devlin's – he was wearing and replaced his fingers with his penis, driving it home. The woman moaned but did not stop kissing the first man.

'It is our job to pass sentence,' Paul said solemnly, trying to ignore what was going on in front of his eyes.

The woman whose mouth was impaled on the first man's cock reached out between the second man's legs. She caught his balls in her hand and pulled them down as he pistoned in and out of the other woman's cunt, his penis slick with her juices. He moaned, his hands holding her hips slipped under the long suspenders of the basque.

'I sentence you, Devlin, to serve Amanda for as long as she so may choose.' Paul's own cock was hardening as he spoke.

'And I sentence you, Stephanie,' Mick said, 'to serve Andrew for as long as he may choose.'

'Is there anything the prisoners wish to say?'

Neither Stephanie nor Devlin moved or tried to speak.

'Good, then the court is adjourned.' Paul banged the poker one final time and then virtually vaulted over the table to join the melee among the jury.

One of the female slaves was watching the little circle of fucking. She was dressed in one of the black satin suspender belts from the wardrobes in the cellar and very sheer shiny stockings, as well as black spike-heeled shoes. She had been wearing a short summer dress too but pulled this off as the foursome developed in front of her eyes. She was not wearing a bra and her big breasts trembled as she sat with her legs wide open and fingered her clitoris with one hand and pinched her right nipple with the other. Her cunt, like the woman who was being fucked in front of her, was almost hairless, its labia thin. Exposed as it was, her cunt looked small and extremely round like lips pouted to say 'oh' and Paul could not resist it. Pulling the tracksuit bottoms he had worn under the black sheets down and the sheets off, he knelt in front of her, his cock sticking up from his loins.

'Well, you're just what I need,' the girl said, hooking her arms round his neck and sliding forward until her wet cunt felt his hard cock on her labia. Using his hand, Paul guided it home.

All around the 'court' the scene degenerated into sex. Andrew headed for the foursome. The woman who was sucking the man's cock had a large plum-shaped arse. She had slipped onto her knees in front of him and the white panties she wore covered only a small triangle of her buttocks. Paul pulled the panties down as far as they would go, which wasn't far, and watched his cock sink into the deep cleft of flesh. She reared her backside up at him and his cock slid effortlessly into her wet sex.

Stephanie watched Molly, the petite blonde, turn to kiss the girl next to her. Almost immediately Molly's hand was rubbing the girl's tits and her mouth followed it, until she got to her knees, opened the girl's legs and pulled the crotch of the girl's panties aside to get at the auburn hair of her labia. The girl responded by hooking her thighs over Molly's shoulders, pressing her sex onto Molly's eager mouth.

Another scene had developed with the two remaining females. One had stripped completely naked and pulled one of the men down onto the thick carpet, clearing away the chairs. He lay on his back as the second woman sucked him to erection, then made way for the first to kneel over him, helping her to guide his cock into her hot wet cunt. At the same time the second woman swivelled round and knelt above his head, her glistening labia right over his mouth. As his cock slid into one woman, his tongue slid into another, and the two women leant forward to kiss each other hard on their mouths, their hands playing with the other's breasts.

But that didn't complete the picture. Mick knelt behind the girl whose cunt was already being fucked. Slowly he nosed his cock into the puckered opening of her anus.

'Yes,' she said enthusiastically. 'Oh yes, do it. I love it.'

She wriggled her arse back at him by way of encouragement. He pushed forward into the tight rear passage made even tighter by the presence of a cock reaming into her cunt.

The second girl saw what was happening and began to feel left out. She caught the hand of one of the only other two men not engaged in sex, both of whom were watching this performance.

'Do it to me,' she said.

He didn't hesitate. His cock was fully erect. He knelt behind her, seeing the other man's head between her thighs, his tongue still working on her cunt. He pushed his cock forward and felt the tongue too. Pulling back he found the entrance to her arse.

'Yes, there,' the girl said excitedly. As he pressed his cock home she moaned, gripping the first woman's breasts more tightly, her finger-nails digging into her nipples.

The last man got up and rid himself of shirt and trousers. The writhing mass of bodies in front of him had taken up a rhythm like some monstrous many-headed animal trying to bring itself off. Three cocks and one tongue plunged home in perfect synchronisation, the two women so full of sensation they were coming almost continuously, almost unable to catch their breath between huge shockwaves of feeling.

The last man stood beside them. Both girls were blonde, one with long hair and the other with her hair cut into a neck-length bob. It was the one with the long hair who had both cocks buried in her body but both girls looked wild, their eyes unfocused, their bodies trembling. They were clinging to each other so tightly it was as if they feared to let go, feared they might drown in sensation.

They kissed each other continuously, not tonguing kisses but little nibbles and sucks. The last man put his hands on the back of their heads and pushed his cock between their lips as they met.

'Mmm . . .' the long-haired woman mumbled at once.

They both licked and sucked enthusiastically, yet another notch to rack up their excitement. They felt the cock throbbing between their lips, just as the other cocks throbbed in their bodies. Their orgasm continued to roll over them. Their cunts were so wet their juices ran out over the men's balls. The man who was licking out the second woman had to swallow her juice, there was so much. The women had never been wetter, nor the men harder.

If it hadn't been for the indulgences of last night they would have all come in seconds. But they held on, wallowing in the feelings of being completely engulfed in sex. It was the man in the long-haired blonde's cunt who came first, unable to stand the excitement any longer, never having seen or felt anything like this. He bucked his hips one final time, then held his cock still as he felt it spasm and jet spunk into her sex. This throbbing, spunking cock, separated from his only by the thin membranes of the woman's body, set Mick off too, plunging him over the edge of a shattering climax, his spunk jetting out into the hot tight passage of her arse, as he felt the other shaft jerking against him.

The man embedded in the other woman's arse felt all this as though it were vibrations directly in her body, the orgasm transmitted from one woman to the other like musical harmony. He too felt his cock spasm and spunk as he felt the other man's tongue still licking underneath him. All the bodies were trembling, all in a kind of shock, all shaking uncontrollably from the aftermath of orgasm.

The last man could stand it no longer either. His penis began to spasm. The other's view was restricted but he could see everything, see the two women, their lips wrapped around either side of his cock, their breasts squeezed tightly in each other's hands, their cunts open, their thighs bent as they knelt over the man's prostrate body. As the shorter-haired blonde felt the cock begin to twitch she moved her mouth round quickly and took it between her lips. Not a moment too soon because just as the cock invaded her throat she felt its spunk pumping out in great hot gobs.

But she wasn't selfish. She waited until the man's crisis had passed and his cock had shrunk slightly, then pulled away from him and leant forward to kiss the other woman, using her tongue to give her a share of the spoils. They both swallowed spunk. Some escaped and dribbled from their mouths.

Amanda decided it was time to join the party. But she wanted to be alone. Quickly she unbuckled the leather strap that held Devlin into the wing chair. She pulled him to his feet.

'Follow me,' she said, striding out of the room. He nearly tripped over one of the slaves as he hurried to follow her.

Stephanie looked around for Venetia. She had slipped away. Not that that gave Stephanie any grounds for hope. After the way Venetia had testified with such venom, any hope she had in that department had gone. Venetia had disappeared for no other reason than she had no desire to see what she did not care to do.

For the moment no one paid any attention to Stephanie. It was just as well. Left to the not-at-all-tender mercies of Andrew and Amanda, she could imagine that her life, and Devlin's, was going to be very unpleasant from now on.

It was going to be a long time before any of the company grew bored of this situation. There was lots of money to buy food from the mainland and enough booze to keep the party going for months. Their sexual appetites would not be satiated quickly either, not with the extra ingredient, for the slaves at least, of being able to savour something that had been so long forbidden.

Tied and helpless, Stephanie cursed herself again. If she had only paid attention to her instincts none of this would have happened . . .

Stephanie had spent the night in her cell. The evening's proceedings after the trial had left the whole company exhausted and in no mood to play further games with their newly sentenced slaves. She had heard Amanda locking Devlin away in the next-door cell and then, once again, silence had descended on the cellars and not a sound was to be heard.

For the first time since the slaves had taken over,

food was provided. A tray of bread, cheese and fruit was left in the cell. Stephanie had not eaten since breakfast the day before and she had consumed avidly everything they had given her.

It was a long time, in the darkness of the cell, before anyone came again and Stephanie could only sleep fitfully. With no mattress the stone floor provided little comfort and even though her arms had been freed and she was bound only by the ankle chain, it was difficult to find a position that afforded a good chance of sleep. Her mind refused to stop working either. Now that she was convinced Venetia had thrown her lot in with the rebels, there seemed little possibility of escape. The future that stretched ahead seemed bleak. The tables had been turned and, effectively and completely, she and Devlin were now the slaves of the castle.

In the morning, at least Stephanie assumed it was the morning since her watch now belonged to Amanda and she had no other means of telling the time, one of the former female slaves came to unlock Stephanie from the ankle cuff and took her to wash and use the toilet. But she was returned to her cell immediately and the ankle cuff was re-attached. Hours later, how many she could not tell as time dragged so slowly, a tray of food – water, bread, cheese and fruit again – was pushed into the cell and the light left on.

Again Stephanie ate everything and the food made her feel better. She had to try and think positively. Andrew and Amanda would inevitably get bored with the castle. The former slaves would all gradually drift away and the castle would become increasingly more difficult to live in with no servants to clean up the mess that was being made. Sooner or later they would be free.

But as much as she tried to be optimistic, there were still nagging doubts. Venetia might go into the village – where they all knew her – and persuade the servants to return to serve a new master. There was plenty of money in the safe to pay them and Venetia knew how, through the computer, to get more transferred to the local bank. Andrew and Amanda could live a life of total luxury for months to come, with Devlin and herself to amuse them and satisfy their every whim.

Stephanie shivered. They had stripped her out of the leather leotard before putting her in the cell and she was naked again. The experience reminded her of the time she had spent in Gianni's cellars after he had kidnapped her: cold and helpless. Then, as now, she had been naked and available for use.

She would have given anything to be able to speak to Devlin. She tried knocking on the stone wall with the links of the metal chain, hoping Devlin would hear and respond. Even a couple of meaningless taps would have been important to her; it would be contact, however limited. But though she listened intently there was not a sound in reply and she sunk back into listless depression, leaning against the cold stone wall and closing her eyes.

She must have fallen asleep because the cell door being thrust open woke her with a start.

'Playtime,' Amanda announced. Again she was dressed in one of Stephanie's outfits, this time a crimson red silk creation. It was backless with a halter neck and a tight knee-length skirt. Her legs were sheathed in sheer black nylon and her feet in red shoes with very high heels, the heels themselves clad in a chrome metal casing. She wore long crimson suede gloves that covered her arms to well above the

183

elbow. She had taken her time with her make-up and hair. She wore a dark red lipstick to match the dress and an eye-shadow in a similar shade that made her light brown eyes look deeper and more alluring. Her short black hair had been brushed out and seemed to have a noticeable sheen to it.

As she got down on her haunches to unlock the metal ankle cuff, Stephanie saw the time on the Patek Phillipe watch, her Patek Phillipe watch, was nine o'clock.

'Up,' she ordered. Stephanie got to her feet. With the high heels, Amanda was taller than her for once. 'Are you going to behave or do I have to cuff you again?'

'I'll do what you want,' Stephanie said.

'Very sensible. Follow me, then.'

Amanda led the way to the small door of the back staircase that led directly to Stephanie's bedroom. The vaulted corridor outside the cells was still a mess, with empty bottles of booze and mattresses strewn about the floor. One of the garden overseers was lying on a mattress, his arms bound behind his back with leather straps and his legs tied together with thick white rope so it was impossible for him to move a muscle. A leather strap had also been tied tightly around his cock and under his balls. Judging from the way it glistened and from the strong aroma of sex, he had been used by one of the females recently, though clearly she had been careful not to let him have any gratification.

Stephanie mounted the stone staircase first, with Amanda following. The stairwell was always cold, getting no sun and being sunk right in the heart of the thick stone walls. Stephanie shivered and felt her nipples pucker as the air chilled her to the bone.

Emerging in her bedroom, she was amazed to find most of the mess she had seen last time had been cleared away. The wardrobes and drawers were closed and all the clothes and items of equipment had been put away. The doors to the terrace were open and Stephanie could see Andrew standing near the parapet, looking over the lake to the mainland where, in the distance, the lights from occasional houses and the one village shone like stars against the dark canopy of night.

Hearing their arrival, Andrew walked back into the bedroom and closed the terrace doors. He was wearing one of Devlin's silk Sulka robes, knotted at the waist.

'Good evening,' he said. 'You look as though you could do with a wash and brush-up, and some make-up. That's no way to appear in front of your master, is it?' He came up to her and twisted a lock of her hair around his finger.

'No,' Stephanie said, resisting the temptation to add that she didn't have any choice.

'No what?'

She knew the answer to that question straight away. 'No, master,' she said unenthusiastically.

Amanda pulled her towards the bathroom. 'So get yourself looking decent,' she said, pushing her inside and closing the door.

Being in her own bathroom was not much of a relief. It reminded her of what she had won and what she had lost. She ran a hot bath, washed her hair and sat down to apply make-up for the first time in three days. She applied a mascara and blusher to her cheeks, which looked pale from lack of sunlight already, she thought, and painted on a very red lipstick. She had not seen herself in a mirror for three days.

With her make-up on and her hair dried and brushed out she looked good: apart from the slight paleness there was no sign, in her face at least, of the deprivations she had suffered.

The bathroom door opened and Andrew entered, closing it behind him. Stephanie faced his cold, unwavering eyes. For once he had the power over her, total power. He could do anything with her and she knew he would. He had been her slave, now she was his.

'Oh that's much better,' he said. 'You're a very beautiful woman aren't you, slave?'

'Yes, master,' she said demurely. It was the role she knew she would have to play. There was no point railing against it. For the immediate future Andrew was her master. He would decide what she ate, what she wore, when she slept and where. She belonged to him and she knew there was nothing else to do but accept it, just like the sensible slaves at the castle had done. The line of least resistance, the line Andrew and Amanda had never learned to follow.

'So what shall I do with you tonight?'

'Anything you want master,' Stephanie said, not looking at him.

'Very good. You learn fast, don't you? Get on your knees.'

As he said the words, Stephanie felt an unexpected surge of excitement course through her body. Andrew was not an unattractive man. She had played the dominant role for so long she had forgotten the thrills of being submissive. But that could be a thrill too. Not being in control. Giving yourself totally to someone else. Letting them have the power to decide what you would do or not do. She had experienced it before. It had thrilled her before. She was a natural dominant – she had discovered that about herself – but submission was the flipside of the coin, the other side of a two-faced mask, and perhaps it was not possible to enjoy one completely without the experience of the other. As she slid to her knees on the cold marble tiles of the bathroom floor she felt her body, the big engine of her sexual sensations, begin to throb.

He came to stand in front of her. 'Undo my robe.'

She reached up and undid the knot of the silk sash. The robe fell open. Andrew's smooth cock was beginning to unfurl from its bed of blond curly pubic hair.

'Get it hard,' he ordered. 'With your mouth.'

Eagerly, Stephanie had to admit, she gobbled the cock into her mouth, her hands moving round to the back of his thighs as her tongue cruised the rim of his circumcised glans and she felt the blood flowing into it. He was soon too big to be contained totally in her mouth, but she tried, feeling the tip right at the back of her throat.

She began a rhythm, bobbing her head up and down, using her saliva to make the movement frictionless, flicking her tongue along the underside of his cock. She heard him moan.

'Lick my balls,' he ordered.

The marble floor was hard on her knees but she concentrated on what she was doing. She dropped her head down under his cock and put her arms up behind him onto the back of his thighs, sucking on his balls one by one just as she'd done the day before. Then she went back to his long hard shaft and plunged her mouth down on it again. Her fingers worked up over his buttocks until she found the little crater of his anus. She paused there, waiting for instructions.

'Yes, do it,' he said.

She obeyed immediately. As her mouth swung up and down on his erection her finger pressed up into his arse, deeper and deeper until it was right up inside him and she could get at the bunch of nerves that lay hidden there. As soon as her finger touched their target she felt his body jerk and his cock pulse in her mouth. It was like a trigger, she knew, like a button that opened the floodgates of the dam, and Stephanie pressed it hard.

'Don't . . .' he said, trying to control himself as he felt his spunk flowing up into his cock.

But she knew he didn't mean it and she pressed again while, at the same time, she sucked hard on his cock.

'Yes . . .' He changed his mind. It was too late to hold back.

'Yes . . .'

Her finger was insistent, it pressed hard, massaging the tiny gland that she had exposed. Her mouth was like a cunt, hot and incredibly wet and clingy. He couldn't believe he could come so quickly again after the experiences of the last three days, but he did. Spunk jetted out into her willing mouth, white gobs of spunk over her tongue and down her throat. She swallowed it all.

His cock slipped from her mouth, glistening with a mixture of saliva and spunk. She withdrew her finger carefully and knelt on the floor, her hands on her knees, her eyes looking down. The perfect slave. If that was the role fate had cast her in, she might as well play it perfectly.

Andrew sat on the edge of the bath.

'You think you're very clever, don't you?' he said, annoyed with himself now for coming so quickly.

'No master, I thought that was what you wanted.'

He got up and pulled her to her feet, leading her by the arm back into the bedroom, his robe still flapping open.

While Andrew had been in the bathroom, Amanda had brought Devlin up from the cellars. He was kneeling at the foot of the bed. His hands were cuffed behind his back and he was naked. Amanda was lying on her back on the bed, still wearing the crimson dress and long gloves. She had wriggled the tight skirt up over her hips to reveal a red suspender belt and tiny matching red panties as well as the thick black welts of the stockings pulled into chevrons on her meaty thighs by the taut suspenders. Her legs were hooked over Devlin's shoulders, the tips of the chrome-clad heels digging into his back between his bound arms, spurring him on to greater efforts like a rider on a horse. His tongue was trying to push aside the crotch of her panties to get at her labia but it was tight, caught under her arse, and kept springing back into place.

'You,' she said as Stephanie emerged from the bathroom. 'Hold this back so he can get at me.'

Stephanie looked at Andrew for permission.

'Do it,' he said.

She went to the side of the bed and pulled the elasticated crotch to one side. It slipped into the crease where the top of Amanda's thigh met her pelvis. Over the bush of her hair, dark and very tight curls of pubic hair, Devlin looked into Stephanie's eyes. It was a tender look, a look that said it all. What else could either of them do? They were trapped. His tongue freed of impediment, licked Amanda's clitoris in long broad strokes.

'Do my tits,' Amanda said to Stephanie.

Stephanie knelt at the side of the bed and reached under the halter top. Amanda's nipples were hard and swollen. She kneaded the soft spongy flesh, then pinched the nipple between her fingernails. She repeated the process with the other breast, watching Amanda bucking her hips off the bed, her cunt undulating against Devlin's mouth.

'Both tits at the same time,' she mouthed breathlessly. Andrew stripped off his robe and came to prop himself up against the headboard alongside Amanda, his eyes on her body.

Stephanie did as she was told, pummelling and pinching Amanda's breasts and nipples under the red silk as Devlin's tongue licked her cunt, moving from her clitoris right the way down to the bud of her anus and back up again, feeling her heels digging into his back like spurs.

She was coming. She bucked herself harder, then her eyes rolled back in her head, she locked her legs tightly, pulling Devlin's mouth hard onto her cunt so he could not move, and her nerves exploded. Devlin could feel her cunt lips contracting and his face was sprayed with her juice as though she had spunked.

But she was not finished. Swinging her legs off Devlin's body, she got to her feet.

'Unhook me,' she said.

Stephanie stood up too and found the three hooks that held the halter in place at the nape of her neck. The silk fell to her waist, baring her breasts. She pulled the rumpled skirt down from her hips and stepped out of it.

'Pull the panties off,' she said, having got used to doing nothing for herself over the last three days. Stephanie skimmed the panties down over her long plump buttocks until they fell around her high-heeled shoes. Amanda stood naked but for the red suspender belt, the black stockings and the long red suede gloves.

'Now you're going to fuck me,' she said, taking Devlin's chin in her gloved hand and forcing him to look up at her near-naked body, the waistband of the suspender belt emphasising her hourglass figure, her firm breasts topped by hard cherry-red nipples. 'Get up.'

Devlin struggled to his feet, his cock erect. However often Stephanie saw it she never quite got used to its size and shape. Devlin was an incredibly ugly man. His face and body were covered with thick wiry hair: his nose and ears were tufted with it too. His skin was pock-marked and his nose bulbous and out of all proportion to the rest of his face. But it was his cock that was his most extraordinary feature. It was massive. Two closed fists could not contained its bulk. It was not smooth and sleek, like Andrew's, but veined and gnarled like the bark of a very old tree encrusted with ivy. Each vein stood up individually forming a huge map, like a relief map of features, one vein running into another. The cock was not quite straight either, it seemed to be slightly crooked halfway down its length so it bowed outward.

Amanda had already experienced this cock inside her. It was like nothing she had ever experienced before. It had taken her to heights she had never dreamt of, and it was going to do it again. Her body ached for it.

She lay on the bed and opened her legs wide, as wide as they would go, the suspenders at the sides of her stockings stretched taut. 'Come on Devlin, I'm your mistress now.' And it was true. She was the mistress of this monster, it was all hers.

191

Slowly Devlin knelt up on the bed. With his hands cuffed behind his back it was difficult for him to position himself properly but Amanda gave him no help. He lowered himself onto her body and then tried to position his cock between her legs.

'Get a whip,' Amanda said as this was going on. Stephanie obeyed at once, going over to the long drawer and pulling out a riding crop. Whether Amanda knew it already or not, being whipped was no punishment for Devlin. It was what he craved.

'Oh . . .' Amanda moaned as the tip of his misshapen cock nudged between her soaking wet labia.

Devlin felt the fold of her labia open. He hesitated.

'Do it,' she ordered. And he did. He drove his huge rod up into her cunt, up into the river of juices that anticipation had created. The lubrication was necessary, essential with the size of him. It stretched her to the limit. Even though she knew it was only half inside her, that she couldn't feel his balls, she was totally filled by it. The sensation was incredible.

The mainspring of her orgasm began to unwind at once. 'More,' she commanded, not really meaning it. He pushed forward again but there was no room for more than a fraction of an inch. He was at the very top of her cunt, at the neck of her womb. Her labia were stretched so far apart that her clitoris was completely exposed, the protection of her cunt lips pulled away by the width of his cock. It seemed to be fluttering like a bird trying to keep airborne but failing. Amanda could do nothing, couldn't think or even open her eyes. Just as Andrew had dreamt of Stephanie, Amanda had never been able to forget Devlin's cock and now it was hers, it belonged to her. And her first orgasm broke over the head of it, making her shudder and convulse with pleasure.

But it did not end there. One orgasm seemed to provoke another and another, her body tossed on waves of orgasm, her cunt, her clitoris, her breasts transmitting unspeakable pleasure. Through the fog of sensation she heard Andrew's voice.

'Come on, give it to him.'

Amanda opened her eyes to see Stephanie raising the riding crop. 'Yes . . .'

The crop slashed down. Devlin's cock lunged into her, driven by the whip, deeper than she'd ever imagined a cock could go and she came again, at least she thought she did but her orgasms were so close together and so intense she just couldn't tell where one ended or another began. She managed to open her eyes again, wanting to see Stephanie slash the whip down across Devlin's buttocks. As it landed she felt his cock power into her, burning with his pain-induced lust.

But then it was too much to do anything but feel. Her eyes rolled back and she wallowed in the orgasms her body produced so freely over the enormous shaft of flesh plunging into her in time to the thwacks of leather on Devlin's hide.

On the fifth stroke Devlin came. He lunged forward, found a place in the streaming wet, sticky, velvety cunt and stopped. His cock pulsed and then began to spasm. At the exact moment white spunk erupted from his glans, Stephanie cut the whip down one last time, sending the shock of pain that he loved so much arching through his nerves to join the fireworks they were already producing.

Andrew had watched this performance with growing frustration, his cock at full erection again by the time Devlin groaned to a climax. He had circled it with his hand and was wanking it hard, smearing the slick of fluid it had produced down its whole length. He knew what he wanted.

Amanda pushed Devlin off her body. She almost came again as his cock disengaged itself from her sex: little aftershocks of pleasure shooting up through her body. She looked over at Andrew.

'Your turn,' she said, smiling.

Andrew stood up, his cock bobbing out in front of him. He had never felt so excited in his entire life. He could have anything his heart desired, anything; any combination, any position, any of the women in the castle, singularly or together. He was the master of all he surveyed. His plan had worked and this was his reward. But he knew exactly what he wanted now.

'What are you going to do?' Amanda asked.

'Get off the bed,' he said to Devlin. Devlin struggled to obey, his cock quite flaccid now. 'You lie down here,' he said, looking straight at Stephanie. 'On your stomach,' he added.

He knew where the suntan oil was kept. He had been sent to get it out of the bedside table so many times as Stephanie lay naked on the terrace, soaking up the hot Italian sun. But his cock had been constricted then, bound by the metal pouch that was chained tightly around his genitals from the first day he had arrived at the castle. He remembered that day well. He would never forget it. His cock surged at the memory. He had been beaten, teased mercilessly by one of the guests, then left, taken to the cells and left, his cock unsatisfied, crammed back into the pouch. But with his arse burning from the welts the whipping had left, someone had come to his cell, had him blindfolded and the pouch removed, and had sunk a hot cunt onto his throbbing erection, allowing him, finally, to spunk.

He had never come so intensely in his life. He remembered that night as though it had happened an hour ago, every detail. He had played it through in his mind like a videotape, over and over again, every detail burned like a brand on his mind.

Andrew looked down at his cock. It was reddened and hard, another tear of fluid running out of the pink slit of his urethra. He opened the bedside table and extracted the sun oil from the drawer. It was in a large round jar and looked like cold cream, white and thick. He smeared both his hands with it.

Amanda had propped herself up on the bed where she had lain, with Stephanie beside her. Andrew knelt between the two women, facing Stephanie's naked back. He started with her shoulders, smoothing the cream over her scapula, then down into the long concave curve of her back. Her arse was magnificent. He had always thought so. It rose from the small of her back precipitously. It was so round and pert, the canyon that ran between its cheeks so deep. He remembered how he had fought not to look at it, fought not to feel it, fought not to notice the thick tufts of hair escaping from between her legs, or the little gap between the top of her thighs when they were tightly closed. But inevitably he had not succeeded, it would be a losing battle, and his erection would strain hopelessly against the metal pouch, agonisingly painful, unable to swell further, unable to get the relief Stephanie's body made it want so badly.

But now it was free. His cock stuck out from his loins as hard as steel, as his hands massaged the so-familiar flesh, the oil making it glisten. As he worked, his cock would brush her buttocks or thigh and that would send a pulse through his body like an electric shock as well as leaving a trail of fluid on her body that dried rapidly to leave a puckered, transparent spoor.

He worked down over her buttocks, taking more sun oil from the jar. His fingers kneaded and gripped the firm, round flesh. He delved down between her buttocks, his fingers opening them so he could see the perfectly spherical, corrugated crater of her anus and under it the first inch of her hairy, thick labia. He massaged oil all around, allowing his hand to stray over the anus itself, and onto her sex, something that would have brought instant punishment before.

'Turn over,' he ordered, his voice almost seized up with passion. As Stephanie obeyed he looked round at Amanda. She was watching him, propped up against the pillows, her legs open, one leg up and bent at the knee. The suspender belt cut across her waist, its long suspenders taut on the leg stretched flat on the bed and loose and looped out on the leg she had raised. Her naked flesh over the stockings seemed, in contrast to the black nylon, creamy and soft. Her hand, gloved in red suede, rested on the triangle of her belly, with her middle finger just moving ever so slightly against the nodule of her engorged clitoris. The wetness there had darkened the suede at the tip of her finger.

Andrew scooped another gob of the white cream from the jar and dabbed it on each of Stephanie's firm, proud breasts. Slowly using both hands, he started by circling his palms over her nipples, so that was the only contact. Stephanie could not help but moan. She moaned again when he changed from this subtle treatment and dropped his hands onto her full breasts, kneading and fingering them, rubbing the oil deep into her flesh.

Stephanie's body was alive. She knew what

196

Andrew was doing and why. Oiling her naked body had been torture for the slaves. They had all been made to do it. Occasionally, on a caprice, she would unchain the pouch and have them fuck her but she had never, never done that with Andrew. He had been too rebellious. She had had to keep him on a tight rein. Except the once. Now, she knew, he was fulfilling his fantasies, doing what he had never been allowed to do before, except on the day he had arrived.

His hands moved over her waist, down to her thighs. He lifted each in turn and massaged the oil with both hands deep into the soft flesh. Stephanie felt his cock nudging against her side again. She looked down at it. Another trail of fluid, leaking from his urethra, slicked over her skin. She looked over to Devlin who was sitting in one of the armchairs to the side of the bed. He looked depressed and uncomfortable, but she could see an excitement in his eyes too.

Andrew finished one thigh and began to work on the other. Working up from the knee, she felt his hands brushing her labia. It made her shudder. Was he going to do to her what she had done to him? Creating a need and leaving it unfulfilled?

But that was not what he had in mind, apparently. As he finished her other thigh he leant across her body now gleaming with oil. He squirmed his chest against her breasts and his hard cock against her belly. He was reaching over her to get into the bedside drawer. He wanted the dildo he had seen there as he'd got the sun oil out. It was big and black, a perfect replica of a circumcised cock.

With no subtlety he rocked back on his heels and positioned the head of the dildo between her legs, then drove it straight up into Stephanie's cunt, as deep as it would go. She groaned at the sudden intrusion, then writhed her body until the dildo was bedded in her sex just where she wanted it.

Amanda got onto her knees so she could get a better view. This she wanted to see. Stephanie's body was shaking, already sensitised by the oily massage. Her mouth was open and she was making little mewing sounds. Andrew didn't move the dildo up and down, he just held it tight inside her, deep and hard. He turned the little gnarled knob at the end and a faint humming filled the air. Immediately Stephanie's body arched over the sheets, her navel uppermost, her buttocks clear off the bed.

Amanda worked her way up behind Andrew until she could press her naked breasts, her nipples as hard as pebbles, into his shoulder-blades and the hard curve of her pubic bone against his buttocks, while one gloved hand snaked round his chest to locate his right nipple and the other circled his rigid cock.

'Do you want me to wank you?' she whispered in his ear, reaming it out with her tongue as soon as she'd spoken.

He did not reply but she knew the answer. She could feel his cock thrusting in the fist she had made of her hand. The suede made it impossible to slide up and down the shaft easily so instead she gripped the cock tightly and let the underside of her thumb move up and down the rim of his glans, the rough suede rubbing the sensitive skin. Andrew moaned.

They could both see Stephanie come. She opened her mouth and groaned, an animal noise, as her orgasm broke over the head of the vibrating, unyielding dildo that seemed to be jammed up against every nerve in her body, exciting them all at the same time. Her body, like a longbow being strung, arched off the bed still further until only her shoulders and heels were on the sheet and every muscle was locked with pleasure.

Amanda's hand squeezed Andrew tight, her suede-covered thumb working faster. Then she felt something against her knee. It was the riding crop. Stephanie had dropped it by her side as she'd lain down on the bed. Amanda picked it up. With her hand still gripping Andrew's cock, she swung herself around to kneel at his side. As Stephanie's body sunk back onto the bed Amanda slashed the crop down on Andrew's white buttocks. She felt his reaction immediately. His cock surged in her hand, jerking so hard it almost escaped her grasp.

'You want it, don't you?' she said.

'Yes, yes . . .' He loved it. He remembered how he had felt that first night in the castle, red welts burning on his buttocks as he had been released from the pouch, blindfolded and helpless, as that hot wet cunt had descended on his cock. He remembered how he had spunked, so hard and so long he thought it would never stop. He would never forget that, the criss-crossed welts on his arse powering his orgasm to heights he had never reached before. Or since. Until now. 'Yes, yes,' he cried.

Amanda raised the crop again. One hard, full cut across the buttocks followed another. His cock jerked again as her thumb rubbed the same place, so sensitive it made him squirm, the fire in his arse making it more so, making it impossibly tender. Even through the glove Amanda could feel how hot his cock was. It was boiling, scalding hot. He was coming, she felt his spunk forcing its way through her tight grip. She raised the crop again.

'Yes,' he screamed.

'This is what you want . . .'

The crop sliced down across the three red welts that had already appeared on his white flesh. It was the hardest stroke of all, burning into him, the pain so close to total pleasure that his cock exploded in her fist, spitting spunk, hot gobs of spunk like a string of pearls, down over Stephanie's tits and navel and into the thick black thatch of pubic hair. Amanda squeezed the shaft, milking it to extract every last drop.

Chapter Nine

It was not a routine but it followed a pattern of sorts.
Days passed slowly. Stephanie and Devlin would
spend most of their time locked and chained in the
cells. Twice a day they would be fed and allowed to
use the shower and toilet facilities but not, as far as
Stephanie could tell, at the same time each day. They
were taken out of the cells as and when it occurred to
someone to do it. To further confuse her sense of time
the light in the cell was sometimes left on all night
and sometimes not. Sometimes it was turned off for
short periods during what Stephanie assumed to be
the day and sometimes it was left on continuously.

With no way of telling the time, or even mark the
passing of a day, time dragged heavily. Days merged
into one another, only differentiated by what Andrew
devised as a means of using his personal slave.

Stephanie had not seen Devlin since the day after
the trial. Presumably Amanda was using him just as
Andrew was her, but they had not been taken out of
the cells together and she had not seen him. As well
as her own, five other cells were bolted when she was
taken out; three for garden overseers, one for Bruno
and one for Devlin. All the other cell doors were wide
open.

Stephanie was taken up to Andrew's bedroom
regularly and always at night. There he commanded
her to perform a variety of sex acts, usually with one

of the other former female slaves in attendance. He too, it appeared, had discovered what Stephanie had experienced on her first visit to the castle; that power is an aphrodisiac and creates seemingly limitless sexual appetites and the energy to satisfy them. Stephanie had been amazed at her own ability to indulge in sexual encounters and clearly Andrew and, from what she had seen, Amanda, were affected by the same phenomenon.

It was at the end of the first week that Mick and Paul had paid serious attention to her for the first time. Since they had 'liberated' the slaves they had been busy receiving the gratitude of the seven females who had been delighted to engage in sex singularly or plurally with the two men, especially when they had been told that the files on the various felonies they had committed against Devlin had been destroyed. They were in a mood to celebrate their freedom.

But though the women were attractive they were no match for Stephanie or Venetia. Andrew had made it clear that Venetia was out of bounds and as Stephanie was his personal slave she appeared to be untouchable too, as much as they thought about her and what it would be like to have her. It was only when Andrew had suggested that they might like to share her considerable talents, that they had been quick to take advantage of the opportunity.

Paul had come to her cell alone. He had taken to wearing a pair of Devlin's shorts, navy blue and very loose, around the castle and very little else. He was carrying a leather body-harness he had found in the punishment room.

'Stand up,' he ordered. Stephanie had been sitting with her back against the wall. 'We're going to have a little party,' he said, kneeling to unlock her ankle from the metal cuff. The harness was comprised of three thick, wide leather hoops attached to a single, much thinner strap. Each hoop was strapped around the body, one above the breasts and under the arms, one under the breasts and the third across the navel, with the thin strap that held them together running down the spine. The hoops were wider as they got lower, with the one around the navel the widest of them all, covering most of the belly. Paul strapped them all into place tightly.

Each of the hoops had a much smaller loop of leather attached to it on either side. The arms fitted into these, buckled in tightly on the biceps, elbow and wrist, making it impossible to move the arms away from the torso.

Stephanie had seen one of the guests use the harness on a slave but had never experienced its effects. She had been bound before but never as tightly as this. But while her whole upper body, with the exception of her breasts which jutted out of the leather hoops, was completely constricted and her arms held rigid; below her hips, in contrast, she was free and exposed and vulnerable. It was an extraordinary feeling of helplessness. Above her hips even breathing was difficult, below her buttocks, thighs and sex were open and unrestrained.

Paul led her out into the corridor and up the back stairs to what had once been her bedroom.

'Well, look at that,' Andrew commented as Stephanie entered the bedroom through the small doorway hidden in the silk panelling of the wall. 'What have you been up to, Paul?' He was drinking champagne, sitting on the large sofa opposite the bed. Mick was sitting next to him.

'Found it in the cellars. Pretty, don't you think?'

Paul spun Stephanie around so that they got the full effect. The pressure of the hoops above and below her breasts had made them redden.

'What a bird,' Mick said, staring at Stephanie's body.

'What an arse . . .' Andrew said. 'Come here, darling.'

She obeyed, standing in front of him. The constriction of the body-harness was making her feel odd: she wanted to take a deep breath but couldn't. The leather had no give in it at all.

'I've told my friends what a special woman you are. They were feeling left out so I suggested they should see for themselves . . .'

'Yes, master.'

Mick, who was wearing a pair of Devlin's Y-fronts, stood up. He pulled the pants to the floor and stepped out of them. His cock was semi-erect.

Whether because of the body-harness or the situation, Stephanie suddenly felt a rush of blood to her head. It was not at all an unpleasant feeling. She felt no fear. After what she had been through in the last months there was nothing these three men could do to her she hadn't already indulged in voluntarily herself. The truth was she wanted them.

'On your knees,' Andrew ordered, clearly relishing his position of power.

'I can't, master,' Stephanie said. With the harness making it impossible to move her upper body, she would have fallen over if she tried to kneel without help.

Paul saw the problem and held her by the shoulders as she lowered herself to her knees. Mick immediately took her by the back of the head and fed his thickening cock into her mouth.

As she sucked on his uncircumcised cock, the strange feeling of excitement she felt increased. She could feel her labia were already wet and was afraid the sap from her body might start to run down her thigh.

Mick was not content with her mouth for long. As Paul pulled his shorts off too, Mick pulled Stephanie up to her feet again. He was a big man, his belly round and fat, his thighs meaty, but it was obvious he was also strong. He picked Stephanie off her feet easily, as if she were an eiderdown, and carried her over to the bed, throwing her down into the middle of the mattress.

That produced a shock of pleasure so intense, so absolute, that for a moment she thought she would faint. It was the helplessness, the feeling of being no more than a plaything, a pawn in their game of sexual pleasure that was doing it to her, she knew. She had experienced it before. The natural dominant was also a natural submissive.

Mick had jumped onto the bed too. In seconds he had rolled on top of her and was spreading her legs apart, his cock pressed down into her labia.

'She's soaking wet,' he said. 'It's running down her legs.' Encouraged, he plunged his cock home and groaned as he felt it sink into the warmth and wetness of her sex. He drove forward like a man possessed, his hand grabbing at her breast between the hoops of leather. She was his at last, the beautiful figure, the haughty looks, the long elegant legs and pert arse, wrapped round his cock. He found her nipple and pinched it between his fingers as his cock powered into her.

She moaned. The constriction of the harness made her nipples extra sensitive. But so, it seemed, did the lack of constriction below her hips. Her labia throbbed. Mick's body, the hard curve of his pubic bone was driving forward right onto her clitoris. Perhaps it was his big belly flattening her navel so her clitoris was more exposed, perhaps it was just her incredible excitement, but she knew she was going to come.

Unfortunately for her, they were not there for her pleasure. Mick pulled out of her and Paul took his place, kneeling between her legs. The shock of his withdrawal sent Stephanie's body into spasm, as Paul leaned forward. His cock was more gentle. She whimpered as it entered her churning sex. Mick's cock was short but wide, Paul's was longer and went deeper. As she felt it slide up into the depths of her sex, slowly in comparison to Mick's speed, Stephanie felt her body contract and her orgasm start again. She could hardly breathe. She panted for oxygen, straining against the leather, but knew that was part of her pleasure too. The spasm caused by Mick's withdrawal had turned into a convulsion of orgasm as her nerves erupted. The constriction of the harness increased the feeling. It was as though the orgasm was unable to escape from her shuddering body, was held in by the straps and instead of dissipating, echoed again and again through her nerves.

She had no idea how many times she came. Her mind was almost blank of everything but feeling. Her cunt and clitoris and her nipples bombarded her with sensation as Paul and Mick took it in turns to fuck her. She found it impossible to do anything but feel. Her cunt seemed to be the centre of her body but she knew, somewhere at the back of her mind where reasoning was still able to work, that it was the feeling of being used, of being had, of being the slave, that was bringing her these exquisite sensations.

In the end she had felt Mick take over from Paul. As he'd pushed inside her she could feel he was about to come. His cock was throbbing and after the third or fourth stroke he stopped, finding his place in the clinging wet walls of her sex. Immediately his cock spasmed and his spunk rocketed out of him, and into her. She tried to hold him there, using all her strength to milk the last drops of come, to keep him sucked up in her. Eventually he slipped away.

The mists of lust had cleared a little. Stephanie opened her eyes to see Paul standing by the bed, his cock, wet from her juices, in his right hand.

For a moment the old Stephanie returned despite her bondage. 'Come on. Give it to me. I want it.'

Paul looked hesitant.

'You want me to suck you?' she said.

But then she could read in his face what he wanted, she could read it in his eyes as they looked down at her body. He didn't want to use her cunt. He wanted to use her other passage. She laughed. Didn't he know she loved that too? Didn't he know they had made her so high on sex, her body pulsing with sensation, that she would do anything, want anything?

Fighting the bonds that held her so firmly and with a supreme effort she rocked herself from side to side until she gained momentum and rolled over onto her stomach.

'There,' she said triumphantly, sweating from the effort, her tender breasts smarting from contact with the sheet and further increasing her sexual temperature. 'Now give it to me. Come on, give me what I want, damn you.' She managed to get to her knees and thrust her tight apple-shaped arse out, her legs apart. He could see the target above the thick fleshy labia, puckered and inviting.

Stephanie wriggled her bottom from side to side.

'Give it to me, damn you,' she repeated.

And, while Andrew and Mick watched, their eyes following every movement, that was precisely what Paul did.

The pattern continued day after day. It was impossible to keep track of the days that passed because Stephanie was never sure, when they came to feed her or take her to the showers or up to Andrew, whether it was once a day or two days or just a few hours. Time passed so slowly that the slightest noise, the slightest disturbance became a major event. In fact there was little of either. For most of the day, it appeared the cellars were desserted, the slaves enjoying the more comfortable accommodation upstairs.

It was four or five days, Stephanie thought, after the experience with the three men, that Amanda strode into her cell. She looked beautiful. Perhaps it had been sunny outside, either that or Amanda had discovered the castle's solarium, but whatever the cause, she looked tanned and fit. She was dressed in a brown leather outfit Stephanie had commissioned from a special shop in Rome, a tight leather body like a leotard with a plunging neckline and a short leather skirt, equally tight but covering no more than three or four inches of Amanda's muscular thighs, and supplied with matching leather boots with high heels. Her breasts created a deep cleavage in the low neckline. Her hair had grown slightly and she had shaped it into soft waves. She carried a riding crop in her leather-gloved hand.

'Well, how are you enjoying the accommodation?' she asked, striding around the bare stone cell.

Stephanie said nothing as Amanda unlocked the metal cuff from her ankle.

'I asked you a question,' Amanda snapped.

'I'm not.'

'I'm not, what?'

'Mistress,' Stephanie added hastily.

'Follow me.'

Amanda turned on her heels and walked out of the cell, her shoes echoing against the stone. Waiting outside in the corridor was Venetia. Stephanie was surprised to see her. It wasn't that she'd forgotten about her but she hadn't seen her at all since the trial. What she had been doing during the endless days since, Stephanie had no way of knowing. She assumed that, having thrown her lot in with the rebels, she had been helping them run the castle, showing them where to get food and fuel for the boat and all the other things they would need to know. As for her sexual favours, so far Amanda had not appeared particularly interested in intimate activities with any of the women at the castle, at least not in Stephanie's presence, so Venetia's expertise in this department had probably not been called for.

To what extent Venetia had been given her freedom was also a question Stephanie had no means of answering. Clearly she had not been held in one of the cells. She was much too elegantly turned out to have been suffering the indignities of the cellar ablutions and she was wearing her own clothes. Stephanie recognised the short black dress Venetia wore. It clung to her body, emphasising the spectacular curves of her opulent body. It was sleeveless but with a full polo-neck that had been slit from throat to waist, revealing tantalising glimpses of Venetia's unencumbered breasts. Its skirt, even shorter than Amanda's, covered only an inch or two of thigh, exposing the rest of her long legs sheathed in nylon Lycra, a transparent black with a slippery-looking sheen. Her height was increased by silver high-heel shoes and the fact that her long hair was pinned to the top of her head.

As Stephanie emerged from the cell Amanda was heading along the corridor to the punishment room. Stephanie seized the opportunity and caught Venetia by the hand, forcing her to look straight into her eyes, trying to rekindle something – loyalty, friendship, she didn't know what – between them. But Venetia looked away, slapped her hand down, grabbed her upper arm and marched her along the corridor. Whatever had been between them, Stephanie thought glumly, had gone.

The punishment room was full of people. Andrew wasn't there but Paul and Mick were, and six of the former slaves. As at the trial all were semi-dressed, two of the men again in Stephanie's panties, their faces, this time, crudely made-up with eye-liner and lipstick. Both men's cocks were being stroked by females. One of the women, naked but for a black bra and high heels, was sitting in the lap of one of the men with his cock buried in her sex. Bottles of booze abounded. The finest clarets and Napoleon brandy were being swigged like soft drinks.

Devlin stood naked in the middle of the room. His hands had been strapped into padded leather cuffs suspended from a rope over a pulley set in the ceiling, and were stretched above his head. His nipples were clamped into a pair of nipple-clips, little springs like bulldog clips but with serrated edges and joined together by a chain plated with chrome. His feet were spread apart about two feet, ankle-cuffs strapped around his ankles and chained to metal rings in the floor.

It was no surprise to Stephanie that Devlin's massive and ugly cock was at full erection. She had discovered Devlin's sexual tastes, unlocked his private fantasies. She had made him her slave. For the last however many days, he had been performing the same role for Amanda: it would not have been something he had to suffer. Devlin's submission was absolute. It was what he craved. The greater his subservience, the more he was excited. That was clear now as his erection throbbed visibly in front of his tormentors.

'Come over here,' Amanda said to Stephanie.

Stephanie obeyed. She looked into Devlin's eyes. For a moment the world stopped. She had had no human contact for so many days, no exchange of emotion, apart from sex, no kindness or concern, that the look of love she could see in Devlin's eyes, a look that spoke of his worry for her, of his despair that all this had happened, a look that told her this was all his fault and that he was so, so sorry, hit her like the headlights of a car on a dark night. She felt a wave of emotion flood through her. She hadn't quite realised before what Devlin, this ugly, misshapen man, meant to her.

'Take this,' Amanda commanded. She handed Stephanie the riding crop. 'He is to have twelve strokes . . .' The audience cheered at this news, '. . . and you will administer the punishment. Do you understand?'

'Yes.' It was the last thing Stephanie felt like doing to him even though, in the past, she had whipped him many times and knew it was no punishment at all. As if to confirm her thoughts a little tear of fluid formed on the slit of his urethra.

'Yes what?' Amanda said, slapping Stephanie's buttock hard with her gloved hand.

'Yes, mistress,' Stephanie intoned.

Amanda took Devlin's cheeks between the fingers and thumb of her hand, squeezing his mouth into a distorted pout. His cock brushed against the hem of her short skirt and the fluid leaked onto the brown leather. 'And you count each stroke, out loud.'

Devlin nodded.

With studied calculation Amanda picked up the chain of the nipple clips and pulled it up towards his chin. The serrated edges bit deeper into the corrugated flesh. His cock twitched so much against the leather skirt that for a moment Stephanie thought he was going to come.

'Get on with it,' the man with the woman on his lap called impatiently.

'Yes, come on . . .' one of the women agreed.

Amanda stepped back. 'Begin,' she said, standing behind Devlin's back.

Stephanie spread her legs slightly and raised the whip. Without hesitation she stroked it down on Devlin's arse, her long black hair streaming out over her shoulders, her naked breasts trembling with the effort. She saw Devlin react, saw the pain turned to profound pleasure as it always did. There was still sorrow in his eyes, but it was sorrow not for what was being done to him, but because they were not doing it under their own volition, that this was a circus where, for once, it was not Stephanie who was the ringmaster, but someone else.

After the fifth stroke Stephanie began to sweat. It was hot in the windowless room with so many people. She tried to concentrate on what she was doing but out of the corner of her eye saw Andrew slip into the room. Venetia, tall and elegant, was standing next to the door. Andrew, in a shirt and slacks, stood beside her.

Stephanie turned back to Devlin's buttocks. The red welts from the riding crop lined his white flesh; there were darker red marks there too, from previous days. She slashed the whip down again, his flesh trembling in response.

'Six,' he cried his teeth gritted.

When Stephanie looked back towards Andrew she could hardly believe what she saw. Venetia had put her arm around Andrew's neck and was pushing her tongue into his ear. At the same time her hand was massaging the crotch of his trousers, gripping the bulge that was growing there.

In all the time Stephanie had known Venetia she had never seen her touch or kiss a man, except on the one occasion she had been forced. She was so astonished that the next stroke of the crop missed the target and landed with no real force on Devlin's thigh.

'Seven,' Devlin grunted.

'No,' Amanda said at once. 'Do that again.'

Stephanie tried to put her mind back on what she was doing. What did it matter anyway? But as she landed the next blow full across Devlin's ample rump she had a feeling it mattered very much indeed.

'Harder,' Amanda complained.

By the tenth blow most of the room had lost interest in the proceedings and when Stephanie looked round Venetia and Andrew had slipped away. The others were all engaged in some form of sex, coupled together by hand or mouth or genitals. Apart from Amanda no one was watching Devlin's punishment any more.

Stephanie delivered the final two cuts in quick succession, sweat running freely down her naked body.

If Amanda had thought this public display would humiliate Devlin, if she thought having Stephanie beat him would make it worse, she had not learnt yet what Devlin was like. His enormous cock was on the point of orgasm. Stephanie felt her own body moisten as she looked at it, her memory of all the times it had reamed into her with such devastating effect, making the process almost inevitable.

The rope that held Devlin's arms above his head was curled around a pulley and tied off on a cleat fixed to the stone wall. Amanda unwound the rope from the cleat and let it fall. Devlin's arms dropped and he moaned with relief.

'Unstrap his ankles,' Amanda ordered.

Stephanie dropped to her knees and obeyed at once. With the tip of his fingers, out of Amanda's line of vision, Devlin touched her long black hair affectionately. Stephanie almost swooned at such tenderness.

'Stop that,' Amanda said, seeing what he was doing as she moved forward. She slapped his cuffed hands. 'I want to be fucked.'

She wriggled the short leather skirt up over her hips. She wore a pair of bright red lace panties that covered the triangle of her belly and the tight curls of her black pubic hair, though the shadow of it could be clearly seen under the material.

Amanda bent over one of the wooden punishment frames, presenting her long plump arse to Devlin, the red silk a slash of colour between her legs.

'Come on,' she said impatiently, 'and make it good.'

But Devlin was too far gone. He moved to stand behind her and poked the tip of his cock forward but the hot pleasure the beating had created in his arse had made his body boil with need. His spunk was heavy in his bails. He knew he could never hold out.

It didn't help that everywhere he looked was sexual provocation. Paul, his cock as hard as a bone, was lying on the frame Amanda was bending over with two women astride his thighs and facing each other. They clung together and bounced back and forward so his cock alternated from one sex to another. Their mouths were locked in a kiss, their breasts pressed together. Or there was Mick enthusiastically tonguing a former slave who had seated herself on a wooden upright chair, normally used to hold its occupant immobile by means of straps on its arms and legs, and had hooked her thighs over his shoulders.

Everywhere there was sex. And there was Stephanie, naked, her body glistening with sweat.

He pushed his cock against the red panties as Amanda reached behind her to pull them aside. He felt her hand brush his cock, and then the heat of her labia and the brush of her tight curls. That was too much. As Amanda wriggled her arse back at him, to get him between her labia, his cock exploded and spunk, white hot spunk, splattered over the panties and the wet flesh of her outer sex.

'You bastard!' Amanda screamed at once. 'How dare you?'

She swung round, bumping against his cock with her hip. 'You're going to have to be punished all over again.'

Stephanie smiled to herself inwardly for the first time in days. There was one thing she knew: there was no punishment Amanda could devise that would give Devlin anything but the extremes of pleasure.

Chapter Ten

Everything was still and quiet. Stephanie had been returned to her cell after being allowed to shower. She had fallen asleep almost immediately and had slept deeply, the best sleep she had had for days on the cold stone floor. But she had been started awake.

Her heart was pounding, pumped with adrenalin from whatever shock her subconscious had perceived. She listened, trying to hear any noise. The little strip of light under the cell door was still there, as it had been every night. No one had ever turned off the corridor lights. But she could hear no reason for her sudden alertness. Everything was as it had been and, as far as she could tell, ever would be.

Shifting her position on the stone floor, Stephanie closed her eyes again. She yearned for the comfort of one of the mattresses that lay abandoned in the corridor outside. However she arranged herself on the floor, after ten or twelve minutes the cold, hard stone was making her body ache anew.

Some minutes later she must have drifted back to sleep because she woke again with a start, but this time recognised the noise that had woken her. The light in the corridor outside had been switched off. She heard footsteps too, which was even stranger. Why would someone turn off the lights and then walk down the corridor?

Almost immediately she heard the bolt on the cell

door being drawn back. The noise sounded like a bullet being shot from a gun in the silence of the cellars. The door creaked open and Stephanie was dazzled by the beam of a torch shining right into her face. It swung away and down onto the floor as the cell door swung closed again and the footsteps walked over to her. She recognised the strong smell of perfume.

'Venetia?'

'Yes.' Venetia knelt on the floor in front of her and shone the torch into her own face. 'Are you all right?'

'What are you doing here?' Stephanie said. There could be only one answer she hoped, her heart suddenly thumping against her ribs, unless this was some cruel game devised by Andrew.

'I couldn't come any sooner.'

'What do you mean?'

'They watched me like a hawk. For the first week they kept me chained up in my bedroom. 'It's only the last three days that I've had my freedom. I didn't come right away in case it was a trap, but I think they trust me now. Oh Stephanie, I'm so sorry . . .'

'They trust you now?'

'I mean Andrew does.'

'Why?' Stephanie saw a shadow of emotion pass over Venetia's face in the torchlight. She already knew the answer to her question.

'Why, Venetia?'

'Because I agreed to go to bed with him. It was the only way. He kept asking me. Over and over. I knew he'd never trust me unless I did.'

'Did he hurt you?'

'No, no. It wasn't so bad. And now he's stopped watching me all the time. They even let me go to the mainland on my own.'

217

'Oh, I really thought you were on their side.' For the first time since the rebellion began Stephanie felt her eyes prick with tears: they were tears of relief.

'I know. I'm sorry. I had to pretend. I saw that on the plane. If they'd brought me here and locked me up I'd have been no use. At least this way I had a chance.'

Stephanie reached out and hugged Venetia in her arms. For a moment they did nothing, Stephanie completely overcome with several strong emotions at the same time; the resurgence of hope which she had suppressed for so long, her gratitude that Venetia had not deserted her, and the feeling of actually being held by someone again, the human contact she had missed so much.

'Listen,' Venetia said eventually. 'I've got to get back before I'm missed. Tomorrow night, when you're taken up to Andrew, you've got to trick him somehow.'

'Trick him?'

'You should be alone. You've got to find a way to overpower him.'

'Why tomorrow?'

'Amanda's going over to the mainland for the day to get provisions. I've got to go and pick her up in the evening. If I can overpower her on the journey back and you can do the same with Andrew, I can release Devlin and we're free. We can take the boat and go.'

'How can I overpower him?'

'You'll think of something. But you've got to do it. If I come back here with Amanda trussed up like a chicken and Andrew's still free, they'll put me down here with you and that's our last chance gone.'

'I'll think of something. Oh Venetia, I'm so glad

... all those things you said. The ways I treated you in London I should never have done that ...'

'Forget it.'

'You wouldn't even look at me.'

'I daren't. I couldn't. I knew if I did I might give something away.'

'I understand.'

'Getting them to trust me was the only chance we had.'

'I know, I know. You knew about the security code for the files then, for the hard copies ...'

'Yes. I knew they wouldn't be destroyed.'

'I couldn't remember if Devlin had told you.'

'Oh yes. If we ever get out of here, the files are all intact. A nasty little surprise for Andrew Harlock. I've got to go.'

'Don't worry, I'll think of something.'

Stephanie embraced Venetia again briefly. She wanted to kiss her, she wanted to pull her down onto the stone floor and press herself into her magnificent body, to feel her warmth again, her breasts and her long powerful legs twining around hers. But there would be time for that later. If the plan succeeded.

Almost as quickly as she had come, Venetia was gone and Stephanie heard the bolt sliding home on the cell door. The sound momentarily provoked a chill of depression in Stephanie's body. She seemed so cold now by contrast to the warmth of Venetia's embrace.

But the chill dissipated rapidly. Now there was hope. Now there was something she could do. She stood up and paced the cell, the chain attached to her ankle dragging against the stone. She tried to remember everything she could about Andrew, everything that had happened when he was at the castle and

219

everything that had happened since. His arrival had coincided with a visit of two newcomers to the castle, a married couple called Clarke, and his display of insolence had been rewarded by the wife, Jacqui, who had teased him incessantly until he had literally begged to be allowed to come – naturally without success. It had been the first of the lessons he had had to be taught. The first, Stephanie now knew, of the humilation he had harboured and cultivated and brooded upon and that he was out to revenge.

But then she remembered something that had happened that same night, after his experience with the Clarkes. It was something that might be very helpful. Stephanie smiled broadly to herself.

By the time the light came on in the morning – at least Stephanie assumed it was morning – and food was pushed in on a tray, Stephanie had a plan. It might not work but at least it was a plan.

She tried not to let her new optimism show. She wanted to appear just as weary as she had been on the other days, and trudged to the shower with her head down and a general air of depression. But it was difficult and she was delighted when the cell door was closed again and she was left to her own devices.

Whether it was the thought of the possibility of escape or the fact that Venetia had not betrayed her that made her most happy, it was difficult to say. She wished she could have talked to Devlin. She couldn't wait for the time to pass before she was called up to see Andrew. Time had always dragged in the cell but today it went by as though in slow motion.

She tried to remember exactly what Venetia had said in their few moments together. Presumably Amanda had gone to the mainland to order supplies. She must be going alone or Venetia wouldn't be so confident about overpowering her. Venetia would drop her off at the jetty and she'd take the Mercedes into town, arranging to be picked up again that evening. Stephanie had done the same thing herself many times. Perhaps she even intended to drive to Perugia. It was not more than an hour's drive and had a good selection of shops.

A sudden depression struck her at the thought that tonight Andrew might not call her to his room. So far he had done so every night. They hadn't always had sex. Some nights he had merely made her stand, watching him eating or fucking Amanda or one or two of the other women. Other times he'd made her masturbate for him or dress in her finest lingerie while he merely watched. But so far, every night, she had been called to his room to perform some service. Venetia had seemed certain he would do so again.

Stephanie knew what a sacrifice it must have been for Venetia, not only to allow herself to be used by Andrew but to pretend to enjoy it. She had never liked men, never had a man before Devlin had allowed a man to take her at Gianni's behest. She had sacrificed herself for Stephanie's sake, and for Devlin's. The first thing they would do in return was to see that Venetia's file, with all the details of her elaborate computer embezzlement scheme, was destroyed. What happened to the other files, the files on Andrew and Amanda and all the other slaves currently in the castle, the files they had thought destroyed, was an entirely different matter.

At the moment Stephanie wanted only to think about escape and how it was to be accomplished. She saw herself sitting at the back of the speedboat next to Devlin with Venetia at the controls, heading away from the castle at high speed in a foaming white

221

wake. They'd take the Mercedes and drive, far and fast.

Stephanie had dozed off to sleep when the cell door was thrown open. It was Venetia, the last person Stephanie had expected to see. She was wearing a white leotard and a small white pleated skirt like a tennis skirt. Her eyes looked straight at Stephanie, her expression terse and controlled. Stephanie immediately saw why. Andrew followed her into the cell.

Stephanie's heart pounded, her mind in turmoil. Had something gone wrong?

'I thought I'd come down and inspect the accommodation. Any complaints?' he said, pacing the cell. He was wearing a white T-shirt and jeans, his feet clad in open-toed sandals.

'I haven't got a mattress, master,' Stephanie said, trying to work out what was going on. Why wasn't Venetia collecting Amanda in the boat?

'That must be very uncomfortable,' he said.

'She doesn't deserve a mattress,' Venetia said, pulling Stephanie to her feet by gripping the tops of her arms. She took a pair of handcuffs, twisted Stephanie's hands behind her back and callously slipped the cold metal loops over Stephanie's wrists, making her wince.

'Careful,' Andrew said. 'I don't want damaged goods.'

'You promised you'd let me have her.'

'I promised I'd let you have her when I'm finished. But I'm not finished by a long way. You'll just have to be patient. Like I was patient with you.'

'I was worth it, wasn't I?' Venetia said, clutching at Andrew's crotch through the jeans and giving his cock a pinch.

222

'Oh yes. And she will be too.'

'You wait till I get my hands on you, you bitch. He's too soft on you. You won't be so lucky with me.' Venetia spat the words out right into Stephanie's face, her eyes full of hatred.

'Hadn't you better go and collect Amanda?' Andrew said, looking at his watch.

Venetia had stopped to unlock the metal cuff at Stephanie's ankle. She got to her feet again and went over to Andrew. 'Save some for me,' she said, kissing his cheek and squeezing one cheek of his buttocks in her hand.

'Don't worry.'

Venetia strode out of the room without looking at Stephanie again. It was such a good performance that Stephanie couldn't help wondering for a moment if last night had just been a particularly graphic dream.

'So you want a mattress, do you?'

'Yes master, please.'

'Anything else?'

'No master.' Stephanie tried to look contrite and obedient.

'We'll have to see what we can do, then.'

Andrew took her arm and led her out into the corridor. One of the other cell doors was open and inside Stephanie glimpsed one of the garden overseers. He was lying with his hand bound to the metal ring set in the floor, the ring that usually held the ankle chain, his arms over his head. One of the former female slaves was crouching over his head. She was fully dressed, one of Stephanie's flowery summer dresses with a very full and long skirt which fitted her perfectly. The skirt had been arranged around his head so it was not visible at all, though it was perfectly obvious from the expression on the girl's face what service he was performing under the folds of colourful cotton. A whip lay on the stone beside her, in case he should flag in his efforts.

Andrew pushed Stephanie through the small door to the back stairs and she mounted the stone steps. Andrew followed her, watching her tight round arse and her long slim thighs as she walked. He could see the thick bush of pubic hair between her legs. Despite Venetia's recent conversion, and Venetia was an extremely beautiful woman, for Andrew there was no one in the castle to compare with Stephanie, her raven-black hair draped over her back, her tight cinched waist, the generous flare of her hips, her shapely calves and pinched ankles, her firm breasts and iron-flat navel, let alone the glories of her tight, controlled cunt. He knew every inch of her body like a map, memorised from the agonising times he had massaged it. Now it all belonged to him. He had seen it perform for him: he had made it do everything he could imagine and it still fascinated him. He had had sex with Amanda and a couple of the slaves, and in the last three days with Venetia who had told him he was the only man she had ever had willingly, but even this thrill did not compare with the feelings he got with Stephanie.

Tonight he wanted to be alone with her, to indulge himself with her. His cock began to stiffen at the idea. He had been stupid, he told himself. He'd spent too much time with the others, too much energy in orgies of multiple sex. He was like a starving man faced with a buffet of food. He'd dived in and eaten everything where he should have selected the things he liked most. Well, now he would be more restrained. Now he would eat and savour his favourite food. There was no hurry after all. The castle had a safe stuffed with money. They could stay here as long as they liked, for at least a year, maybe two. They could certainly spend next summer basking in the sun. Meanwhile Devlin's business empire would come crashing down without him at the helm, and that would be yet another slice of his revenge.

Stephanie stepped into the lushly carpeted bedroom through the concealed door. The windows out onto the terrace were open and a pleasant breeze drifted in from the lake. It was warmer than it had been for days. The sun had almost set, the first time Stephanie had seen it since the trials, and she thought she could see a great white wake stretching out across the water in a long arc, the wake of the speedboat. Her heart missed a beat. It carried all her hopes.

Andrew closed the terrace windows, pulled his white T-shirt over his head and unzipped his jeans. The days of indulgence had done nothing for his already unmuscled body and Stephanie thought she saw definite signs that he had put on weight. His cock poked through the fly of a pair of white boxer shorts.

'Get on your knees,' he said. He'd said it to her before. The words thrilled him; they represented power, power over the woman of his dreams, the woman still in his dreams.

Stephanie sank to the floor a little unsteadily, with her arms cuffed behind her. She had her plan, knew what she was going to say and do. He held her head in both his hands and directed his cock, still flaccid, into her mouth. She gobbled it up easily, taking the whole length between her lips and his balls until it grew too big and his balls escaped one by one.

'Lovely cock,' she mumbled with it still in her mouth.

'What did you say?'

She pulled her mouth away. 'Lovely cock, master.'

'You're lucky then, aren't you?'

'Yes master, very.'

She was about to press her mouth back onto his now fully erect phallus but he prevented her with his hands.

'Do you know what I'm going to do with you tonight?'

'No master.'

'I'm going to fuck you. Long and hard.'

'I'd like that, master,' she said trying to make her eyes show excitement. 'I liked it before when you were my slave.' That was the bait. She held her breath, hoping he would take it.

'You never allowed me to fuck you then.' He pulled her face up to look into her eyes.

'Didn't I?' she said coquettishly.

'When?' he snapped.

'Don't you remember? I thought you'd always remember that? Or didn't you think it was me?'

'When?' he asked insistently, confused now.

'On your first day. You must remember. When the Clarkes were here. After Jacqui had beaten you and teased you. I came to your cell after they'd gone. Surely you remember . . .'

'You, that was you. I thought it was that bloody prick-teaser.'

'It was me, Andrew. I felt sorry for you. No, that's not true. I wanted you. You felt how I came, I just melted over you. That's why I couldn't risk letting you fuck me again. I thought I'd lose control.'

Andrew sat on the edge of the bed. He remembered every detail of that night. But he had no idea it had been Stephanie that had had him hooded and released from the pouch, no idea it was her sex that had impaled itself on his rock-hard erection, no idea it was her who had ridden him to the crescendo of pleasure he would never forget. His cock throbbed at the thought.

'You do remember then,' Stephanie said, seeing the movement of his cock.

'That was you?'

'Yes.'

'My God . . .'

'Let me do it again,' Stephanie said quietly and a little breathlessly. 'God, I'd love to do that again. Take you like that. I'm getting hot just thinking about it.'

There was an agonising pause. Stephanie felt she'd overplayed her hand and Andrew was not going to be drawn. In fact he was rapt in thought.

'I even remember what you were wearing,' he said finally, almost to himself.

'Do you?' she said eagerly. 'Tell me.'

'A black lacy bra, strapless, very low cut, tiny little panties, and black stockings, hold-ups with wide lacy tops . . . you had your hair up . . .'

'Let me find them, let me put them on again . . .'

'You had me wear a hood, a leather hood, very tight. I couldn't see you . . .' His voice was hoarse with passion.

'That's right.'

Andrew's cock was twitching so much and looked so hard, Stephanie thought for a moment he might come spontaneously.

'Get up,' he said in a harder tone of voice.

Stephanie struggled to her feet again, frightened that the mood had been broken. Andrew got up too and took the keys to the handcuffs from his jeans pocket. He came round behind her and unlocked the metal hoops, letting them fall to the floor.

'Do it . . . find what you were wearing. Put your hair up . . .' he ordered.

Stephanie rubbed her sore wrists and went over to the lingerie drawers. Everything had been put back in a different order and it took some time to find what she was looking for. But she found it. She used the big bedroom mirror to gather her hair up and pin it to her head. Her little white porcelain jar of hairpins was untouched on the dressing-table. Without asking permission she quickly lined her eyes with make-up, smeared her lashes with mascara and traced a dark red lipstick over her fleshy mouth.

Andrew sat on the edge of the bed again. Stephanie pulled the strapless bra up over her breasts and reached behind her to fasten the clip between her shoulder-blades. She drew the silky lace panties, no more than two triangles of lace front and back joined by a black satin cord at each side, up over her thighs until they nestled over her sex and halfway over her bottom. Then she sat on the dressing-table stool, unwrapped the black hold-ups from their cellophane packet and rolled one up into a pouch around the toe. She extended her left leg, pointing her foot, and inserted it into the stocking. She rolled the nylon out over her leg, playing it out slowly, suddenly remembering how she had done this for the Baron what seemed, now, to be a lifetime ago. As she leant forward the bra touched her raised thigh. Her hands spun the nylon out, encasing her creamy flesh until it was high on her thigh and the band of elastic under the black lace welt held it securely in place. She repeated the process with the other stocking, not looking at Andrew but aware of his eyes following her every movement.

'Shoes too,' Andrew said, '. . . black high heels.'

Stephanie found what he wanted and squeezed her

228

feet into them. The lingerie, soft and silky against her skin, made her feel better and stronger. It was practically the first time her breasts and sex had been covered since the start of the rebellion. It made her feel confident. The plan was going to work. Without asking permission again she took out a riding crop, carefully selecting one from the long drawer where the whips were kept. She swished it experimentally through the air. She felt a sense of elation, it was all flooding back to her, the old Stephanie, dressed to kill, proud and haughty on her spiky heels, dominant again.

She said nothing but slapped the whip against the palm of her other hand. Andrew looked sheepish. She knew. She knew what he wanted, what she had made him want. He wanted it as badly as he had wanted it that night when she had sneaked into his cell.

He lay on the bed and turned over onto his stomach. There was a silent complicity between them. Master was allowing himself to be the slave.

Stephanie strode over to the bed, the tops of her stockings rasping against each other.

'Bruno had beaten you, hadn't he?' she said, wanting him to remember that night, to keep it uppermost in his mind.

'Yes,' he breathed excitedly.

The crop lashed down on his buttocks. He moaned, his hard cock trapped between his navel and the sheets. Stephanie raised the whip higher, brought it down harder, a red welt appearing immediately.

'How many times? How many strokes did he give you?'

'Six.'

'Six . . .'

The whip fell again. Each stroke enflamed a new

strip of flesh, created a new red welt. Andrew thought for a moment he was going to come over the sheet. The pain from the whip burned into his nerves, and turned to instant intoxicating pleasure, a pleasure so sharp and intense it was, in turn, almost like pain.

At the sixth stroke Stephanie threw the whip down. She went over to the chest of drawers and pulled out the leather hood. She had found it when she was looking for the lingerie. She had found the leather strap she needed too.

Andrew turned around, his arse on fire just as it had been that night, just as it had been time and time again at the castle, the fire filling his body with sensations he had never had before but had wanted, had craved for, ever since. It made his cock burn, it made his blood race, and it would, he knew, make his spunk jet from his body in a climax of exquisite pleasure. He had been whipped twice since he'd been master of the castle and each time he experienced the incredible feeling again. But that was nothing like this. This was Stephanie. This was his mistress. This was his wet dream of pleasure. He wriggled his arse against the sheet, delighting in the *mélange* of pain and pleasure this created.

He watched as Stephanie walked back towards the bed, her body divided into areas of creamy bare flesh and silky black lace. She held the leather hood in one hand, its laces dangling down. The leather strap was hidden behind her back.

'Yes,' he said enthusiastically. That was what he wanted now. To be laced tightly into the hood, enveloped in darkness, gagged and blinded, able only to feel, only to moan, only to be nothing but a throbbing, spunking cock. He was throwing caution to the wind, he knew, but what did it matter? There was nowhere for Stephanie to escape to, nowhere to go. They would soon capture her if she tried it and she knew better than anyone the price she would have to pay for the attempt.

'Take your last look . . .' she said, standing over him. And he did, drinking in the deep cleavage hugged by the bra, the curve of her pubic bone in the black lace, the long, contoured thighs banded by the lacy stocking tops, the calves shaped by the high heels.

Stephanie pulled the hood over his head and darkness descended, accompanied by the strong aroma of leather. Expertly Stephanie stuffed the large rubber ball attached to the inside of the leather into Andrew's mouth, then pulled the hood down to his neck, then laced it on tightly, pulling the soft leather into the features of his face, holding the ball-gag firmly in his mouth, cutting out all light.

Satisfied he was unable to see, she dropped the leather strap on the bed by his ankles. She hooked her hand around his cock and he moaned, though the sound was no more than a muffled murmur. His cock was so hot it felt like it was on fire. She wanked it slowly.

'Do you remember how I got astride you that night?'

He nodded vigorously. In his entire life he didn't think he had ever been so turned on as he was now. But he had once. That night when Jacqui Clarke had strung him up and teased him, teased him until he was on the brink of coming, then pulled away. She did it over and over again. He begged her, pleaded with her, but to no avail. His cock was so swollen he thought it would burst. Just as it felt now.

'Fuck me,' he tried to say but the words could not get past the gag.

Without losing contact with his cock, Stephanie reached out with her foot and caught the handcuffs that lay on the carpet where Andrew had discarded them. She reeled them in until she could pick them up with her other hand, all without breaking the rhythm she had started on his throbbing phallus.

'Don't you want me to rub your arse with my nice cool hands?'

He replied by rolling back onto his stomach. He wanted that very much. She had done that too on that incredible first night at the castle. He could remember exactly how her cool hands had felt after she'd freed him from the metal pouch, soothing the welts that were burning across his arse.

Stephanie laid her hands on his buttocks, criss-crossed with red welts. They were radiating heat. She smoothed her palm over them and heard another muffled moan of pleasure and pain. She pulled his left hand up into the small of his back. He did not resist. This was it. This was the moment. She reached for his right hand. Again he did not resist as she pulled it backwards until both hands were behind him. He did nothing but wallow in the sensations prickling from his tortured buttocks.

This was it. Stephanie readied herself, her whole body tense. In one smooth movement she dropped the open loops of the handcuffs onto his wrists and clicked them shut. Instantly, before he realised what had happened, she picked up the thick leather strap on the bed by his feet and sat astride his legs with her full weight, winding the leather around both ankles tightly and buckling it, just as he began to realise what was happening and tried to buck her off.

It was useless. He was hers. Helpless, captive. She ran over to the chest of drawers that contained the bondage equipment and pulled out a tangle of leather straps. In minutes she had wound them around his body, round his knees and elbows and around his chest. He was hers. Bound, gagged and blindfolded. A neat package.

Stephanie's heart was beating ten to the dozen. She tried to calm herself down. She had done it. She had done it. Now it was up to Venetia.

For the moment Andrew had stopped struggling. He lay quiet, trying to hear what she was doing. But the leather hood made it difficult to hear anything above the throbbing of his own pulse.

Stephanie went to the bedroom fridge and looked inside, needing a drink to stop her heart beating with such ferocity. There was no champagne left but there was a bottle of brandy on the tray with the glasses. She poured herself a stiff tot and drank it down in one.

She thought she had heard the speedboat return some minutes before but couldn't be sure with the terrace door closed. The boat must have returned in any event because it was too dark to navigate the lake by now. She sat and waited nervously while Andrew began to struggle against his bindings again, disconcerted by the silence. For all his efforts he only managed to rock his body slightly from side to side.

It was probably only ten minutes later that Stephanie heard footsteps but it seemed like hours. They came up the corridor to the bedroom. Some instinct, some unconscious recognition, told her it was not Venetia. This time she listened to her instincts. Jumping onto the bed she rolled Andrew on to his back and buried his cock in her mouth, swinging her body over his so her buttocks were over his hooded face.

The bedroom door opened and Amanda strode in. It was the last person Stephanie expected to see. What on earth had happened? Had she turned the tables on Venetia, discovered her plot, had her taken down to the cellars?

With no urgency, Amanda walked over to the bed. She was wearing a yellow silk dress – one Stephanie did not recognise – belted at the waist but with a very full pleated skirt and matching yellow leather gloves.

'You've having a good time, then?' she said. 'Don't mind if I watch.' She sat in an armchair opposite the foot of the bed.

Stephanie tried to concentrate on what she was doing while her mind struggled with the new situation. What on earth was she going to do now? Despite his position, or perhaps because of it, Andrew's cock hardened again in her mouth. She lowered her buttocks onto his face, the silky lace rubbing against the leather hood. While she sucked and tongued his cock she tried to think. Where was Venetia? What had gone wrong? Clearly Amanda wouldn't have been so relaxed if she'd discovered Venetia's treachery.

Andrew was coming. If he came Stephanie would have to pull away and she couldn't justify keeping him tied up. She tried to put less pressure on his cock, but at the same time appear to be doing a good job. She felt the shaft tense, and squeezed his balls in her hand in an effort to delay him. Unfortunately this had the opposite effect. His cock spasmed and spat spunk out into her mouth. Equally unfortunately there was too much spunk for her to contain. She tried desperately to swallow it all but there was just too much and it dribbled out of the corner of her mouth and down into his pubic hair.

'Well, look at that,' Amanda said, getting up and coming over to the bed. She pulled on Stephanie's shoulder to make her sit up, then stooped to kiss her full on the mouth, savouring the taste of spunk. 'Tastes good,' she said finally.

Reluctantly Stephanie climbed off Andrew's trussed-up body. Amanda reached for the laces that held the hood in place.

That was it, Stephanie thought, the whole plan wrecked. She was so desperate, so depressed at having her freedom snatched from her when it was so nearly in her grasp she acted without thinking. Amanda was picking away at the tight bow which held the lacing in place. She had managed to loosen it a little. The top sheet of the bed had fallen on the floor with all the activity and Stephanie picked it up. Behind Amanda's back she held it with both her arms extended and looped it over Amanda's head, bringing it down to her waist so she was enclosed in a tent of material. Her arms had been drawn into the sheet too and Stephanie held it tightly around her middle.

Amanda started to struggle. Stephanie felt the strength in her arms pulling the sheet out of her grip. She felt Amanda's powerful legs kick out and a searing pain erupted from her calf. She would never be able to hold on, let alone wrestle Amanda to the floor and overpower her.

Suddenly Stephanie felt rather than saw another presence. Arms linked around the sheet, holding it down against Amanda's efforts to pull it up. It was Venetia.

'Get a strap,' she shouted.

Stephanie let go of the struggling package while Venetia clung on. The tangle of straps she had not used on Andrew were still on the floor by the bed. The first one she pulled free was big enough. She looped it between Venetia and Amanda and cinched it as tight as she could, binding Amanda's arms inside the sheet. As soon as they released her she fell to the floor.

It took them nearly twenty minutes to get Amanda secured. Just as she had done to Andrew, they swathed her body in straps then cut the sheet away with scissors from Stephanie's dressing table.

'You bitch . . .' she screamed at Venetia when the sheet was pulled from her eyes. 'I told Andrew not to trust you . . . you wait, I'll . . .' But the rest was lost as they forced a ball-gag into her mouth.

'We've got to be quick,' Venetia said.

'What happened?'

'Paul insisted on coming on the boat with me. Quick . . .' Venetia began to lift Amanda's feet, '. . . take her shoulders.'

Together they manoeuvred Amanda onto the bed.

'Put her on top of him so it looks like they're doing it. It won't look so suspicious if someone looks in.'

'Good idea.'

They rolled Amanda on top of Andrew. With two more straps around both their bodies they were held firmly in place. Even if they rolled over it would look as if they were still engaged in some form of sexual bondage. In the castle, that shouldn't seem unusual.

'Come on,' Venetia urged.

'What are we going to do?' Stephanie calmly undid the Patek Phillipe watch from Amanda's wrist and clipped it back onto her own.

'The boat's still at the jetty. We've got to get to it before Paul decides to put it away. I don't know where they keep the keys.'

They decided it would look better if Stephanie remained as she was. A dress would look suspicious after she had been kept naked for so long. If they were stopped, Venetia would say she was taking Stephanie down to the cellars. To complete the picture they found a collar and leash amongst all the equipment stored in Stephanie's bedroom. Quickly buckling it around Stephanie's neck, Venetia took the leash in her hand and led the way out of the bedroom.

As they walked through into the corridor and down to the stairs Stephanie, who had only seen her own bedroom since the trial, always having been brought up the back stairs, saw the house had been wrecked. The slaves had used every guest room. Though Andrew had kept Stephanie's room tidy none of the others appeared to have bothered. Open doors revealed unmade beds, uneaten food and half-empty bottles everywhere. Clothes and lingerie littered the floors. Paintings had been torn and ornaments smashed.

They got to the marble staircase and began to walk down it. As they did, Mick appeared from the main reception rooms with one of the females, a rather dumpy redhead dressed curiously in a black one-piece swimsuit.

'What's she doing here?' Mick said abruptly.

'Andrew's just been . . .' Venetia couldn't think of the word.

'Why didn't you use the back stairs?'

'Oh, I forgot. Andrew and Amanda are at it like rabbits. Slipped my mind . . .'

'At it again. They never get enough.'

'Neither do you,' the female slave said, running her hand over Mick's penis covered by his striped white and blue shorts. 'She looks good enough to eat. If Andrew's finished with her let's take her with us, Mickey.' The redhead was looking straight at Stephanie.

'Yeah, good idea.' Mick grabbed the leash from Venetia's hand.

'Paul wants her,' she said quickly.

'Paul can bloody well wait.'

'You can tell him then. He's waiting down in the cellars. I'm not going to take the blame,' Venetia said calmly, though she felt anything but calm.

Stephanie's heart was in her mouth. She saw Mick's eyes looking at her body in the black lingerie, sizing up whether it was worth the trouble of going down to explain to Paul.

'Oh, we'll have her tomorrow. I'm too randy.' He dropped the leash.

'Please . . . I really fancy it,' the redhead whined.

'You'll get it tomorrow,' Mick said with annoyance, grabbing her hand and pulling her up the staircase.

'I'm going to get you, bitch,' the redhead snarled in disappointment. She resisted Mick's pressure and ran her hand over Stephanie's navel to the strapless bra. Pulling it in the middle between the two cups, she tore it down off her breasts.

'Tomorrow,' Mick insisted, pulling her harder this time. They set off upstairs.

Venetia picked up the leash and led Stephanie to the cellar doors as they listened for the footsteps to disappear above them.

'Listen, go to the boat. I'll get Devlin.'

'What if someone sees me? Where's Paul?' Stephanie pulled the bra up over her breasts again.

'I don't know. Just hope . . . he's probably otherwise engaged by now . . .'

Venetia opened the cellar door tucked under the corner of the huge tapestry that hung from the main wall.

'Good luck,' she said.

'You too.'

They were so close and yet so far. The next few minutes would tell.

Stephanie ran over to the main door as Venetia disappeared down the steps into the cellar. Gingerly she picked her way across the courtyard and through the tunnel of foliage that led to the stone steps down to the jetty. There was no one around. She kicked her shoes off so they wouldn't clack on the stone and started down the steps as stealthily as she could.

The boat, no longer gleaming and highly polished, bobbed up and down in the slight swell in the single light that hung from the castle wall. For the umpteenth time that night Stephanie's heart sank. Sitting on the long bench seat in the transom, a bottle of brandy in his hand, was Paul. His other hand trailed in the water.

He had seen her before she had seen him.

'Come aboard,' he said, apparently not at all phased by her presence. His voice was fogged with drink.

'I can't, sir,' Stephanie straightened up. 'Andrew sent me to find you,' she lied, hoping he would believe she was on a genuine errand.

'Come aboard,' he repeated.

'Please sir, don't make it hard on me. He'll beat me again if you don't come.'

'Oh, I'll make it hard on you if you come aboard,' Paul laughed. He unzipped the shorts he was wearing and pulled them down his legs. They were all he was wearing.

Seeing no alternative, Stephanie stepped aboard. His cock was flaccid.

'Come on, make it hard.'

239

'Andrew wants you. It's important . . .' she tried one last time.

'I'm not at his fucking beck and call.' He lunged out and caught the waistband of her panties using it to pull her towards him. 'I want to fuck you.'

There was no point trying to get him off the boat now. It was too late. He would run into Venetia and Devlin on the way down and even in his condition would realise something was wrong.

'You've got such a big cock. I loved it last time you fucked me.'

'Did you?'

'Well, you didn't actually fuck me did you . . .?'

'No . . . I didn't, did I?' She saw his cock stir slightly at this.

'Shall I take my panties off?'

'Yes . . . yes get them off.'

She rolled the tiny panties down her thighs until she could step out of them. Bunching them in her hand, she rubbed them against his cock. She felt it pulse.

'Nice?'

'Yes. More . . .'

She spread the silk out over his hardening shaft, rubbing it against his glans. What she was going to do she had no idea. But at least this was better than him raising the alarm. With her hand she reached up to pinch his nipple. She felt him react, his cock swelling and stiffening.

'Like stockings . . .' he said, running his hand up the back of her thigh and over the lace welts. 'Very sexy . . . super sexy . . .'

'I like them too, they make me feel very sexy . . .'

'Do they?'

'And available. Shall I suck you?'

'Yes. Give me head, baby . . .'

She dropped to her knees, opened his legs and moved her mouth down to his cock, still covered with the silky black lace panties. She sucked it all into her mouth, then used her tongue to work the fabric against his tender flesh. He moaned and closed his eyes. It was just as well he did.

Stephanie saw Venetia and Devlin step onto the jetty. She sucked harder and Paul moaned again, his head right back on the aft rail of the boat. Stephanie saw her chance, her only chance. She sucked again, using her tongue to probe the escarpment of the glans under the now-soaking wet silk, then ran her arms up under his thighs and gathered all her strength. With one huge effort she raised herself up from her haunches, lifting his thighs until they were above the level of his waist, and he was somersaulted backwards over the stern and into the water.

Venetia saw what had happened and came running with Devlin behind her. They ran to the lines holding the boat to the jetty, Venetia to the forward line and Devlin to the aft. So anxious were they to cast off that the boat almost drifted away before they could jump aboard, but they made it. Venetia flicked the ignition switch and the engine hummed into life just as Paul grabbed one of the loose lines and began to pull himself out of the water, the cold water having a sobering effect.

The boat swung round and headed out into the lake. Venetia dared not gun the engines too strongly for fear of hitting one of the many rocks dotted near-by that couldn't be seen at night. Paul pulled himself hand over hand along the rope.

'The cleat . . .' Devlin shouted, running towards the brass cleat where the rope was secured. But Stephanie got there first. As Paul pulled himself even closer

Stephanie unwound the other end of the rope. As Paul's hand was within inches of the stern rail the rope came free, scorching Stephanie's hand as Paul's weight pulled it out of her grasp. Paul was tossed into the water again, and into the huge white wake of the boat.

Stephanie and Devlin hugged each other tightly. Venetia slowed the boat as soon as they were sure they were clear of Paul. It was not going to be a quick trip back to the mainland. There were rocks and shallows in the lake that it was difficult to navigate at night. Taking two torches from the locker, Devlin and Stephanie watched from either side, shouting directions to Venetia at the helm. Eventually they spotted the wooden jetty on the mainland and the Mercedes parked in the lean-to alongside.

The rest was simple. Venetia had taken the Mercedes keys and with the use of its carphone the Learjet was ordered to return to the landing-strip the following morning with six of Devlin's security guards. Meanwhile a hotel was booked and Venetia drove them through the night to the hilltop town of Perugia. Clothes were a problem. Devlin was naked and Stephanie had only her bra and stockings, her panties having gone overboard with Paul. But when they got to the hotel Venetia explained that there had been some sort of accident and clothes were found, a maid's outfit for Stephanie, a porter's for Devlin, and they walked through the foyer and up to their rooms so dressed.

They did not return to the castle for a week. The Learjet arrived and the security men were ferried out to the island. But they were unnecessary. When Venetia had got down to the cellars she had found them deserted. Freeing Devlin, she had also freed the garden overseers and Bruno.

The four men, armed with the element of surprise, had gone through the castle room by room, quickly overcoming the slaves and returning them to their cells. Andrew and Amanda were the easiest of all. They were still bound and gagged on the bed in Stephanie's bedroom, having made no impression on the tightly buckled leather straps. Only Paul and Mick escaped the net, though no one was quite sure how.

After a week's rest Stephanie and Devlin returned to the castle. The servants had been brought back in and had already made an impression on the chaos the slaves had wrought. Paintings and furniture were sent away for repair.

Of course there were other arrangements to be made. The news that their files had not been destroyed came as very unpleasant news to the slaves and, of course, most of all to Andrew and Amanda. Copies had been sent from London to allay any doubts.

Stephanie ordered an area to be prepared just as it had been by Andrew. There would be a court again in the castle and a trial. This time it would be Andrew and Amanda in the dock and Stephanie conducting the prosecution. Again there would be no defence, but this time there would be no jury either and Devlin would be the judge. Only the sentence was yet to be decided in this trial, Stephanie's trial.

Letter from Esme

Dear Readers

It's a bit cold for this, I know, but I couldn't resist taking
a last look at the view from my favourite window. Yes: it
breaks my heart, but I'm leaving!

It's not that I don't enjoy my job. I mean, apart from
the kick I get out of editing all these horny books, it gives
me an electric thrill knowing that I'm giving pleasure to
thousands of readers too. No, I'm quitting on the advice
of my doctor. Who, as it happens, has also invited me to

emigrate with her to the balmy shores of the West Indies.

So how will Nexus fare without me? That's for you to judge. Dreadful though it is of me to say this, I don't think they'll miss me too much. I'm leaving you in good hands (and they *are* good hands — I should know, I've been in them myself). There may not be any sexy photos of me in the back any more, but I've managed to persuade some of my friends to model in my place. And it pains me to say it, but they're almost as gorgeous as me!

Before I go, I've got some specially tasty treats in store for my loyal fans. First of all, there's the new cover image. From now on, if you're looking for Nexus books, remember — they'll all be in their smart new uniform!

But while the covers have changed, the stories remain as steamy as ever. If you don't believe me (or, come to that, if you do) read *Stephanie's Trial*. It's the fourth adventure for the dark-haired enchantress, who we find taking a well-deserved break from her exertions at Devlin's castle. Having left as a domineering mistress, Stephanie returns to find that the tables have turned, and she is soon standing in the dock facing the wrath of her former sex slaves.

Stephanie's bedfellow this February is a book I hold very close to my heart — because I put it together myself! *New Erotica 2* is a tightly packed compilation of extracts from 13 of the best recent Nexus and Black Lace titles, including *Adventures in the Pleasurezone*, *Web of Desire*, *Linzi Drew's Pleasure Guide*, *Paradise Bay*, *Wild*, and *The Dungeons of Lidir*. And they all boast a personal introduction from yours truly! I trust you'll have as much fun reading it as I did compiling it. If that's possible!

And for this frosty month of February, Black Lace proudly presents *The Senses Bejewelled*. It's the sequel to *The Captive Flesh*: the next instalment in the licentious life of Marietta. She's now sitting pretty as Kasim's favourite in the harem, but things soon turn ugly. She is kidnapped by her master's greatest rival, and subjected to all manner of humiliations. Not surprisingly, she turns to her fellow slaves for solace.

Well gird my loins, we're off to mediaeval England for *Avalon Nights*, to join King Arthur and his famous Knights in a tale of saucy sorcery. A new arrival causes great upheaval at court, and the noble lords find themselves revealing some very embarrassing secrets. If the plot sounds familiar, you must've read *Knights of Pleasure*, which is very similar. So keep your purse strings pulled 'til next month!

Haring into Mad March, we find *Elaine*. Secretary to a hugely wealthy aristocrat, the young lady of the title is seduced by her boss's wife, recruited into a kinky establishment providing sexual services, and drawn into a sinister plot to blackmail the rich with videos of their filthy antics. Who's a busy girl then?

Now what else have I got up my sleeve . . . *Witch Queen of Vixania*? What is this? I'll tell you. It's a thumping good sword 'n' sorcery tale about the good but naive Brod and the efforts of the wicked Queen Vixia to subjugate him. Unbeknown to the sorceress, though, the young man has a formidable weapon to use against her . . . Sex with Brod is magic, in more ways than one.

Stand by for a Black Lace double whammy in March — and that's just in *Gemini Heat*. Deana and Delia Ferraro are a pair of scrumptious identical twins (yum yum!), yearning for sexual release in the searing heat of an early summer. Unfortunately, they both set their sights on the wealthy Jackson de Guile. It is soon far from clear who's manipulating who, and Jackson is eventually forced to choose between them. A decision that I personally would defer as long as possible.

Have you ever wondered what goes on in the jet-setting world of classical music? Because that's the background to *Virtuoso*. Mika's career as a solo violinist has come to a premature end, but his old friend Serena, another musician, is only too willing to help him get over it. With so many skilled mouths and fingers in one group, nobody's symphony is going to stay unfinished for long!

Ah well, time to fly. Mm, I can feel the cream being rubbed into my skin already . . . but I mustn't get carried away. I've still got to send a big wet kiss to all of you who have been reading Nexus under my editorship. It's been fun, and I'm sure you'll continue to enjoy the books. I shall be keeping an eye on things — I'm getting copies of all new books air-mailed to the West Indies!

Lots of love, and goodbye,

Esme ♡

$$\left(\overline{\textit{Nexus}}\right)$$

THE BEST IN EROTIC READING – BY POST

The Nexus Library of Erotica – almost one hundred and fifty
volumes – is available from many booksellers and newsagents. If
you have any difficulty obtaining the books you require, you can
order them by post. Photocopy the list below, or tear the list out
of the book; then tick the titles you want and fill in the form at
the end of the list. Titles with a month in the box will not be
available until that month in 1994.

CONTEMPORARY EROTICA

AMAZONS	Erin Caine	£3.99	
COCKTAILS	Stanley Carten	£3.99	
CITY OF ONE-NIGHT STANDS	Stanley Carten	£4.50	
CONTOURS OF DARKNESS	Marco Vassi	£4.99	
THE GENTLE DEGENERATES	Marco Vassi	£4.99	
MIND BLOWER	Marco Vassi	£4.99	
THE SALINE SOLUTION	Marco Vassi	£4.99	
DARK FANTASIES	Nigel Anthony	£4.99	
THE DAYS AND NIGHTS OF MIGUMI	P.M.	£4.50	
THE LATIN LOVER	P.M.	£3.99	
THE DEVIL'S ADVOCATE	Anonymous	£4.50	
DIPLOMATIC SECRETS	Antoine Lelouche	£3.50	
DIPLOMATIC PLEASURES	Antoine Lelouche	£3.50	
DIPLOMATIC DIVERSIONS	Antoine Lelouche	£4.50	
ELAINE	Stephen Ferris	£4.99	Mar
EMMA ENSLAVED	Hilary James	£4.99	May
EMMA'S SECRET WORLD	Hilary James	£4.99	
ENGINE OF DESIRE	Alexis Arven	£3.99	
DIRTY WORK	Alexis Arven	£3.99	
THE FANTASIES OF JOSEPHINE SCOTT	Josephine Scott	£4.99	

Title	Author	Price	Month
FALLEN ANGELS	Kendall Grahame	£4.99	Jul
THE FANTASY HUNTERS	Celeste Arden	£3.99	
HEART OF DESIRE	Maria del Rey	£4.99	
HELEN – A MODERN ODALISQUE	James Stern	£4.99	
HOT HOLLYWOOD NIGHTS	Nigel Anthony	£4.50	
THE INSTITUTE	Maria del Rey	£4.99	
JENNIFER'S INSTRUCTION	Cyrian Amberlake	£4.99	Apr
LAURE-ANNE TOUJOURS	Laure-Anne	£4.99	
MELINDA AND ESMERALDA	Susanna Hughes	£4.99	Jun
MELINDA AND THE MASTER	Susanna Hughes	£4.99	
Ms DEEDES AT HOME	Carole Andrews	£4.50	
Ms DEEDES ON A MISSION	Carole Andrews	£4.99	
Ms DEEDES ON PARADISE ISLAND	Carole Andrews	£4.99	
OBSESSION	Maria del Rey	£4.99	
THE PALACE OF EROS	Delver Maddingley	£4.99	May
THE PALACE OF FANTASIES	Delver Maddingley	£4.99	
THE PALACE OF SWEETHEARTS	Delver Maddingley	£4.99	
THE PALACE OF HONEYMOONS	Delver Maddingley	£4.99	
THE PASSIVE VOICE	G. C. Scott	£4.99	
QUEENIE AND CO	Francesca Jones	£4.99	
QUEENIE AND CO IN JAPAN	Francesca Jones	£4.99	
QUEENIE AND CO IN ARGENTINA	Francesca Jones	£4.99	
SECRETS LIE ON PILLOWS	James Arbroath	£4.50	
STEPHANIE	Susanna Hughes	£4.50	
STEPHANIE'S CASTLE	Susanna Hughes	£4.50	
STEPHANIE'S DOMAIN	Susanna Hughes	£4.99	
STEPHANIE'S REVENGE	Susanna Hughes	£4.99	
STEPHANIE'S TRIAL	Susanna Hughes	£4.99	Feb
THE TEACHING OF FAITH	Elizabeth Bruce	£4.99	Jul
THE DOMINO TATTOO	Cyrian Amberlake	£4.50	
THE DOMINO QUEEN	Cyrian Amberlake	£4.99	

EROTIC SCIENCE FICTION

Title	Author	Price	Month
ADVENTURES IN THE PLEASUREZONE	Delaney Silver	£4.99	

RETURN TO THE PLEASUREZONE	Delaney Silver	£4.99	
EROGINA	Christopher Denham	£4.50	
HARD DRIVE	Stanley Garten	£4.99	
PLEASUREHOUSE 13	Agnetha Anders	£3.99	
LAST DAYS OF THE PLEASUREHOUSE	Agnetha Anders	£4.50	
TO PARADISE AND BACK	D. H. Master	£4.50	
WANTON	Andrea Arven	£4.99	Apr

ANCIENT & FANTASY SETTINGS

CHAMPIONS OF LOVE	Anonymous	£3.99	
CHAMPIONS OF DESIRE	Anonymous	£3.99	
CHAMPIONS OF PLEASURE	Anonymous	£3.50	
THE SLAVE OF LIDIR	Aran Ashe	£4.50	
DUNGEONS OF LIDIR	Aran Ashe	£4.99	
THE FOREST OF BONDAGE	Aran Ashe	£4.50	
KNIGHTS OF PLEASURE	Erin Caine	£4.50	
PLEASURE ISLAND	Aran Ashe	£4.99	
WITCH QUEEN OF VIXANIA	Morgana Baron	£4.99	Mar

EDWARDIAN, VICTORIAN & OLDER EROTICA

ADVENTURES OF A SCHOOLBOY	Anonymous	£3.99	
ANNIE	Evelyn Culber	£4.99	
THE AUTOBIOGRAPHY OF A FLEA	Anonymous	£2.99	
CASTLE AMOR	Erin Caine	£4.99	
CHOOSING LOVERS FOR JUSTINE	Aran Ashe	£4.99	
EVELINE	Anonymous	£2.99	
MORE EVELINE	Anonymous	£3.99	
FESTIVAL OF VENUS	Anonymous	£4.50	
GARDENS OF DESIRE	Roger Rougiere	£4.50	
OH, WICKED COUNTRY	Anonymous	£2.99	
THE LASCIVIOUS MONK	Anonymous	£4.50	
LURE OF THE MANOR	Barbra Baron	£4.99	Jun
A MAN WITH A MAID 1	Anonymous	£4.99	
A MAN WITH A MAID 2	Anonymous	£4.99	
A MAN WITH A MAID 3	Anonymous	£4.99	

Please send me the books I have ticked above.

Name   . . . .
Address   . . . .
          . . . .
          . . . . Post code   . . . .

Send to: **Cash Sales, Nexus Books, 332 Ladbroke Grove, London W10 5AH**

Please enclose a cheque or postal order, made payable to **Nexus Books**, to the value of the books you have ordered plus postage and packing costs as follows:

UK and BFPO – £1.00 for the first book, 50p for the second book, and 30p for each subsequent book to a maximum of £3.00;

Overseas (including Republic of Ireland) – £2.00 for the first book, £1.00 for the second book, and 50p for each subsequent book.

If you would prefer to pay by VISA or ACCESS/MASTERCARD, please write your card number here:

Please allow up to 28 days for delivery

————— ————— ————— —————

Signature: _____